The League of Heroes

The League of Heroes
Or
How Lord Kraven Failed To Save the Empire

by
Xavier Mauméjean

adapted by
Manuella Chevalier

A Black Coat Press Book

Acknowledgements: I should like to thank Jean-Marc Lof-ficier for his suggestions and notes and David McDonnell for proofreading the typescript.

First published in France by Editions Mnémos, 15 Passage du Clos-Bruneau, 75005 Paris, France.
http://www.mnemos.com

Visit our website at www.blackcoatpress.com

ISBN 1-932983-44-9. First Printing. November 2005. Pub-lished by Black Coat Press, an imprint of Hollywood Com-ics.com, LLC, P.O. Box 17270, Encino, CA 91416. All rights reserved.

Life is infinitely stranger than anything which the mind of man could invent. We would not dare to conceive the things which are really mere commonplaces of existence. If we could fly out of that window hand in hand, hover over this great city, gently remove the roofs, and peep in at the queer things which are going on, the strange coincidences, the plannings, the cross-purposes, the wonderful chains of events, working through generations, and leading to the most outré results, it would make all fiction with its conventionalities and foreseen conclusions most stale and unprofitable.

Sherlock Holmes

Thanks to Jules Verne, Herbert George Wells, James Matthew Barrie, Arthur Conan Doyle and Edgar Rice Burroughs.
Also thanks to Stan Lee, who created a world, and to Alan Moore, who rocked its foundations.
But. above all, thanks to the Three Fairies, and to the Master of the Air.

XM

PART ONE

The League of Heroes

Excerpt from A Young Child's Guide To History
by J. M. Barrie,
Hodder and Stoughton, London, 1902

We will probably never know how it happened. Some historians claim that it was the earthquake in Sanriku, others that it was the Fairy Folk themselves who, with their strange spells, opened the path between our universe and theirs. And others believe that the hole in the aether was created by Professor Cavor's early efforts to synthesize the prodigious substance now known as Cavorite in June 1896. Whatever the cause, the world has never been the same since that fateful day when the inhabitants of Neverland arrived in Kensington Gardens. Everyone knows the autobiographical story of symbolist sculptor George Frampton, the first man to have established contact with our "neighbors."

"I was trying to come up with an idea for my Lamia *for the next Art Nouveau exhibition," declared Frampton. "It must have been about 5 p.m. when* she *appeared in front of me, wrapped in luminescent beauty. At first, I saw only her, until one of the 'children,' all grumbling and hairy, stole my hat. I tried to catch the cheeky boy, but then the fairy smiled at me, I couldn't say a word."*

That same evening, the Gardens were surrounded by the Royal Army. Upon reflection, one might be surprised by such strong measures, but who could guess at the time that a new age would soon dawn for Albion and the rest of the world!

Around 11 p.m., reporters dispatched by The Times *and* The Daily Telegraph *noticed the appearance of a galleon in the Gardens' great, circular pond–a genuine pirate* ship,complete with sails, rigs and a Jolly Roger flag flying at the top of its misen mast. The most adventurous of the journalists even ventured as far as the Indians' tent village, which had been pitched on the lawns, and watched the dance of Tiger Lily. To see this savage girl gesticulate wildly around the fire, while intoning prayers to her ancestors, was a terrifying and enchanted spectacle.

The next day, Her Majesty's Home Office took a census of the newcomers, then dispatched them to various camps, according to their ethnic origins. The Indians were sent to the Isle of Dogs–a proposal to relocate them to America having been rejected by the United States Government. The so-called "Lost Boys" were placed in various asylums. The spokesman for the pirates, a man later identified as James Hook, later Lord Hook of the Admiralty, negotiated permission for them to moor near the docks. As for the Fairy Folk, depending on whether they were sufficiently pleasant and of gentle disposition, they were either adopted by various families, or relegated to live amongst the prostitutes of Whitechapel.

These disconcerting events began an era of prosperity and abundance for the Empire, the full effects of which have not yet been assessed. The Royal Navy bore Albion's banner to the far ends of the world–and beyond. The Fairy Folk, in full cooperation with our scientists and engineers, opened wide the Gates of Progress.

What remained unsettled was the difficult case of the boy known as Peter Pan. The boy who would not grow up also refused to become part of society. He chose to remain in Neverland, displaying his spite and trying vainly to tarnish Albion's image. His repeated failures, far from calming his rage, only increased his resentment.

And that is why it is necessary that all of our Kingdom's children, before they go to bed, to be utterly convinced that Peter Pan is truly evil.

The Prisoner of Ingolstadt
(*August 1900*)

Half a moustache suited Lord Kraven perfectly. It had, nevertheless, been a close shave–Prince Spada's blade having nearly run him through the throat.

The foremost hero of Albion fixed his tie, looked at himself in the mirror one last time and proceeded to shoot his attacker in the head. The bullet, which was powerful enough to stop a raging bull (according to the gun manufacturer who had, in all probability, never set foot outside Camden) continued through the wall, ricocheted against the Tower's metal frame and went on to kill Ambrosio Terracota, the Prince's henchman, splattering his brains across the floor.

Two-for-one is not so bad, thought Lord Kraven. After wiping some cerebral matter off his boots, he looked at his timepiece. He didn't have much time left. Spada was an imbecile. Not only was the self-dubbed "Lord of Pain" a fraud (Lord Kraven knew all the genealogical trees of all the Great Families of Europe by heart and "Prince" Spada was nowhere in sight) but he had also made the mistake of trusting a Corsican shepherd boy–the simple-minded Matarese youth–to program a Cavorite Bomb.[1]

One thing was certain: if English Bob didn't arrive soon, there would no longer be an Heir to the Empire. Also, the map of a significant portion of the surrounding countryside would have to be redrawn. It was useless to try to flee. Kraven could clearly hear Spada's mercenaries beyond the door, spouting insults as to his mother's sexual preferences and his lack of manly prowesses. Better to take his chances outside.

Kraven tore down the magnificent Aubusson tapestry (not surprisingly, a fake), attached one of its ends to the barbi-

---

[1] The knowledgeable reader will recall that Prince Spada made the same mistake in *The Venice Affair*, and that it cost him his right hand. For this story and others, see the *Appendix*.

can with his nail gun, grasped the fabric and jumped. *It was time to remember Lord Greystoke's advice*, he thought, as he swung through the air. Moving like a pendulum, left to right, faster and faster, he felt as if he was a monkey dressed in the Royal Uniform of a Colonel of the Guard. At the precise moment, he leapt, feet forward, and crashed into the ground floor window.

The stained glass exploded into thousands of colorful shards, tearing the clothes of the operators of a Gatling machine gun who had been posted there as sentinels. Kraven ran straight into a gallery that went around the banquet hall. His mad dash was accompanied by the continuous rattling sound of the machine gun tearing holes into the plaster ceiling and the wooden beams. Kraven veered off towards the Prince's apartments where he suspected the prisoner was being kept. He opened the door wide–and immediately fell into a deep pool of dark, freezing cold water.

The Savior of the Empire, as he had been dubbed by the Press, held his breath at once–an exercise he had practiced a thousand times in the Danger Room at the League's Headquarters. He tore off his utility strap and pulled out a tiny oxygen mask. But already, a giant moray eel was rushing him, a single, terrifying creature with only one purpose: to tear through its victim's flesh. Kraven stuffed the oxygen mask into the beast's mouth, aimed his pistol and shot it at point-blank range. He barely had time to pull his head out of the water to avoid having his eardrums punctured by the resulting explosion. It almost blew him out of the pool. Slightly groggy, he managed to pull himself out and emptied his gun into the two powder-wigged servants who guarded Spada's bedroom.

When Kraven got his breath back, he found himself facing three duelists. The first was Edward-Albert, Prince of Wales and Heir to the Imperial Crown of Albion. His second and third adversaries were also Edward-Alberts! Kraven managed to block a low feint by Edward-Albert I, grabbed Edward-Albert II's sword and ran Edward-Albert III through with it. God help him if he had made a mistake in assessing the true identities of his opponents. Then, he succeeded in knocking out the other "fake" (Edward-Albert I) and loaded the surviving Prince of Wales on his shoulders.

He started to climb up the spiral staircase. Halfway to the dungeon, however, he knew that the fateful moment of this adventure had finally come. Prince Spada stood before him, completely dressed in black, a Toledo blade in his left hand, the priming mechanism of the Cavorite Bomb tied to the end of his right stump.

"You didn't think that you could escape so easily, did you, Lord Kraven? Come, my dear enemy, it's time for that duel that I've desired for so long."

Spada had been quite brief. Normally, he would have declaimed some boring poem about the ravages of syphilis by Girolamo Fracastoro or showered his opponent with a barrage of caustic comments. But, this time, the Calabrese Crime Lord seemed in a hurry to finish up.

Lord Kraven deposited the Prince of Wales on the granite steps and pulled out his own sword. The two men were of equal skill. Both knew that, by the end of this duel, an era would come to an end. The winner, whoever he was, would probably miss their reckless chases throughout Europe, never knowing who would lose and who would win.

The two combatants' shadows danced on the walls by the light of the chandeliers, a fitting allegory of the eternal struggle between good and evil. Kraven was suddenly distracted by the buzzing of the alarm in his waistcoat. Spada used this advantage to pierce his foe's shoulder with his blade–but found that he was unable to pull it out. The Lord of Pain immediately realized his defeat. Smiling his last, cruel smile, he opened his arms and willingly offered his chest to his adversary. Kraven severed his head neatly. Then, he cut off Spada's right stump and threw the detonator into the castle's moat, praying that the water would short-circuit the device.

The buzzing alarm indicated the presence of English Bob just above the Tower. Kraven pulled the Heir to the Crown all the way up the stairs and stopped a brief moment to admire the magnificent *HMS Albion Ascendant*.

The airship was 416 feet long from its nose to its rear propeller. It had a diameter of 38 feet and could reach a cruising speed of 18 miles per hour, which would soon be sorely required.

Kraven handcuffed the Prince of Wales' wrists around his neck, grabbed the rope ladder that English Bob had thrown him and climbed the rungs four at a time. Spada's men were gathering around the battlements but could not aim accurately. However, one shot managed to cut off a tuft of Kraven's hair before ricocheting on the ship's hull. *Better not linger*, thought the Savior of the Empire.

The airship's envelope contained 15,000 cubic meters of hydrogen, which could easily turn it into a giant flying bomb. Once inside the gondola, Kraven took the gangway to his cabin and put Prince Edward-Albert down on his bed. The telephone light was blinking, indicating that English Bob was busy talking. Lord Kraven yelled the itinerary to follow into the acoustic pipe–and nearly fell over. He looked outside: English Bob had hit one of the watchtowers when redirecting the airship. At the rate things were going, there would be soon nothing left of Ingolstadt Castle, a daring architectural folly, combining Magyar rigor with Ottoman affectation. Kraven ordered English Bob to turn right; he made sure they were truly getting away before heading towards the bridge.

For someone who didn't have any pilot qualifications, English Bob was not doing too badly after all, he reflected. Prior to this mission, Holmes had taught the teenager a few basic facts about piloting. One of the wings was a bit crumpled and they had lost an accumulator, but the ship was basically operational. Kraven took the controls and headed towards Albion.

Now, Lord Kraven could only wait, hoping that he had made the right choice. When the ship was far enough away from danger, he switched on the automatic pilot and returned to his cabin. Prince Edward-Albert was turning in bed, sweating heavily, dreaming loudly of Parisian orgies spent drinking champagne from La Goulue's shoe. *So he was the right one after all*, thought Kraven. He lifted the Prince's eyelids, noted the unusual dilatation of the pupils and wrote down a preliminary diagnosis, which he then tied to a carrier pigeon's paw. The bird flew through the porthole and would soon reach Sir Phileas' medical team.

"Here you are, My Lord. This will buck you up," said English Bob.

The Savior of the Empire accepted the cigar and the glass of cognac gratefully. He then proceeded to get a few hours' sleep.

Lord Kraven was awakened by loud, creaking noises. The airship had come dangerously close to the mooring pylon, located on a bare plot of land near Customs House, secretly purchased by the Reform Club, a.k.a. the Empire's Intelligence Service. If English Bob crashed the *Albion Ascendant*, the two daring heroes and the Heir to the Kingdom would drown in the Thames–a shameful end. Bob took off his goggles. The Great Detective had been a good teacher. With great care, the youth managed to pull the airship up so that the ground crew could grab the mooring cables. When they did so, he sighed deeply. Mission accomplished again!

Sir Phileas Fogg was waiting for them in the warehouse. Their superior had been keen on being there in person to take reception of the "royal parcel." He insisted on accompanying his two agents on the rest of the night's expedition. The two men squeezed inside a cab, the Prince of Wales lying over their knees. English Bob took the wheel and the car drove towards Limehouse.

One could always count on the teenager to find his way through the fog, along the railway and through the maze of back alleys, which were deserted at this time of the night.

"We've arrived."

Lord Kraven helped his superior get out of the car. Then, he knocked on the door–three short knocks, then two more.

The woman who opened the door was less than five feet tall. In her time, she had been beautiful, with fine, white skin, like a miniature from Dresden, but now, she looked more like a crone. The immoderate use of white and black magic, undoubtedly.

"Vulpinia, the time has come for you to help me."

The Enchantress watched Kraven. Since her defeat in Anvers, she owed him her life.[2] Today, he was offering her an opportunity to pay back her debt, and above all, to recover some of her past dignity. The woman opened her shawl, leaned over the Prince of Wales, who was dribbling as he slept, did a few magical passes and announced her verdict:

"A level-2 curse. A Continental rush job. I should be able to remove it easily. Come back tomorrow."

Fogg sighed with relief. All he had to do now was to inform the Office of Information Management. He took a red handkerchief, nearly as large as the sail of a small ship, and wiped his forehead.

Later, home at last, Lord Kraven emptied his pockets; they held a few sleeping pills, a derringer, a Malaysian dagger and a wad of foreign currencies. He swallowed one of the pills and fell asleep.

Interlude at the League of Heroes

When Lord Kraven awoke, the bells of St. Pancras told him that it was 11:30. His mind felt addled–the after-effects of the sleeping pill.

He walked towards the gymnasium, located on the second floor, to devote himself to his daily hour of intensive exercise: a long series of abs, a few stretches at the bar, some weight-lifting and a sequence of katas. Then, he took a shower, put on a large collar shirt from Capper & Waters,

---

[2] See *The Return of Lord Kraven*.

chose Ralph & Norton suit from the wardrobe (original but without affectation), took ten minutes to knot his tie perfectly, put on a fine pair of Spanish leather boots, brushed his hair and went down to have breakfast.

Kraven lived in a majestic four-story house on Drummond Street. He had a small but very efficient staff, who had previously worked for Sir Phileas. Stilson, the butler, whose jaw had been broken by a mutated primate during a mission in Sudan, served him a kidney pie, then left the room quietly.

While wolfing down his breakfast–he felt famished every time he returned from a mission–Lord Kraven scanned the headlines of the morning papers. *The Times*, *The Daily News* and *The Standard* were all announcing that the Prince of Wales would not appear at the Crystal Palace ceremonies next month due to a case of acute appendicitis that had required the intervention of the Royal Surgeon himself, Doctor Frederick Treves. The Office of Information Management had done a good job. Kraven contemplated eating a couple of hard-boiled eggs sprinkled with paprika, but looked at his watch and decided that it was time he left.

His 1900 Dunhill was waiting in the garage. More than a masterpiece of Albion engineering–which it was to Kraven's eyes–the vehicle symbolized the endless possibilities of the human mind. It was built around an x-shaped, tubular chassis, reinforced at the front, and sported a half-floating hypoid differential with hydraulic power steering, double action Delco shock absorbers, automatic transmission and, to top it all off, a powerful 283-horsepower engine that could do 6,000 revolutions per minute. Kraven got inside the car, wiped an imaginary stain from its ash-white interior trim, opened the automatic garage door that let out on Tottenham Court Road and drove out.

A jaded reader, knowing that Londoners were used to seeing Pirates and Indians walk their streets, would be justified in believing that they would remain equally indifferent to the wonderful spectacle of a 1900 Dunhill roaring at full speed along its busy thoroughfares. But he would be wrong. Reaching the corner of Whitcomb Street, Lord Kraven turned right without bothering to downshift and, by so doing, nearly collided with a pedestrian looking wistfully at a poster of the new *Eleanor Rigby* musical playing at the Alhambra. He stopped abruptly before the headquarters of the League of Heroes.

The building was a 13-story glass and steel contraption that looked like a gigantic Archimedean mirror. It had been built near Piccadilly by the Krupp Company out of a special polymer so that it was impossible for anyone outside to see inside–and it was bulletproof to boot. There was a mooring pylon on the roof. The building was equipped with a surveillance system designed by Cavor himself. According to *The Inventor's Review*, a magazine generally well informed in such matters, the notorious scientist had requested the architect to include three underground levels capable of withstanding the full blast of a Cavorite Bomb.

Lord Kraven went inside the marble lounge that was open to the public, walked by the counter of the Thos. Cook & Son Agency and, without paying any attention to the lobby elevators, checked in at the security counter. As soon as the voice recognition system–an Afghani war veteran with devilishly sharp ears–identified him, he inserted a punch-card into a special elevator and pressed the only button inside. The cabin went up directly to the next-to-last floor.

As usual, Plunder was waiting for him with a cup of tea. The butler, who refused any assistance and generally ignored the advice of Her Majesty's Secret Service, managed the Council Rooms of the League of Heroes by himself, making sure that everyone felt at home. In fact, he was just like a father, proud of his children, even if he never forgot that they were more than ordinary children.

"The gentlemen have decided to hold their meeting in the Danger Room," he declared.

Kraven left his coat in Plunder's good care and stepped across the bronze threshold.

The Danger Room was a clever, if somewhat sadistic, but always useful, contraption. Resting on hydraulic jacks that enabled it to fully rotate on its own axis, it had been designed to simulate any perilous environment that had either been visited, or might someday be visited, by the League. It included hidden arrows, secret machine guns, numerous traps and even live black mamba snakes brought back from Africa by Lord Greystoke. Sherlock Holmes was usually in charge of programming new sequences to make sure that his associates were not becoming complacent. Because of the Detective's eagerness, Kraven still had an ugly scar made by a drill that had unexpectedly sprung from a wall just as he thought he could safely leave the Room to go and take a shower.

Right now, however, the Heroes were resting.

Lord Greystoke had just returned from a difficult mission in which he had made contact with a giant gorilla on an island near Sumatra. His body was covered in bandages. Lord Kraven had heard him mutter something about giant prehistoric rats as well, but had not inquired further.[3] The Lord of the Trees seemed to be in a dark mood. The Great Detective, on the other hand, was half-sunken into his favorite armchair, his body wrapped in a ritual Indian blanket, quietly smoking his calumet. Neither took any notice of the technicians who were busily working in the center of the room.

"Gentlemen," said Lord Kraven, "this evening, we shall toast the passing of Prince Spada, Monarch of Thieves. He is no more. Now, could someone tell me what's going on here?" he asked.

Cavor's team–the only men with the authority to work inside the Council Room–were assembling the last bits of what looked like a armor suit suspended by a winch. One of the engineers opened its chest plate and connected two pipes coupled with a generator; another loaded some darts into a gauntlet. Then, they left without a word.

"I'm glad to see you're back alive, Lord Kraven," said Holmes, drumming his fingers on the sheath of his pipe. "But we don't know any more than you do. We've been asked

---

[3] See *The Giant Gorilla of Sumatra.*

merely to wait." The Great Detective gestured Kraven to sit. "Our friend who can't keep still," he then added, "believes that it's a new weapon."

"More like some kind of trickery," said Greystoke. The Lord of the Trees stopped swinging on his trapeze, let himself fall down to the ground from eight feet in the air, did a somersault mid-way, landed on a pommel horse, and finished off with a double-backward somersault, faultlessly landing on the tips of his toes. Then, he sniffed at the air. "They're coming. Cavor and a man who reeks of gin."

A few seconds later, two men walked into the room. One would have had to have Greystoke's keen sense of smell to detect the light fragrance of alcohol around the younger man.

Cavor, as usual, wore a cricket cap and cycling knickerbockers and stockings. He looked like he was having difficulties controlling a series of nervous twitches about his face. Everyone was familiar with his small, nearly rotund shape and skinny limbs. His famous portrait at the Wallace Collection made him look like a cannon ball. But his bright eyes burned with genius. An uncanny energy constantly ran through his body, giving him an appearance of being compulsively agitated.

To the great relief of his audience, who cared little about the niceties of etiquette, and frankly disliked the lies put out by the Office of Information Management, Cavor began his presentation at once.

"Gentlemen, in many significant ways, we here are all cut from the same cloth. Of course, I'm not referring to our, er, divergent backgrounds, or unique and varied skills; I'm talking about the bonds which unite us and our common desire to serve Albion to the utmost of our abilities. So it is in that spirit that I have the honor today of introducing you to my latest and greatest creation: MechaMan!"

Just like a stage magician, Cavor made a half-turn and stretched his left arm to point at the bizarre, man-shaped machine, the wheels of which were now being oiled by the younger man, his assistant.

"I know what you're thinking: it's not an android, nor is it merely an ordinary suit of armor, more a combination of both. Never mind the science. What you should know is that it will allow you to safely explore the fiery depths of a volcano, to safely stroll beneath an ice field. It comes equipped with stand-alone batteries and thermal regulators. In short, Mecha-Man will guarantee your comfort and your safety."

"You mean, one of us must get inside that thing?"

The scientist stared at Holmes before replying.

"Yes, of course, otherwise how do you expect to make it work? Did I mention that MechaMan man also comes with a prodigious range of ground-breaking weapons: nerve gas, curare darts, guns and, above all, a power-coupling system that greatly magnifies its wearer's physical strength. It guarantees total invincibility. And I can prove it!"

The assistant gave Cavor one of MechaMan's boots and gauntlets. Cavor took off his shoe, put his foot inside the heavy metal boot and put on the glove. Then, the man who was Newton's successor at the Royal Society limped towards the bronze panels of the Danger Room and, with barely a flick of his hand, smashed the wall.

One was almost reminded of a fairground attraction. For just a second, Kraven pictured the comical-looking inventor in his striped sweater using his new-found, mechanically-amplified strength to smash a pile of plates.

Meanwhile, Lord Greystoke sent Plunder away; the butler, alerted by the noise, had come to see what was going on. After that, the Lord of the Trees asked the question that was on everyone's mind.

"Is there any Cavorite in your metal suit?"

The great scientist looked as innocent as a village maiden. For several months now, responding to a request from some of the Empire's top-ranking Ministers, the Office of Information Management had launched a propaganda campaign stressing the spirit of cooperation that existed between all the various branches of its Administration. This was aimed at debunking a numbers of rumors spread by Peter Pan and his allies. Despite this, everybody, from the lowest clerk to the highest minister, knew that the celebrated League of Heroes detested having to serve as guinea pigs to test Cavor's inventions.

"Well, yes, but only in the engine."

Lord Greystoke leaned towards the Professor.

"If that is so, then try it yourself."

Looking like a dwarf in a Wagner opera, Cavor maneuvered the winch. The upper part of the armor rose about ten feet above the ground and revealed the inside of the suit: red velvet stretched over the steel frame. The scientist, purple from exhaustion, waved to his assistant to climb into Mecha-Man. The young man hesitated, looked at the Protectors of the Empire all watching him intently, and decided to do as he was told.

"Are you settled inside, Flanders? Ready?" asked Cavor. "I'm going to switch on the generator."

Immediately, a long, hissing burst of steam came whistling out of the suit, followed by several sparks that ran across the armor like will-o'-the-wisps. Through the porthole, they all saw Flanders screaming. His very body was boiled alive, his skin sticking to the glass like molasses, until the pressure caused his skull to explode like a melon.

Nobody could have done anything to save him.

Cavor took out a slide rule, whispered a few figures under his breath, probably to hide his emotions, then declared in a very serious tone:

"It's merely a small problem with the thermal insulation."

Excerpt from The Traveler's Guide to London,
by Karl Baedeker, Leipzig, 1900 edition

During the past year, many tourists have expressed the desire to end their stay in London by a visit to the people of Neverland. We can only advise them to be exceedingly cau-

tious. *A mistake, or even a simple misunderstanding, could prove very risky for the unprepared traveler and lead him into a variety of perilous situations. For example, to suggest trading jewelry for a tapestry would offend the Indians. It is also strongly recommended to not mingle with any of the Pirates, from the cabin boy to the boatswain. A simple "my dear man" could cost the unwary visitor his life. Tourists wishing to brighten their journey with a walk though Kensington Gardens do so at their own peril. In a joint statement, the Crown and the Neverland Delegates stated that there would be no public prosecution in the event of any children being taken. Visiting hours vary and are posted at the Caretaker's Office.*

Ceremonies at the Crystal Palace
(September 1900)

The orchestra had just begun to play the first notes of *Nimrod* when the special Imperial Train arrived at Crystal Palace Station.

At a signal from the Head of Protocol, two guards located at the end of the red carpet unfolded a small, ornate wrought iron staircase before withdrawing.

Victoria, Queen of Albion, Empress of India and recently proclaimed Majestrix of the Fairy Folk, appeared.

She stood straight and proud, looking magnificently regal, despite the recent stroke that had left her partially disabled, with a twitch to her face. While the King attended orphanages and brothels, the Queen kept an eye on the Empire, and liked it that way.

The Queen walked slowly down the red carpet, followed by her ministers. The Neverland delegation was waiting for her. There were the Pirates and the Indians, led by Tiger Lily, and the so-called Lost Boys, all of them standing under the gigantic crystal dome embedded in steel.

The Queen stopped a few feet away from the delegates to welcome their speaker, Lady Wendy Moira Angela Darling.

Victoria's choice had been criticized by many. Some had publicly said that they were surprised to see the mistress of the Renegade being made a Lady of the Kingdom. However, the Queen's strategy was quite simple: by welcoming Lady Darling to her entourage, Victoria was buying peace. She knew that Peter Pan would never try anything that could put his friend's life in danger, and would limit his opposition to a few acts of mischief as usual.

Lady Darling bowed before her Queen and presented her with the traditional symbols of her allegiance: A holly leaf, evoking a kiss, and an ice dagger, symbolizing death. Love and death, the cardinal values of the Fairy Folk. Victoria accepted the presents, kissed the young woman on her forehead and motioned her to get back to her feet. The cortege then continued towards the conservatory, up to the grand staircase.

Since its construction in 1851 by Sir Joseph Paxton, the Crystal Palace had been retrofitted in order to become suitable as the Courts of the Fairy Folk. Of course, its general style had been preserved, as well as its spidery work of wrought-iron and its perfumed fountains. But in order to keep the public away and to guarantee her safety, the Queen had called on the services of the greatest engineers and enchanters in the Kingdom.

From 5 p.m. until dawn, the Crystal Palace's gardens were swept by polyvalent spells designed to turn any unexpected visitor whose weight exceeded three pounds to stone. If that wasn't enough, mediums posted as sentries all around the building could detect any unusual cerebral activity. Finally, for good measure, a system of hidden deadly blades guaranteed its security. Nevertheless, incidents still occurred from time to time, usually caused by the Fairy Folk themselves.

We would be wrong to think that the Fairies are wise and quiet folk. They live only for the moment, are unable to remember in the morning the events of the day before, which often causes them to start their work all over again; they don't care about anything and spend most of their time thinking they are flowers. Carefree and frivolous, they are unable to do anything but flutter around aimlessly.

When he was in charge of Royal Security, Cavor had, more than once, risked being turned to stone, removing their golden ribbons from machine guns or scratching the sweet surface of their poisoned darts. It had been a nightmare for the scientist, then one day a Lost Boy had died. The foolish Boy had believed he could catch a speeding bullet with his teeth– and had been proven wrong. They had found the remains of his head, still looking quite amazed, in the pond. That very night, Cavor had been transferred to Sir Phileas and the League of Heroes–much to his relief.

The League stood at the bottom of the stairs. Sherlock Holmes, his face covered with ritual paintings, Lord Greystoke, who on this special occasion, had agreed to wear pants, and Lord Kraven, whose bravery was being rewarded that day.

Victoria whispered a few words in Sir Phileas' ear. The Queen smiled at the retelling of the Lord of the Trees' latest exploits, congratulated the Great Shaman on his part in the curious case of Caldwell's Living Dead,[4] and thanked Kraven for bringing her son back. The Savior of the Empire puffed out his chest and grumbled some incoherent nonsense about duty and motherland. Everybody applauded, except Cavor and English Bob, who had had too much to drink.

English Bob was, in fact, quite shy, and neither his fame, nor his Union Jack could remedy that condition. His real name was Rupert Hammerstein; he was the son of Prussian immigrants and had first learnt the tough lessons of life in the grimy back alleys of Spitalfields, until the day Lord Kraven had taken notice of him. Under the miserable appearance of a kid with a crumpled face, a crooked cap and clothes too large for him, he had seen the ideal assistant, the complement for whom he had searched. Young Rupert had just forced Kraven's car door, intending to rob it. Without a word, the hero had sprung

---

[4] See *The Strange Case of the Living Dead of Caldwell*.

behind him, opened the door, thrown the little rascal onto the backseat and driven off. Since then, they had never been parted.

The first few months had been quite difficult. Rupert, who had become Robert Hammerstone, or simply Bob, didn't understand that people could just be nice without asking for something in return. More than once, he had run away from Drummond Street. Since Kraven lacked the time to look after the boy properly, not being able to both save the Empire and teach him table manners at the same time, he had entrusted his care to Plunder. At first not thrilled with the task, the old servant had quickly become very fond of the youth. In a few months, the fearful and unhealthy boy was transformed into a tough, determined individual, disciplined in his studies as well as in sports, quite capable of assisting Kraven in his battle against evil. However, there were still things that made him uneasy.

For example, dealing with Sir Phileas Fogg still frightened English Bob, much more than the villains conspiring to rule the world from Soho to Hong Kong. Still, he wasn't the only one afraid of Sir Phileas. The man inspired immediate repulsion in most of the people he came in contact with, and even quite a few heroes, even though they would be understandably reluctant to admit it. More than his physical appearance–Fogg was morbidly obese–it was his unchecked taste for devious intrigues and elaborate schemes that drove people away.

He directed the Empire's Secret Service from the Blue Room of the Reform Club, far from human passions, laughter and tears, purposefully reducing individual and collective destinies to simple logical patterns that only he could understand. In his eyes, the heroes were nothing more than mere extensions of his own intelligence, to be dispatched here and there, to shape the world. No one could even guess at the totality of Sir Phileas' schemes: a revolution in Mexico, a great painting to be saved in Austria, a delivery to be made in Hong Kong–it was wise not to ask too many questions. The Queen was satisfied, and that was the only thing that mattered.

English Bob felt fingers ruffling his hair. It was Holmes who stood apart from the others, quietly smoking his pipe.

"You should do like them, take some time off and have fun."

The Great Detective was looking at the Lost Boys, who were sliding along the banister, balls of fur and hair not intimidated by any protocol.

"Sightly, Nibs, Tootles and Curly... I wonder if they're really that happy, away from Peter."

"Why do you say that?" asked English Bob.

"Because when they are brought too close to men, the folk of Neverland start losing some of their identity. Peter likes change, but only when he commands it. The other creatures have decided to play by the rules set by the Boy Who Would Not Grow Up, but they're adult. These are children. I'm not sure they're aware of the stakes..."

English Bob then saw the ribbon hidden under the Detective's collar. It was a scarlet ribbon, the symbol of the Resistance.

One could be hanged for that.

Holmes saw the boy's look and turned away.

Excerpt from L'Echo de Paris, (January 23, 1901)

"I will be good" were Princess Victoria's first words when, in 1830, the Regency Bill made her the heir to the throne of William IV.

According to a news bulletin just released by Buckingham Palace, Queen Victoria passed away last night, January 22, her children and grandchildren at her side. She was born in 1819.

With her death, the oldest European Monarch has now left the scene. She will be remembered for her appointments of formidable statesmen such as William Lamb, 2nd Viscount Melbourne, Sir Robert Peel, Henry John Temple, 3rd Viscount Palmerston, Benjamin Disraeli and William Ewart Gladstone, to name but a few.

She had come to incarnate the Empire of Albion and was the witness of a magnificent era that has now passed. This new century is fraught with uncertainties. The reign of her successor, King Albert-Edward VII, has begun inauspiciously, some claim, mostly due to the as-yet unsolved problem of the integration of the denizens of Neverland into the Empire.

One feels that Albion and her people will soon come to miss the glories of the reign of Queen Victoria.

The Queen's Funeral
(February 1901)

The funeral cortege walked through the silent rain, except for the sound of the cannons. Sir Phileas and the League of Heroes were there; so was Kaiser William, grandson of the late Queen, walking seven feet behind the casket, as prescribed by protocol. The carriage was drawn by four fretful horses that had almost slipped four times because of the rose petals that the Fairy Folk had thrown in their path.

Finally, it arrived at Westminster Cathedral. The Archbishop of Canterbury stood in the entrance, next to Edward-Albert, the new King of Albion. The monarch, who could barely contain his sorrow, had asked his nephew William to take charge of the ceremony.

At Sir Phileas' signal, the Captain of the Steam Guard, the new unit of MechaMen equipped by Cavor, stopped the cortege to enable the League to carry the casket. The Guards' steam covered Victoria's body with a fine mist. She had expressed the wish to be buried in her wedding dress. Seeing the Queen's peaceful face, one no longer doubted that she was at last reunited with her beloved Albert. The Kaiser and the League stood on both sides of the casket, Lord Greystoke and

Sherlock Holmes on the left, Lord Kraven and the Kaiser on the right. Edward-Albert deposited a last kiss on his mother's forehead.

Then, to the sound of Beethoven's *Funereal March*, the Empire of Albion escorted its dead sovereign to her final resting place.

Excerpt from The Times, *(June 26, 1902)*

A huge crowd, gathered since dawn along the route of the procession, was waiting to cheer its new King, Edward-Albert VII. In their state coach, the monarchs reached Westminster Abbey where, before an audience of Princes, Lords and Sultans, they were crowned with the 3,000-diamond crown.

Today, Albion is filled with joy. It reflects with pride on its ancient ceremonies symbolizing centuries of tradition. The Empire praises its new King for he is the one who guards that tradition and guarantees its freedom.

The Deadly Doctor Fatal *(September 1906)*

Lord Kraven was in a difficult position.

He was lying on a dissection table, naked, his hands and feet handcuffed, his body closely shaved and covered with some kind of greasy substance. To his chest were attached several cables connected to a cardiograph that controlled the release of a large tank filled with acid, located only a few inches above his mouth.

Elsewhere in the room, a scientist–utterly mad–who had once been the Pride of the Empire [5]–was badly botching a Bach fugue on an organ while telling him in great detail his lunatic plans for the improvement of the human species.

Kraven sighed deeply, then interrupted his enemy.

"Do you know that the Jade Mask said virtually the same thing to me last year? [6] What were his plans? Ah yes! To use Feng Shui to cause the collapse of the Towers of San Francisco. The truth is that I left him packed inside a crate on his way to the Forbidden City, duly stamped."

Looking clearly vexed, Sir Reginald Plumdritch, a.k.a. Doctor Fatal, stayed silent for several minutes. Suddenly, he jumped off his stool and rushed towards the table. His face was only a couple of inches away from Kraven's.

"How dare you compare me to that senile scientist, barely capable of dissecting a bird's nest with his overgrown nails? You disappoint me, Lord Kraven. When Peter Pan injected me with Fairy Folk genes, he unwittingly turned me into the New Messiah. Soon, Doctor Fatal will rule Albion and his will shall be supreme to Men and Fairy Folk alike. But, unfortunately, you won't be here to see it. Believe me, I regret that deeply."

Doctor Fatal then went back to playing Bach, leaving Lord Kraven to meditate upon his grim destiny.

The tank's release mechanism was controlled by his heartbeat and every pulsation, diastole and systole, only caused its beak to open slightly wider. Doctor Fatal had given him the choice of dying from a sudden heart attack or having his face melted by the acid. With his tongue, Kraven took the cyanide capsule hidden in his hollow tooth and bit it, letting the sour almond taste spread in his throat.

A few seconds later, his heart had stopped beating.

That was the signal.

---

[5] See *Albion Mourning*.
[6] See *The Wharves of San Francisco*.

A high-explosive shell went through the back of Doctor Fatal's head, spreading splinters and fragments of brain matter onto the organ keyboard.

English Bob gave a sharp knock to release the roller skates hidden in his boots. The floor was probably booby-trapped, but he hoped there was a way to navigate it safely. When he had been heading the League's metaconditioning program, Sir Reginald had set up a similar simulation in the Danger Room. With Plunder's help, Holmes had located the program in the archives. The thinking was that they would provide a clue as to the traps protecting Doctor Fatal's lair. Sir Phileas believed that his former colleague didn't like innovations. English Bob was going to have an opportunity to test that theory right in the real world.

The teenager began skating on the checker-like pattern, weaving in and out of the squares, careful to avoid the black ones. He did this enthusiastically, remembering the sunny afternoons spent playing on the lake located near Lord Greystoke's Scottish manor. He especially liked it when the League forgot their status as heroes and became just men.

Becoming distracted, Bob skimmed past a black square and had to quickly jump aside to avoid a club that fell from the ceiling. The black squares were booby-trapped–Sir Phileas had been right. English Bob finally reached the other side of the checkered pattern. He ran to the dissection table which, luckily, was on wheels. He pushed Lord Kraven towards the exit after pouring the contents of a small glass vial down his throat.

Nobody questioned the medical wonders that came out of Neverland anymore, especially in the field of toxicology. Everyone, for example, knew of Lord Hook's stone rings, which contained a mysterious yellow substance, unknown to any scientist, and without question, the most powerful poison ever known.

During their complicated lifetimes, it was not unusual for the inhabitants of Neverland to poison each other–mostly as an elaborate joke. Conversely, they had also devised nearly-magical medicines that would bring them back to life. The ancient Greeks, who were used to receiving gifts from the Gods, had called such cures *pharmakos*.

Even if not all of the Neverland medicines worked on humans–no ointment had yet succeeded in growing back a severed limb–the doctors never hesitated to prescribe a "magical" *pharmakos*, even if their patient had already been pronounced dead. *Cyanosis pectrax*, for example, combined the miraculous qualities of Neverland magic with the latest medical discoveries.

It had a wide variety of applications that allowed it to react to most of the poisons known to man–arsenic, strychnine, cyanide, prussic acid, thallium, nicotine, phosphor, veronal, caffeine, hydrochloric morphine and mercury, plus a few more still unknown–and spread throughout the body, absorbing and destroying the toxic molecules.

The small glass vial that English Bob had emptied down Lord Kraven's throat contained such a substance.

Suddenly, the Savior of the Empire sat upright and violently threw up all over the Afghan carpet.

Excerpt from The Amazing Story of Nikola Tesla
by Hugo Gernsback,
Modern Electrics Publ., New York, 1926

In 1880, when Nikola Tesla first arrived in the United States of America, he had four cents to his name, a book of poetry and a letter of recommendation to Thomas Alva Edison. Eventually, Tesla earned the respect of Edison and offered to undertake a complete redesign of the Edison Company's continuous current dynamos. After Tesla described the nature of the benefits from his proposed modifications, Edison offered him $50,000 if they were successfully completed. Tesla worked for nearly a year to great success. When he inquired about the $50,000, Edison told him, "Tesla, you don't under-

stand our American humor" and reneged on his agreement, offering a raise in Tesla's salary of $10 per week. Tesla resigned on the spot. In 1882, Tesla formed his own company, Tesla Power & Light, and thanks to the financial backing of the Shangri-La Electric Company, moved to Indonesia, building a secret factory on the Island of Krakatoa, announcing his intention to provide humanity with unlimited power.

The Eggs of the Roc
(February 1909)

"Ho there! Passengers, run for your lives! Hasten back to the ship and leave your gear! Save yourselves from destruction, Allah preserve you. For this island whereon ye stand is no true island, but a great fish stationary a-middlemost of the sea, whereon the sand hath settled and trees have sprung up of old time, so that it is become like unto an island. But when ye lighted fires upon it, it felt the heat and moved, and in a moment it will sink with you into the sea and ye will all be drowned. So leave your gear and seek your safety ere ye die!"

Captain James Hook closed his copy of Sir Richard Francis Burton's translation of *The Arabian Nights* and looked at the flotilla of enemy dhows sailing towards his *Jolly Roger*.

He sat comfortably on the upper deck of the ship, completely at ease and in control, striking as ever a dashing figure with his long, black hair and his red-and-gold frock coat. Red, some said, to better hide the blood of his enemies.

With experience born of a thousand battles, he studied the enemy forces through a spyglass. The ships were crewed by Singh, hirsute, hairy gnomes with filed, pointy teeth, their bodies covered with tattoos, fanatically devoted to their Lord and Master, Prince Sinbad. Murder and piracy was second nature to them, something to which he could easily relate.

He then looked at his own crew. Everyone was fit and trim, and holding to his post.

"Mister Smee," said Hook.

"Yes, Captain?"

"Hoist the flag."

"Aye aye, Captain!"

Soon, the Union Jack of Albion with, in the upper left-hand corner, Hook's skull and bones, began to flap in the wind at the end of mast. Hook felt a sense of pride swell within him.

"Mister Cecco?"

The handsome man with the perfect pigtail, who had cut his name in letters of blood on the back of the warden of the Prison of Goa, fed the ammunition belt into the Gatling gun.

"Ready, Captain!"

Hook turned towards his Second, Shala Khan, a man who, in his time, had caused the China Sea to run red with blood. Shala Khan had not been part of the *Jolly Roger*'s original crew, but he, too, hated Peter Pan with a passion. When swearing fealty to Hook, he had cut off his right hand, which had endeared him at once to the Captain.

"The guns are ready, Captain," said the Mongol.

"Excellent. Grapeshot in the bow guns and explosive shells for all the others."

The Mongol shouted the order. At once, the men rushed to load the guns.

"Fire only on my command," added Hook.

The dhows were getting closer. Hook appreciated the elegance of the long, flat vessels with triangular sails. *Too bad they chose to side with the enemy of the Empire*, he thought.

The Singh began firing at the *Jolly Roger*. The bullets flew between the sails without harming anyone. Hook snorted contemptuously. *Makeshift rifles undoubtedly smuggled from the Bengali*, he thought. It was either stupid respect for tradition or desperate economic measures on the part of Prince Sinbad. In any event, it would take more than a few volleys of lead to cause serious damage to the *Jolly Roger*.

Captain Hook put out his tongue; it was as thin and pointed as that of a Komodo lizard. He licked his forefinger and felt the breeze.

"Raise the guns three degrees," he barked.

The gunnery men obeyed as one. The Captain lit up two Cuban cigars, took a puff of smoke, then grumbled:

"Now we'll see which of the two of us is truly the King of the Seas, Prince Sinbad."

He raised, then lowered his hook.

All the guns fired simultaneously, a thundering conflagration that shook the ship. A devastating wave of hot metal slammed into the Singh, tearing their bodies to shreds and destroying everything in its path.

Hook put his hand to his ear to better hear the cries of pain and suffering that, almost immediately, erupted from the dhows. As was his habit, he sniffed the air, filling his lungs with the smell of gunpowder and blood. Smee smiled. He knew that nothing could put Hook in a better mood.

"Smell that, Smee," said the Captain. "There is no better scent on Earth!"

As if they were acting in a Chorley & Sullivan play, the entire crew of the *Jolly Roger* nodded and sang "There is no better scent on Earth!" echoing Hook's own words. The moods of their Captain were something to which they had learned to be sensitive.

The acrid cloud of death started to dissipate, revealing the extent of the carnage and damage that had been inflicted on the dhows.

Beyond the wrecked ships, the true enemy finally appeared: the metallic, cigar-shaped form of the *Siddhârta*, the private submarine of Prince Sinbad.

"Ah-ha! The lion appears after his jackals have been slaughtered," said Hook. "Prepare for a second volley!"

Hook pointed his spyglass at the ship: it was about 230-feet long and could reach speeds of up to 60 miles per hour. If he could capture it, it would make a royal gift for King Edward-Albert. Since Queen Elizabeth I, Albion monarchs had loved the spoils of sea battles.

"Guns ready, Captain," said the Mongol.

Hook took another puff from his Neverland cigar. He hated the taste of Indian tobacco but had found that there was no adequate substitute for it. He had always hated the Indians, too, because they had been allies of his personal nemesis, Peter Pan. He swore that, one day, he would recapture their Queen, Tiger Lily, and would sell her into slavery to... To the Singh, why not? If they survived the encounter, he smiled evilly.

"Guns ready, Captain," repeated the Mongol.

Hook nodded to show he had heard his Second.

"Aim for the prow, low on the water."

The cannons fired their deadly shots, but only suucceeded in denting the reinforced, steel-plated hull of the *Siddhârta*. Hook grudgingly admired Prince Sinbad's ship. He was about to order that "Long Tom," the *Jolly Roger*'s mightiest cannon be reloaded with heavier artillery, when someone behind him coughed to attract his attention.

"Cap'n?"

It was Gentleman Starkey who had left his post to talk to Hook.

"Yes, Mister Starkey?" said the Captain in his softest and most dangerous tone.

"Well, er, it's the dhows, Cap'n. They're trying to go around the ship."

"And Peter Pan is a baby snatcher. Do you have something new to tell me, Mister Starkey?"

"I think they're preparing to board us."

"I'll deal with them when the time comes."

"But they look dangerous!"

A vein began throbbing in Hook's temple. His eyes acquired a faint red haze. He put his arm around Starkey, feigning friendship.

"Mister Starkey, how long have we been sailing together?"

"Well, er, a long time, Cap'n."

"A long time indeed." Then Hook violently pushed the man forward, slamming his face against a mast. While keeping the sailor immobilized with his right hand, he put his hook around his throat. A drop of blood seeped from beneath the razor-sharp implement. "Then if you wish for this long and mutually-rewarding relationship to continue unimpeded, I strongly suggest that you never again question one of my orders, Mister Starkey. Understood?"

The Captain released his grip; the pirate dropped to his knees, grabbing his neck, breathing with difficulty. The others conspicuously ignored the scene. Hook held his 150 men-strong crew in an iron grip.

"Mister Khan, are the gunners ready?" barked Hook.

The Long Tom had been loaded with Cavorite shells; it was a dangerous gambit due to the unpredictable nature of the alloy. They could just as well explode upon firing, blowing the *Jolly Roger* to Kingdom come.

"Aim for the propellers," shouted the Captain. Then: "Fire!"

The shells zoomed through the air and hit the rear of the *Siddhârtha*, blowing up its twin propellers. The crew of the *Jolly Roger* roared with satisfaction. The submarine was now crippled, unable to dive.

"*Avast belay, yo ho, heave to, A-pirating we go, And if we're parted by a shot, We're sure to meet below!*" sang the pirates.

"Now, let's take care of the rest of the Singh," said Captain Hook, stroking his frilly cravate. "But first, Mister Smee, please ask His Lordship to join me on the bridge."

The fat little man ran towards the Captain's cabin. He soon returned, accompanied by Lord Greystoke, Hero of Albion. As usual, His Lordship was naked, except for a loincloth and a huge cutlass hanging on a belt.

"I wouldn't have wanted you to miss this for the world, Your Lordship," said Hook.

The first dhows bumped into the Jolly Roger's hull. The surviving Singh, daggers clenched between their yellow teeth, were preparing to board the ship.

Hook looked contemptuously at them and gestured to Cecco.

"Fire at will!"

The pirate began to fire the Gatling gun at the blood-thirsty mob, cutting them to pieces. But more followed as grapplers began to fall on the bridge.

Hook pulled out his sword and sliced one of the assailants from the sternum to the throat. But other Singh were already clinging to the rigging and swarming the ship. Shala Khan fired his pistol twice and three attackers fell dead. Mister Smee, looking for all the world like an uncle kindly disciplining an errant nephew, used "Johnny Corkscrew," his favorite knife to politely eviscerate one Singh after the other.

Blood ran freely across the *Jolly Roger*'s bridge as Hook's pirates met the attackers, matching ferocity with savagery. Lord Greystoke easily held his own against the murderous horde, avoiding potentially fatal blows with the grace of a dancer while delivering swift and merciless death to all with his cutlass. There was something feral about him that kept even the most fanatical Singh at bay. They were as afraid of him as if he had been a phantom.

Suddenly, something caught his attention from the corner of his eye. It was a straight foaming line rapidly crossing the waves.

"Hook! What's that?" he asked.

The Captain coolly parried a blow that would have sliced him open and neatly decapitated his opponent.

"It looks like a torpedo," he answered calmly.

The Lord of the Trees grabbed a Singh who was trying to bite his ankles and threw him overboard.

"If it hits the powder magazine, we're done for."

Hook kicked a Singh back while thrusting his blade through another.

"It's not armed," he said.

"How can you be sure?" asked Greystoke.

"Because I know Sinbad," said Hook, smiling his predator's smile. "It'll be much worse."

Indeed, the projectile hit the *Jolly Roger* without exploding. Instead, it began releasing a foul-smelling, yellow mist.

"The Prince hates technology. He sent his goddamn Jinn!"

They heard screams of terror near the stern and felt the ship creaking and bending as if under some fantastic weight. A gunner ran onto the bridge; his right arm had been torn off and a geyser of blood spurted from the wound.

"Capt–" He barely had time to croak a last warning when a huge hand grabbed him like a doll. The Jinn was a huge creature with a bald head, except for a long pigtail, slanted, green eyes, pointy ears and hands with fingers like talons. He was bare-chested and his pants disappeared into billows of golden smoke. He grabbed men and swallowed them whole in his impossibly large mouth, sometimes spitting back a wooden leg.

Bill Jukes appeared, looking haggard.

"We're taking water downbelow. It's bad!" he shouted.

"Man the pumps!" barked Shala Khan.

Hook waved a perfumed, laced handkerchief under his nose to dispel the Jinn's foul smell. He pointed to a dot just on the horizon.

"I think we've arrived at your destination, Your Lordship," he said.

"It seems you're right," said Greystoke. Then, he turned and looked at the Jinn. "Are you sure you don't need my help, Lord Hook?"

The Terror of the Seven Seas laughed.

"I'm only afraid of one thing, and since I don't hear any ticking, I know it's not nearby. We've used spells to shrink ships into bottles for centuries. A Jinn is a bit harder, but not impossible. No, Sir Phileas impressed on me that your mission is far more important. Go, Milord, go!"

Lord Greystoke hung his cutlass back on his belt, then jumped into the air, did a somersault, landed on the prow, waved good-bye to the Captain, and from there executed a perfect dive into the water.

"Good luck!" shouted Hook.

But the Lord of the Trees was already swimming rapidly, with powerful breast strokes, towards his destination: the Island of Krakatoa.

After setting foot on the shore, Lord Greystoke looked at the *Jolly Roger* in the distance. He could not tell whether Hook's optimism had prevailed and the Pirate turned Lord of the Admiralty had succeeded in bottling the Jinn. *Hook is an extremely resourceful individual*, he thought. *My money is on the Pirate.*

If Sir Phileas' information was correct–and it invariably was–Krakatoa was the lair of Prince Sinbad, who had plagued the Imperial Navy of Albion with his dreaded electric submarine, the *Siddhârta.*

Twenty-six years before, the island had been devastated by a formidable explosion, which had literally destroyed half of its landmass. The cataclysmic conflagration was distinctly heard as far away as Perth in Australia. Atmospheric shock waves reverberated around the world. Forty thousand people died in the tsunami which followed.

At first, most scientists had blamed a volcanic eruption, until it had become known in certain circles that Krakatoa was where the ever-mysterious Shangri-La Electric Company had relocated the scientist Nikola Tesla after he had parted company with Thomas Edison, only a year before. Tesla had been seeking, in his own words, *"to provide humanity with unlimited power,"* and no doubt, he had succeeded–but at what cost! However, the tree had already given up its poisonous fruit...

After the Sepoy Rebellion of 1857, Edward George Bulwer-Lytton, 1st Baron Lytton, then Governor General of India, reinforced the grip of the Albion East India Company, and crushed proposals to replace it with direct rule under the Crown. Shocked by the extent of solidarity amongst the Indian soldiers during the rebellion, Lord Lytton also recruited a corps of mystics, the Black Lodge, renegades from the Aggartha, to crush any future revolts. They proved mostly successful, but India, more than ever, suffered under Albion's yoke.

In 1899, the year Lord Kraven had tried to retire from the League of Heroes, a new threat had risen to defy Albion's power in the very place where it believed itself to be the strongest: the seas. Something–or someone–had been attacking and sinking Her Majesty's destroyers and preying on commercial shipping lines to India and the Far East.

The Press had blamed a sea monster, a theory created by the Office of Information Management. But Sir Phileas' services knew better. It was the work of the mysterious Prince Sinbad, who used a submarine craft of revolutionary design, the *Siddhârtha*, to attack Albion. Intelligence about the Indian Prince had been scarce at first. But thanks to the diligent work of his agents, in particular Sandy Arbuthnot, Lord Clanroyden, a thick file had been compiled at the Reform Club.

Additional evidence was unearthed by Sir Phileas' League when, in 1902, they came across the enigmatic Shangri-La Electric Company in the baffling case of Anton Banacek's deadly toy.[7] Directed from afar by the powerful Chinese Doctor Natas, the Shangri-La Electric Company, as it turned out, was the entity that had financed and equipped Prince Sinbad.

Then, in 1908, the Indian Prince struck a major blow: Calcutta, then Bombay, two jewels of the Albion crown, were destroyed with new bombs of almost unimaginable power. The Black Lodge, led at the time by Numa Pergyll, identified it as the *vril*, a force that he claimed had first been discovered by the ancients of Atlantis. Obviously, Sinbad had now dis-

---

[7] See *Robotor*.

covered how to store and release vast quantities of *vril* and his new *vril* bombs made him virtual master of the world.

The Empire was shaken to its very foundations. Questions were asked in Parliament. Sir Phileas was threatened with forced resignation. More manpower was expended to try to locate Sinbad's lair, but Lord Kraven was beyond the Earthly sphere [8] and Sherlock Holmes was in France, fighting a being whom even Peter Pan feared.[9] It was only when Professor Cavor made a link between the Krakatoa explosion of 1883 and the *vril* bombs that the whole picture began to emerge. The conclusion was obvious: the Shangri-La Electric Company, which had financed Tesla, had rebuilt Krakatoa and, after salvaging some of the late scientist's discoveries, had put them at the service of Prince Sinbad.

One more highly disturbing piece of information was discovered. A defector from Sinbad's crew revealed that the Prince had made not two but *three* egg-shaped *vril*-bombs in what he had poetically called his "Roc's nest." The third bomb's target was–London! The defector had not only confirmed Cavor's analysis, but provided Sir Phileas with detailed plans of Sinbad's underwater lair on Krakatoa.

Lord Hook had immediately volunteered to lead the expedition that would defang the murderous Indian once and for all, and he would be joined by the only League member available: Lord Greystoke.

The Lord of the Trees walked across the petrified island. There was some sparse vegetation, whatever had managed to regrow since the 1883 explosion, but–strangely–no signs of life: no birds, no small animals, not even insects. It was oddly disturbing.

Greystoke reflected that a portion of the island had been blown so high that some of it was probably still orbiting the Earth.

---

[8] See *The Sow*.

[9] See *The Claws of the Horla*.

Thanks to the information provided by the defector, Greystoke managed to find one of the secret entrances into Sinbad's subterranean lair. The hatch was cunningly hidden behind a dragon-shaped rock formation. He unscrewed it using his cutlass and started to climb down a metal ladder, arriving in a small tunnel which had been dug out of the rock and reinforced with metal beams. Lighting was sparse, but the keen eyes of the Lord of the Trees could easily pierce anything but the most total darkness. His sense of smell told him he was alone.

Walking along the tunnel, Greystoke arrived at a large cave that had also been excavated out of the rock. Large, bolted together metal plates had been affixed to its walls, which were otherwise bare, except for a large sculpture representing Prince Sinbad's emblem: the Lion of Sarnath, the symbol of the Indian insurgency and the sworn enemy of the Lion of Albion.

The Lord of the Trees sniffed the air but detected no human odor. Was the base empty? Had Sinbad left in another submarine and Hook fought only a diversion? He feared the worst. Prince Sinbad was a single-minded automaton with one goal and one goal only: revenge.

During the last rebellion in 1890 in the Bundelkund region of India, the Black Lodge had located Prince Sinbad's refuge and Albion had mercilessly executed his wife, the beautiful Lailah, and all his children. Swearing eternal revenge, the Prince had vanished from the surface of the Earth. It was not hard to speculate that he had eventually joined forces with the Shangri-La Electric Company which had provided him with his spectacular tools of revenge.

The *Siddhârtha* carried a crew of 40, all former thieves recruited by Sinbad. During his so-called "third journey," Sinbad had found himself trapped in a terrible storm which had lasted for several days and had finally carried him to harbor on a strange island. It was inhabited by the Singh, hideous savages, not more than two feet high and covered with reddish fur. Throwing themselves into the waves, they had surrounded the *Siddhârtha*, swarming up the ship's sides with such speed and agility that they almost seemed to fly.

That day, Sinbad had been rescued by the unforeseen arrival of Peter Pan and his diminutive fairy companion. Peter had brokered a truce with the Singh, who quickly became some of Sinbad's most trusted allies. The Boy Who Would Not Grow Up and the Indian Prince had soon discovered the rightness of the old saying, "The enemy of my enemy is my friend." And from that day onward, Prince Sinbad the Sailor had joined forces with Pan's Resistance.

A door hidden in the rock slid out and a man appeared. Greystoke recognized him at once: it was Prince Sinbad: tall, burning coal-black eyes, but this time, he looked sickly, pale and sweating. He seemed to even have difficulty staying on his feet as he staggered forward.

"Welcome to my humble abode, Your Lordship," said Sinbad, bowing his head. "Your reputation precedes you. It makes me proud that Sir Phileas thought me worthy of such an opponent."

The Lord of the Trees relaxed. Oratory jousts before a battle were almost an accepted convention; Sinbad would not strike as long as the banter went on.

"The pleasure is all mine, Your Highness," said Greystoke. "Some thought you might have died in the Calcutta explosion."

Prince Sinbad laughed, a laugh tinged with regret.

"Alas, it was my faithful Hindbad whose body you recovered. He fulfilled his destiny and repaid his karma."

Greystoke noted that Sinbad's turban barely covered several abscesses filled with pus.

"Repaid his karma?"

"Yes. Hindbad was a coward. When the sorcerers of Albion came, he was afraid and abandoned Lailah and my children, whose protection I had entrusted to him. He repaid that blood debt in Calcutta by sacrificing himself for the Cause. As you have doubtless gathered, my *vril* bombs must be activated by a human being... Soon, it will be my turn, and your proud capital, too, will be incinerated..."

The Prince remained silent for a moment, as if envisioning and relishing in advance the moment of his revenge. Then, he continued:

"If I may ask you a question, Lord Greystoke... The Empire is no more yours than it is mine. Why do you serve it so loyally?"

The Lord of the Trees feared that question, with which he had often grappled. But he had an answer.

"I don't want History to repeat itself. I saw what happened to the Great Apes when Man first invaded the jungles of Congo. The same might happen now that the Fairy Folk have crossed the aether. And Albion is the bulwark of Humanity's defense."

"Then you bear them no ill will? How wonderful. I cannot say the same. They are like an evil octopus reaching its tentacles throughout the world, sucking up life wherever it finds it. I am sworn to destroy it—and so I shall. Open Sesame!"

At a gesture from the Prince, another, larger door slid open and the 40 thieves came out. Lord Greystoke crouched, cutlass in hand. But his weapon was suddenly torn out from his grasp. The blade flew through the air and hit one of the metal plates, where it remained stuck.

"Electro-magnets, Your Lordship," said Sinbad. ""I'm afraid we all know your prodigious fighting abilities."

The 40 thieves raised their own ceramic scimitars and launched themselves at the Lord of the Trees. The first man aimed at cutting the Hero's head off with a swift stroke of his blade, but Greystoke rolled down and, with a fast kick, broke the thief's ankles. The man collapsed on the rocky floor. Swiftly, the Lord of the Trees grabbed the man's scimitar and eviscerated the next two men who were rushing him. Then, with skills mastered in the Halls of Ancient Kôr, he proceeded to mercilessly cut down his assailants, one after the other.

He thought to himself that he expected better from Sinbad's notorious 40 thieves. His opponents, far from being the threat they might have been, were weak, disorganized. *Even Kraven might have won such a fight*, he smiled grimly. It was obvious that they were suffering from the same affliction that was ravaging their master's body.

Lord Greystoke dispatched the last two men, then counted the bodies.

There were only 39.

Looking at Sinbad while grabbing back his cutlass, he saw that the Prince was attempting to flee. Obviously, his diversion had failed and he was now retreating towards the *Siddhârta*, which must be carrying the last *vril* bomb. *A chance that Hook's attack had disrupted Sinbad's last journey*, he thought.

Greystoke ran after Sinbad, but the Prince had already entered an open shaft elevator that took him down.

As he rushed down the metal stairs to catch up, Greystoke shouted:

"You're dying, Your Highness. Just as are the rest of your men."

Sinbad wiped some ichor from his eyes.

"It's the *vril*, Your Lordship. Long-term exposure is always fatal. Doctor Natas probably knew it, but failed to mention it. No matter, I still have enough life in me to carry out my final mission."

Beneath his feet, Lord Greystoke saw a vast, underground basin. The *Siddhârtha* was moored there, waiting. There was obviously an underwater tunnel that connected directly with the ocean. Sinbad was almost in reach of the submarine. The Hero knew that if he managed to escape, all would be lost.

He jumped from the last metal landing, grabbed a chain hanging from the ceiling above and swung through the air. He managed to land only a few feet from the Prince, within yards of the *Siddhârtha*'s hatch.

Sinbad reached in his garments for a Malay kriss and threw it at the Lord of the Trees. The Hero avoided it easily and lunged at the Prince. Despite his sickness, Sinbad was still a dangerous foe. He pulled out a thin dagger and struck Greystoke, burying the blade in his arm. But the Lord of the Trees, grabbing the chain that he had used to catch up with the Indian, quickly wrapped it around his opponent's neck and pulled.

Sinbad was still wrestling, trying to free himself. The pilot of the *Siddhârtha*, the last of the 40 thieves, rushed out to aid his master. There was a gunshot. A bullet whizzed by. *It is time to finish this*, thought Greystoke. He gave a mighty pull on the chain and heard a gruesome snap.

Prince Sinbad the sailor was dead, his neck broken.

Without exhibiting any outward sign of pain, Greystoke pulled the blade from his arm and threw it at the pilot. The last thief fell into the dark waters of the basin, blood spurting from his throat.

Lord Greystoke knew that he now had to dispose of the *vril* bomb. Cavor had come up with a plan, but first he had to find the deadly device.

He climbed through the *Siddhârtha*'s hatch and began searching the submarine. There was no egg-shaped device on the bridge, just various instruments of navigation. He ran through the metal corridors, briefly looked through the crew's quarters, before reaching Sinbad's cabin.

The metal walls were lined with shelves containing numerous books and samples of the most amazing-looking marine fauna and flora in glass jars. The floors were covered with thick Persian rugs. There even was a large piano organ decorated with pearls and sea shells which occupied one end of the room. Electric light flooded everything; it was shed from four unpolished globes half sunk in the ceiling panels–but one of the globes seemed to have burned itself out.

Greystoke broke the opaque glass cover and, inside, found what he was seeking: the *vril* bomb, a grey, metallic ovoid. If the mission was successful, Sir Phileas and Cavor had agreed that it was best to destroy the bomb in the safe confines of Krakatoa. But to do it without sacrificing one of their best agents had been a quandary, until Greystoke himself had suggested the perfect solution.

Grabbing the deadly device, the Lord of the Trees ran from the submarine. He had no problem locating an exit elevator that deposited him in a cave, just outside a sandy beach on the island's southern shore.

There, Greystoke took two miniature implements that had been manufactured at his request and which he had kept inside the handle of his cutlass.

One was a small *vaporisator*, a device that could spray white paint, and the other, a silver whistle. Quickly, he spray-painted the bomb a pearly white. Then, stepping back inside the cave, he blew the whistle.

He barely had time to hide before a gigantic shadow passed over the beach. It was a Roc, the legendary bird that Prince Sinbad had found and domesticated during one of his "journeys." The nightmarish creature could easily lift an elephant. Sinbad had used it during his attack on Bangalore the previous year.

Mistaking the bomb for one of its eggs, the towering bird grabbed it in its claws and began to fly away, ever upward.

Greystoke did not have to wait long. An apocalyptic silver-blue lightning bolt burst from the sky, tearing apart the very atmosphere. For a brief second, the Lord of the Trees even saw the stars.

Then, everything returned to normal. It was as if nothing had ever happened.

Half-an-hour later, a row boat from the *Jolly Roger*, commanded by Mister Smee, came to pick him up. As they approached the ship, Greystoke saw that it was in sorry shape, all its sails badly torn, but basically sea-worthy.

"Another week of repairs," said Smee, "and we'll be on our way, Your Lordship. Which is a good thing, as far as you're concerned."

"Why?" asked Greystoke.

"The Captain just received an aethergram from London. You're needed at the League of Heroes."

Excerpt from The Encyclopaedia Albianenses
1912 edition

After the House of Lords rejected the Fairy Folk Pension Act of 1909, Herbert Asquith and his chancellor, David Lloyd George, asked King Edward-Albert VII to create a large number of new Liberal peers to give their Government a majority. But the King refused, insisting that the issue should be put to the electorate in a General Election.

In the middle of this dispute, the King fell ill. Edward-Albert VII died at Buckingham Palace on May 6, 1910, leaving the throne to his son, King George V.

The Sons of the Pharaoh
(March 1911)

Lord Kraven was crouching above the Turkish toilet, a smelly hole dug in the floor of his cell. A small-minded man would have said that he was emptying his guts, but one with a greater perspective would have known that he was waiting to see Doctor Auguste de Grandin, an Agent of the French Government.

The Savior of the Empire had arrived in Cairo a couple of weeks before. He had settled in a discreet guest house and had been met by Dr. Moreau, who had been dispatched to Egypt by Sir Phileas for the occasion. That evening, despite the blistering heat, Kraven had undergone brain surgery. The purpose of the operation was to disable his speech functions. Moreau had assured him that it could easily be reversed when they returned to London. Before the journey, Holmes had taught Kraven sign language, so that he could communicate undetected even in a crowd of Egyptian beggars. The success of his new mission depended on it.

Lord Kraven had since then spent his days wandering through Cairo's maze of dark alleys and narrow streets, dressed in rags, looking wretched. He was tired of the nagging, monotonous song of the zumarra, of begging for a few piasters in this dusty atmosphere, full of the smell of spices and leather, of having his skin bitten by the acarids that dug deep in his flesh to deposit scabies.

He had come to Cairo because, just before Christmas, a young researcher from the Ministry of Defense had come to the attention of his superiors. His name was Thomas Lawrence–a young man with piercing blue eyes. He had stated his concern in a report over the number of explosions that had lately happened in Egypt. An amount which, according to Lawrence, was above the norm and could not be explained by negligence and fate. Sir Phileas, whose attention was, at the time, focused on the disappearance, near Gibraltar, of a ship transporting Cavorite had taken notice of the report and had sent Lord Kraven to investigate.[10]

The secret service agent finished wiping himself, put his sarouel back–a very practical garment in these circumstances–and dragged himself to his straw mattress. Lord Kraven, together with some 5,000 other patients, was locked in Cairo's Lunatic Asylum! Most of the other patients were rapists and murderers waiting for an improbable trial date. His task was to find the mysterious author of these terrorist bombings–and then eliminate him.

The information that Kraven had gathered during his wanderings through the city had enabled him to locate the source of the explosions. They were the work of a network of terrorists working under cover for an ultra-nationalist politician. In the bazaars, they had been dubbed the "Sons of the Pharaoh." Their purpose was to threaten the interests of the great foreign powers in Egypt–mostly France and Albion. To

---

[10] See *The Werewolf of Gibraltar*.

achieve its goals, the Sons had enlisted the help of a sorcerer, who could psychically and remotely detonate bombs made with the Cavorite stolen from the ship hijacked near Gibraltar.

Until now, there had been only a few minor explosions to create an atmosphere of fear amongst the population. Anonymous posters on the walls of Cairo even blamed Albion. Kraven had managed to pry a list of future targets out of an informer. One was a diplomatic banquet at the Shepheard Hotel, another, the Assouan Dam.

Lord Kraven had immediately gotten in touch with the French Embassy. That had not been easy, as the guards had refused to believe that the filthy beggar who smelled of hashish was the same man who, five years earlier, had graced the front page of *Le Figaro* when he solved the case of the Marquis de Charançolles.[11]

Since then, Lord Kraven had been waiting for Auguste de Grandin to arrive. The Frenchman was a world-renowned alienist who would, from time to time, help the Deuxième Bureau. Some whispered that his services were provided more due to blackmail than out of a strong sense of patriotism. The man was reputed to love women and gambling, but from past experience, Kraven knew that he was a very effective agent. De Grandin had joined the Asylum's medical team after they had heard rumors of an inmate capable of opening the doors of his cell from a distance.

His mission was to inform Kraven as soon as he had located the sorcerer. The Hero, on the other hand, had had no difficulty, after days spent outside starving and being baked by the Sun, faking insanity. To amuse himself, the Savior of Albion was building a cockroach trap based on those used by Malaysians to capture tigers alive. It was nearing completion when the door opened wide.

De Grandin stood before him, thin and straight in his white coat, his face decorated with a well-trimmed moustache. He was accompanied by a giant, whose chest glistened with

---

[11] See *The Case of the One-Armed Marquis*.

49

sweat. The Frenchman made a face, took out a perfumed handkerchief and said that he wouldn't be long.

The punch caught Kraven right in the face. He hit the wall and fell at the giant's feet. The man tried to kick him, but Kraven managed to avoid the blow by rolling away quickly. He glanced at the Frenchman who was yawning, looking bored. Kraven got up and waited; as the giant stepped forward, he kicked the legs out from under him and delivered a powerful *atemi* to his shaved skull. The man fell down face first–on the very nail that anchored the cockroach trap. He screamed, tore the bottom of his trousers and pressed the fabric against his bleeding eye.

De Grandin offered his hand to Kraven and indicated that he should follow him.

"Mes compliments, Monsieur Kraven! I had to make sure you were the man I expected. I hope you still have some strength left in you, for I now know where to find our patient."

When they reached the end of the corridor, the alienist handed a big copper key to Kraven.

"He's in here. Forgive me for not staying with you, but I have another case to attend. The daughter of a very wealthy merchant. They say the poor girl suffers from nymphomania. But she can be an asset for France–if properly handled. I congratulate you again for your perseverance. You men from Albion have resolve second to none. Please close the door behind you when you leave."

Inside, the cell was completely dark. It took a few seconds for Kraven's eyes to adjust so he could see the sorcerer.

He was sitting in a corner, drawing intricate patterns on the muddy wall. His face was covered with a ragged beard and he was dressed in rags. Young Lawrence had warned them about spells, a millennia-old tradition in Cairo, where some of the practitioners of the Dark Arts used magic dating back to the great Im-Ho-Tep himself. Under certain circumstances, a spell of protection could rot a man's soul in mere seconds.

The sorcerer whispered:

"I was waiting for you. But remember that, even if you kill me, you will not win the fight. The Sons of Im-Ho-Tep will go on. Others will come after me and will throw you out of Egypt."

The sorcerer uttered an incantation. But before he could finish it, Lord Kraven pictured the counterspell in his mind, crossed the mystic's protective barrier–now rendered useless– and quickly broke the man's neck.

The Empire had been saved once again.

Breaking News from Reuters,
(August 4, 1914)

Albion Declares War On Prussia!

Albion is in a state of war with Prussia. It was officially stated at the Foreign Office last night that the Empire of Albion declared war against the Holy Prussian Empire at 7 p.m.

The Albion Ambassador in Berlin has been handed his passport. War was Prussia's reply to our request that she should respect the neutrality of Belgica, whose territories we were bound in honor and by treaty obligations to maintain inviolate.

Speaking in a crowded and hushed House, King George V yesterday afternoon made the following statement: "We have made a request to the Prussian Kaiser, William, that we shall have a satisfactory assurance as to Belgican neutrality before midnight tonight. The Prussian reply to our request, officially stated last night, was unsatisfactory."

A Council of Heroes
(August 1914)

"Would you like us to bend over an' let ourselves be reamed, too?"

Dressed in a fringed leather jacket and leather trousers, wearing a Stetson on his head, Kid Colt stepped away from the conference table.

Lord Kraven and Lord Greystoke were already tired of arguing with the fiery American, but felt it their duty to do so.

"That's how you are, you limey bastards! You let the Darkies kick yer asses out of Egypt and you keep beggin' for more! Well, don't count on the good ole U.S. of A. to bail you out this time!"

The well-known American hero had made the trip from Washington to announce the Senate's decision: the people from the United States did not wish to get involved in a European conflict.

"We understand your Government's position," replied Kraven, "but we were hoping that you, personally, might join us in a communiqué of support. Considering our past association in San Francisco, I thought that a token of solidarity would not be unwarranted."

"Well, OK. Lemme have your com-mew-nee-kay, pardner, and ah'll tell you what ah think."

Kid Colt took the sheet of paper Holmes handed him, threw it in the air, drew his gun and, with lightning speed, shot a hole right through its middle.

"There! Ya kin add that to yer fancy speech. An' you, monkey boy, ya better stay put, if ya wanna stay airtight. Yer balls are showin' under that loincloth of yers, that's disgustin', man! Lissen to me, all, and lissen good. We don't give a flyin' fig about yer pansy Empire an' its fairies and its faggot magic. I know some guys back home who wouldn't be sorry if them Krauts kicked the hell outta you. The Boche, at least, are like us. None of that la-di-da. Call me after yer war's over. If you guys make it all in one piece, you an' yer blasted Empire, then mebbe we can talk agin. Like real men."

The Bertram's Incident

"Yes, he is still inside, but I must warn you, gentlemen, it isn't a pretty sight."

Major James West III of the U.S. Secret Service and the Bertram's Hotel's Manager stepped aside to let Lord Kraven and Lord Greystoke pass.

West had had his men cordon off the floor and question the hotel staff. Dressed in dark suits, they stood guard motionless at both ends of the red corridor like tin soldiers fresh out of their boxes.

Earlier that evening, Sir Phileas Fogg had also arranged for a security cordon to be set up around the Bertram's Hotel, preventing anyone from either entering or leaving.

Normally, the Albion and American secret services did not cooperate well with each other, but this time, the extraordinary aspects of the situation had forced Major West to ask for Sir Phileas' assistance. He had been seen immediately at the Reform Club and had told Sir Phileas the facts. The latter had quickly issued orders to quarantine the Bertram's and evacuate its guests, who were all being interrogated individually.

Then, he had gone to the League's headquarters. Kraven and Greystoke could hardly refuse the mission, even though they both felt it was beneath their dignity.

Lord Kraven observed Major West. The handsome Secret Service man looked embarrassed, almost ashamed. The Savior of the Empire liked the American and could well understand how he must have felt. To be obliged to ask Sir Phileas for assistance must have been quite a blow to him.

The two Lords had come by cab so as to not attract any attention. Kraven had tried to calm Greystoke, whose temper was growing out of control. His eyes ablaze with anger, his long black mane unkempt, the Lord of the Trees' fury remained in check, but for how long?

"What has that fool done this time?" he muttered between his clenched teeth.

Greystoke could barely contain himself. Sir Phileas' news had not surprised him, and Major West's warning did not faze him either.

"You can go in now, gentlemen," added West. "But be careful. He's armed."

Kraven signaled his companion that he would go in first. He had emptied his gun and replaced its bullets with stun darts in the cab.

He walked into the suite.

The dark atmosphere was oppressive; the room reeked of tobacco, alcohol and sex. It was a mess: leather clothes thrown everywhere, cigar butts had burned holes in the Persian rug and newspapers covered the floor. There were also dozens of empty bottles on the coffee table: they had once held gin, bourbon, brandy and whisky. Without paying attention to those, Kraven grabbed a much smaller bottle, this one full of a milky white liquid and immediately spotted the syringes with their bent needles.

Cocaine, from the London firm of Curtis & Co., which legally sold a 10% solution.

Kid Colt, the Lone Star of Texas and All-American Hero, had been having quite a party, far from the prying eyes of the press and his countrymen.

Lord Greystoke sniffed the air.

"Colt is still here–and he's not alone."

The Lord of the Trees stepped forward, itching for a fight. But Kraven was ready. He blocked his way.

Kid Colt sat in a comfortable armchair, his dressing gown half-open, a bottle of whisky in his hand and a sawed-off Winchester rifle on his knees.

"Ah! Lord-Almighty-Kraven has arrived in full Chorley & Sullivan uniform with his pet monkey. Have a seat, boys! As we say on the border, *mi casa es su casa*."

The American kicked a stool across the room.

"Come and have a look, Kraven," said Greystoke.

The Lord of the Trees was kneeling by the foot of the bed. There was a Fairy Girl crumpled between the sheets, her cheeks wet with tears. Of course, it was impossible to guess her age but she looked very young. Feathers from a tear in the mattress drifted around her like angels trying to bring her comfort. She was naked and covered in cuts and bite marks. A huge bruise on her tiny chest prevented her from breathing normally, and one of her arms looked broken. Kraven gently turned her over and saw that her wings had been partially torn off.

"My God..." he whispered.

"Our Father-Who-Art-In-Heaven had nuthin' to do with this, pardner. It's the work of a man. A real man."

Kid Colt stood up. The American began parading around the room, his dressing gown now completely open, dressed only in a pair of boxer shorts. He was massively drunk and stoned. Greystoke took off his coat and laid it over the poor girl. As usual, he was naked beneath it, except for his loin-cloth.

"Come on, monkey-boy, give her a try!" the Texan taunted him. "But lemme warn you, after me, she probably won't feel a thing."

The Lord of the Trees did not respond. He walked to the window and opened the blinds. He stayed there for a long moment looking at the Moon–not Peter Pan's star but the goddess that looked after his tribe in Congo.

Suddenly, he threw back his head and cried out loudly.

"What's wrong, monkey-boy? Ain't she hairy enough for ya? Well, then mebbe you should try..."

The American stopped in mid-sentence. Lord Greystoke had rushed him and grabbed him by the throat. Then, he threw the Texan against the wall. Kid Colt went through the partition, rolled on his side and got his hands on a Bowie knife.

"You wanna play?" asked the Texan. "I've been wantin' that for a long time."[12]

The Texan was playing with the Bowie knife, throwing it from one hand to the other. Suddenly, he sprang forward, but

---

[12] See *The Ghost of the Hudson.*

the Lord of the Trees easily avoided his attack and punched him in the ribs.

Colt moaned softly and hit his opponent from behind. His drunkenness, however, kept him from delivering a fatal blow. The blade caused only a superficial wound. The Lord of the Trees turned and struck the American on the temple, twice. Colt dropped his knife and collapsed onto the carpet. Lord Greystoke seized the weapon and grasped the Texan by the hair, holding his neck to the blade.

Suddenly, he felt the barrel of Kraven's stun gun on his shoulder.

"Please, my friend, don't force me to do this," said the Savior of the Empire.

The American Secret Service men walked into the room, their guns pointed at Greystoke. The Peer of Albion made a low roar; he was ready to fight. He most probably would have won as well. But Kraven whispered in his ear:

"Forget about it. There's nothing you can do and he isn't worth it."

Kid Colt got up, blood running from his ears.

"He's right. I've got diplomatic immunity. They won't charge me. And I'll tell you sumthin' else. You'd all better do like me, fuck them Fairies an' give 'em all a lot of bastards–if they can be got pregnant, that is. That would keep that faggot Peter busy and he wouldn't be after yer kids anymore."

Major West asked them to leave the room.

"Thank you very much for your assistance, gentlemen. We'll take over now. And we'll see to the, er, girl."

The two Heroes found themselves back on the street, outside the Bertram's. The fresh air revived them.

"Kraven, would you have shot me?" asked Lord Greystoke.

The Savior of the Empire smiled and handed his friend a pack of cigarettes.

"No. But I would have had to knock you out. And the Office of Information Management wouldn't have been happy. Bad publicity, that."

Sir Phileas Fogg was waiting for them in his private Rolls-Royce, hiding behind its windows' tinted glasses. Lord Greystoke turned towards his companion.

"Do you have a pen and paper?"

Kraven handed over his leather-covered notebook and a silver pencil. The Lord of the Trees tore out a page and scribbled a few lines down. Then, he gave the piece of paper to Sir Phileas.

"My resignation letter."

The fat man ignored the paper.

"It's not as simple as that, Lord Greystoke. Need I remind you that you volunteered to serve the Empire? Nobody leaves the League of Heroes, except on my terms. You know too many secrets, dangerous secrets, to be allowed to quit now. And as a further motivation, may I add, Your Lordship, that the Reform Club is presently the only thing that stands between a certain tribe of anthropoids in Congo and a well-organized safari..."

The Lord of the Trees straightened up, took a deep breath, and crumpled the letter, which fell to the ground. Sir Phileas smiled benevolently and patted his hand.

"There, there. That's much better, Your Lordship. I understand that you're tired; you do need a bit of rest. We run a quiet and peaceful village in Northern Wales where our agents can relax and forget their stress between missions. Why don't you go there for a holiday? You'll find it very soothing. The future looks quite difficult and my Heroes must be ready."

Communiqué from the League of Heroes
(published in The Times, *August 1914)*

In order to prevent a catastrophic war, we have tried every possible avenue of compromise, listened to every offer of negotiation. It was always the League's goal to help reach a peaceful settlement in accordance with the rules of Honor and Law. Alas, such a settlement was not to be found.

Having failed to secure the peace, we must, regretfully, now prepare for war, on the ground, in the air and above the water, throughout the Empire.

We, the League of Heroes, call on every able-bodied man to join us and serve, all united together under the Union Jack, all united together in the service of peace and freedom.

God Save the King!

The Lusitania Affair
(May 1915)

"We're sinking!"

When he heard the cry, English Bob opened the door, which gave onto the cabin next to his, picked up his rucksack at the bottom of Lord Kraven's bed and started running towards the upper deck.

In the corridors, the passengers were mobbing a Cunard steward to learn the reasons for the terrible shock they had felt, which had shaken the "Queen of the Seas" so violently. They didn't look as if they were as yet aware that she had just been torpedoed.

English Bob walked past the officers' quarters, took a gun from the gun rack and headed towards the radio operator's cabin.

"I'm an agent of His Majesty's Secret Service. Can you tell me what's going on?"

"If you can read Morse code, you're welcome to have a look for yourself," replied the man.

The cable read: *SUBMARINE ACTIVE IN SOUTHERN PART OF IRISH CHANNEL. LAST HEARD OF 20 MILES SOUTH OF CONNINGBEG LIGHT VESSEL.*

So he had been right, thought English Bob. The *Lusitania*, with her 2,000 passengers, had just been torpedoed off the Old Head of Kinsale in Southern Ireland by a Prussian U-boat.

The sea journey had started rather well. He and Lord Kraven had left New York on May 1, their only concern being to recover the secret Royal Navy plans stolen the month before from the Admiralty. They had quickly identified the thief: a stage magician hired by Cunard to entertain the passengers, who had hidden the documents in one of his props. But English Bob had been struck by sea sickness and had had to stay in his cabin most of the way. He had been swallowing quinine pills as if they were Cadbury sweets. The youth managed to control a new attack of nausea and spoke to the radio operator:

"Why didn't the Captain change course?"

"We'd received another cable telling us the danger had passed and there were no U-boats in the vicinity."

English Bob left the radio operator and dashed along the gangways, bumping into sailors running from the engine room. Water was already reaching his ankles. He took a ladder and arrived on the upper deck. At port side boat station No. 2, a junior Third Officer was in charge. Standing on the after davit, he was trying to keep order and explain that, due to the heavy list, the lifeboats could not be lowered. English Bob realized that meant getting the passengers already in the lifeboats to get out so they could lower the boats to the rail, but he doubted the Third Officer would be that lucky. A disaster was clearly under way.

"English Bob, I presume?

The youth turned towards the woman who had spoken. She was dressed all in black. Through her veil, her fine features were just visible.

"Yes?"

"I think you'll find Lord Kraven on the bridge with Captain Turner."

"You should go to the starboard side, madam. The way things are going here, they'll never succeed in launching these boats, and it won't be long before the ship sinks."

The woman smiled in a resigned way.

"I already lost my husband on the *Titanic*. Professor Augustus Van Dusen. The so-called 'Thinking Machine.' One can't always escape one's fate, I suppose."

Meanwhile, seemingly indifferent to the panic sweeping through the ship, Lord Kraven stood straight, facing the sea. He was nearly naked, dressed only in a pair of swimming trunks and smoked a cigar that Alfred Vanderbilt had generously offered him.

Earlier, before the Prussian torpedo had struck, the ship's band had been playing *The Blue Danube*, then *Tipperary*, and for a moment, Lord Kraven had found himself transported back to the magic days of Brighton Beach. He still heard the music in his head.

Watching events through the periscope of the U-20, Kapitan-Leutnant Schwieger could not believe that so much havoc could have been wrought by just one torpedo. He noted in his log that an unusually heavy detonation had taken place and observed that a second explosion had also occurred which he put down to boilers, coal or powder, not suspecting that the *Lusitania* had actually been carrying 1,248 cases of live three-inch shrapnel shells (each case containing four shells) destined for use by the Royal Artillery. He also noticed that the torpedo had hit the ship forward of where he had aimed it. Schwieger brought the periscope down and the U-20 headed back to sea.

English Bob made his way as fast as he could, even signing an autograph or two along the way, before finally reaching the Savior of the Empire.

"Ah! Here you are, my boy!" Kraven pointed at the periscope. "That is a U-boot of the Prussian Imperial Navy, propelled by two 600-horsepower electric motors with armament consisting of four 19.7 inch torpedo tubes, plus one 4.1 inch deck gun. Ships like these have sunk many Allied ships in the past few months. But, by Jove, that's enough rambling for now. Did you bring me my little toy?"

English Bob took the magnetic Cavorite Mine out of the bag he had been carrying and helped Lord Kraven attach it to his back.

"See you later in Queenstown!"

The Hero threw his cigar into the sea, climbed onto the railings, and under the awe-filled eyes of the passengers, who momentarily forgot their panic, executed a perfect dive into the ocean.

"Is he always like that?"

English Bob looked at the small man who was pulling on his sleeve. He wore a derby hat and a checkered jacket that made him look like a Cubist painting; he puffed on a cigarette and held out a card.

"Allow me to introduce myself: Charles Frohman, theatrical producer. The stage magician you nabbed was one of my clients. If ever your boss decides to go into show business, tell him I'm ready to take him on."

English Bob ignored him; his eyes remained fixed on the grey ocean.

Two minutes later, there was a huge explosion not far off starboard, followed by a rain of debris and an oil slick. English Bob guessed accurately that the predator U-Boat was now sinking towards the bottom of the sea, where it would soon be joined by its prey.

Toast of Rittmeister Baron von Tod
before Prussian Chief of Staff Paul von Hindenburg
(August 1915)

We will stop fighting only when the House of Windsor is again called Saxe-Coburg—and when all the Fairy Folk speak Prussian!

Albion Is Burning!
(January 1916)

"The Flying Dragons are back!"

The crowd, screaming and running, was blocking traffic along Piccadilly. Lord Kraven decided to leave his now useless car where it was. He got out, taking his binoculars. From where he stood, he could clearly see the shapes of the Prussian pilots, dressed in black leather overcoats, in the cabins attached to the crimson bellies of the zeppelins. The three airships loomed above the avenue, waiting for the order to fire.

Suddenly, everything stopped. Everyone looking up saw the zeppelins drop their fatal eggs at exactly the same time. A minute later, three conflagrations erupted along the street, forming a fiery wall of molten debris and charred flesh.

Lord Kraven held his breath to avoid inhaling the burning air. An almost unbearable wave of heat slammed him against a brick wall. Only his asbestos uniform saved him from becoming welded to it, like the other hapless bystanders who were being turned into puddles of melted flesh and bone. Kraven repressed the urge to throw up as he saw hard-boiled eyes, teeth and body parts floating along the gutter.

The Prussian attack had been meticulously coordinated; it had begun with the destruction of St. Paul's Cathedral, then of the Crystal Palace. The last message sent by Sir Phileas mentioned that there had been heavy losses among the King's entourage, but the Monarch was safe. Peers of the Kingdom had perished under the melting lead of the Cathedral's once proud dome; many Fairy Folks had been crucified by crystalline shards during the destruction of the Palace. Kraven thought that was ironic, as Ice Daggers were ordinarily among the Wee Folk's favorite weapons.

The zeppelins were moving towards the Houses of Parliament. Kraven decided to follow them. Although he was slowed by the carnage and the molten tar that made walking difficult, he managed to reach Piccadilly Circus–a veritable sea of corpses–circled the ruins of the Criterion Club and began walking along Whitcomb Street.

The war killed with no hint of racial discrimination. Here, he saw a Lost Boy, looking like a repulsive pile of burnt leaves; there, he spied a man, mad with grief, still singing a lullaby to a lump of coal that had once been a baby.

Lord Kraven trekked on, despite the black, acrid smoke that burned his eyes and throat. He walked towards Queen Victoria's Embankment. On Northumberland Avenue, he spotted firemen trying to create a firebreak by blowing up several buildings. They were assisted by survivors of the Steam Guard, protected inside their MechaMen suits. They smashed the empty houses with their steel-clad fists and feet. But it was too late.

The Kaiser's *Fliegenden Drachen* had reached the air above Whitehall and Parliament Street. Kraven turned his head to avoid being blinded by the explosion. The Admiralty, the Treasury, New Scotland Yard and the Ministry of War, the lifeblood of the Empire, were all swallowed by a gigantic fireball which broke through the clouds and reached to the Heavens.

Perhaps because of it, rain began to fall. *Evil provides its own cure*, thought Kraven.

No one had seen the Flying Dragons arrive. Undoubtedly, they had been cloaked by a protective spell cast by the Fairy Folk who had decided to join forces with Prussia.

Kraven could no longer really feel pain; his body was burned in multiple places, his lips were cracking at the corner of his mouth. He had decided to return to the docks when he was nearly knocked over by a running man from the Homefront Volunteers. With his flat, silver helmet, he looked like Hermes sent by Zeus–not an inappropriate analogy under the circumstances.

"Did you hear King George's speech?" he asked. "His Majesty spoke directly to our minds through magical means, according to what they said–it's even better than the radio! He wants us to remain cool-headed–bloody funny right now, ain't it?–and find shelter in the Underground. I don't know what you're planning to do, but me, I'm not dilly-dallying up here."

Kraven hadn't heard the King's telepathic broadcast. He only knew that Sir Phileas had organized the evacuation of His Majesty, his wife and their six children, towards Balmoral. He looked as the man ran on, overwhelmed by a feeling of defeat.

The fire was progressing towards Westminster Abbey. Hundreds of Londoners, men and fairies alike, had gathered on the docks in a vain attempt to escape. Some had thrown themselves into the Thames, but had been boiled alive, for the Prussians had set it ablaze with Grecian fire. The firemen watered down the few survivors, and by sheer mercy, some had drowned instead of being consumed alive.

Then Kraven, like all the others, saw Lord James Hook's magnificent ship, his *Jolly Roger* flag still flying defiantly, collapsed, sails burning, a twisted wreckage. Her captain stood proudly on her bridge, lighting two cigars at the flame of his own funeral pyre. Rising his hook up in the air, as if to burst the hydrogen-inflated bellies of the zeppelins, or perhaps consign them to a Hell known only to him, he uttered a series of curses, followed by a few, final words to Peter Pan that no one but he could hear, then he, too, was engulfed by the flames.

Kraven continued walking along the Thames towards Waterloo Bridge and saw crowds of Indians and Lost Boys running away from the Isle of Dogs with no belongings other than the few items they could carry with them. People were massing on the piers and a well-known stockbroker was offering the surviving Pirates an incredibly high price for a simple barge. In vain. The Terror of the Seven Seas, among whom Kraven recognized Mr. Smee, Cecco and Bill Jukes, were crying while singing the *Jolly Roger* Song. The crocodile would have at last prevailed if it, too, had not been boiled alive.

"This way!"

Lord Greystoke stood in front of a pub by the river. He looked to be seriously drunk. At the time, Lord Kraven did not notice, but later he would remember the odd way the Lord of the Trees was dressed. For the first time, as far as he could remember, he was wearing a shirt, a tie, a jacket and striped trousers. The tie was even adorned with a tie pin.

"This way, my friend, but be mindful of the bottles of gin; they fly quite low tonight!"

Lord Kraven joined his friend at the counter. Greystoke sat on a stool that could have been made of baobab, and looked at the urban jungle with supreme aloofness. He proceeded to fill two glasses with gin and drank a toast:

"To the end of one era, and the beginning of a new one!"

The Savior of the Empire let the liquid wash away his exhaustion.

"Don't you find it all rather ridiculous, Kraven?" asked Greystoke.

"What do you mean?"

"The League of Heroes, Prince Spada, Doctor Fatal and all of that rigmarole."

Lord Kraven was used to his friend's changing moods. More than once, with Holmes' help, he had checked Greystoke's anger to prevent him from being found out by the Press. The Lord of the Trees was being slowly suffocated by his contact with civilization, and for some time now, he had been drinking far too much.

"We are the Protectors of the Empire, my friend," replied Kraven. "The soldiers of good in the fight against evil. Surely, that is both moral and useful."

Lord Greystoke nodded.

"Yes, of course, I always forget that we are the good guys," he said with irony. "Always ready to defeat a new threat, to foil a new convoluted plot, to stop a new would-be world conqueror. But it all sounds very hollow right now. Consider our foes, Kraven. They always tell us their plans in great details after they capture us, they always make a last minute mistake which enables us to escape and defeat them... Yes, we win, but only until the next time, for they always return..."

"Sometimes, they die. Like Spada."

"Well, yes, but it doesn't seem to change things, does it? The evil prince is replaced by the idiot doctor or the crazy scientist. Instead of kidnapping the Prince of Wales, they'll seek to poison London's drinking water or create a race of giant dwarfs or God only knows what other absurdity! We're not evolving, my friend, there is only an illusion of change. All the dangers, our battles, our victories are the same, repeated over and over, as if somehow it was meant to make us feel safer."

"You forget Peter Pan."

Lord Greystoke filled his glass to the brim, letting the alcohol spill onto the counter.

"Ah, yes, the Boy Who Would Not Grow Up. No, I didn't forget him. A mischievous brat who, alone, would justify our existence? So much effort and money spent to stop a baby snatcher when, every day, our streets are filled with murders and rapists that no one cares about."

"What are you getting at?"

The Lord of the Trees shrugged.

"I don't have a clue. But tonight, my mind is made up. I'm returning to the Congo to live amongst my people. Remember my words, my friend. This war is real, this slaughter is real. But for the rest, the Fairy Folk and all of the crazy schemes of that fat tub of lard–I mean Fogg–it's up to you to decide when the time comes."

Suddenly, Greystoke dropped his glass, jumped over the counter and landed near a trap door that led to the basement.

"Did you hear that?" he asked.

"Hear what?"

The Lord of the Trees sniffed at the lock, then forced it open with one hand.

"There's a child crying. Follow me!"

The two heroes went down the stairs carefully, listening to every noise.

"Behind the barrels."

Kraven and Greystoke each lifted a barrel of Guinness' best ale and moved them aside.

Behind them, a small barefooted girl, dressed only in a nightgown, was curled up in a recess in the wall. She smelled of beer and looked scared.

"Come on, little one," said Greystoke. "I'll return you to your parents."

The child did not move.

"Let me try," said Kraven. "You must've seen us before, in the magazines? We're from the League..."

Suddenly, the main beam that held up the ceiling snapped in two, like a matchstick. Lord Kraven threw himself on top of the child, protecting her with his body. Lord Greystoke held up the crumbling ceiling and shouted:

"Hurry up! Get out of here! I won't be able to hold this for long! I'll see you later!"

Kraven grabbed his friend's cloak, wrapped the girl in it, rushed up the steps and was barely out of the pub, when the building collapsed in a terrifying tumult of sound.

The next day, Lord Kraven commandeered a squadron of civil engineers to dig through the ruins. But despite moving tons of rubble and smoking debris, they never found Lord Greystoke's body.

Had he truly perished, or was it, somehow, an elaborate ruse that had enabled him to escape undetected and return to his beloved Congo?

The undisputed fact is that, after the London bombing, no one ever saw Lord Greystoke again.

Many later agreed that that day marked the beginning of the end of the League of Heroes.

Selected Headlines from The Daily Herald,
(*January-April 1916*)

"The Triumph Of Hell!"
"Time: Seven In The Morning: Will They Get A Job To-day?" (Over pictures of workers in threadbare clothes.)

"No Money For Our Children, But Plenty To Burn."
(Over pictures of shoeless children next to images of brand-new airships being churned out for war.)

"Revolt Against Servitude Is Good, Fighting For Our Place In The Sun Is Good, The More Revolt And The More Fighting The Better."

"Calling For One And A Half Million Strike. All Businesses To Be At A Standstill!"

Bloody Friday
(May 1916)

"Break it up! Disperse! Go home! King's orders!"

For nearly two hours now, Lord Kraven had been standing at the top of a hastily assembled barricade, and yelling at the crowd of workers gathered on George Square–the only result had been the beginnings of laryngitis.

The day before, he had been sent by Sir Phileas to Glasgow to stop the 35,000 striking engineering workers and Clydeside munitions workers who were threatening to cripple the Empire's war effort; the strike had been ordered by the Triple Alliance which had brought together miners, railwaymen and transport workers. It was a non-rewarding task that Kraven wished to finish quickly.

"Come on, the party's over, get back to work."

The strikers had gathered in the square with their wives and children. They drank from iron mugs full of boiling tea and gin; some were nibbling on cheap sausages. Nobody looked as if they were willing to move.

One man finally stepped away from the crowd and climbed the barricade near Lord Kraven. The hero recognized the notorious anti-war socialist, John Maclean.

"What do you want?" asked Kraven.

"You can stop shouting, Milord. We can all hear you perfectly well. I only hope that you can hear our demands just as well."

Kraven took the paper that the man handed him and read it carefully. It was the standard request for a 40-hour week, accompanied by the usual anti-war propaganda. The Hero found himself filled with anger.

"Shame on you, John Maclean! While men like you live sheltered lives with assurances of honest work and a hot meal on their tables everyday, our boys are fighting and dying at the front, in the cold, dirt and vermin of the trenches. The League constantly faces new threats from the Kaiser, whose hordes threaten to invade our beloved island. And you, you dare show this rag to me! You should be hanging from the highest lamp post on this square!"

Maclean looked at Kraven for a while before replying:

"With all due respect, Milord, that's all a load of bollocks. Up here, we don't give a damn about your fancy exploits and your fights with baddies in colorful costumes. The only fight we're interested in is our own–against poverty. Our poverty."

Kraven could feel the crowd watching him. The strikers, of course, but also the police and the armed soldiers from the South. There was a full battalion of Scottish soldiers stationed at Maryhill, but Sir Phileas had ordered them confined to their barracks for fear that the fellow Scots would go over to the workers' side. Everyone expected him to say or do something. Even English Bob, who had joined him behind the barricade.

"Please, listen to me. Return to work. The cities of the Kingdom are on their knees. They lack everything. Food and coal. After the fire-bombing of last January, it's Hell on Earth in London."

"Can't say that I don't sympathize," replies Maclean. "Maybe now is the time to destroy capitalism for good."

"You don't care about the 40-hour week; you want a revolution. It won't happen, not here, not today."

"And how would the high and mighty Lord Kraven know what will happen here in Scotland on this day? I say, ask your English troops to withdraw, leave our beautiful city and take your war back with you!"

Whistling and clapping accompanied Maclean's declaration. Kraven tried to address the crowd and pushed the unionist away, but Maclean was not Prince Spada and the Savior of the Empire had misjudged his strength. The Scotsman fell, rolled down the barricade, his neck hitting the pavement with a sickening, fatal snap. Used to fights when opponents routinely experienced worse falls and then helped each other to get back on their feet with some smart repartee, Lord Kraven reflexively extended his hand to the union leader, as if he expected the man to rise from the dead.

Another union leader, David Kirkwood, was the first to realize what had happened. Almost like a bad dream, moving in a slow motion, he turned towards his companions and screamed that "they" had killed John Maclean. Next to him, William Gallagher urged the men to stay put and not respond to the provocation, but he was too late. Too many could no longer find it within themselves to swallow their tears and their rage.

The first blow, delivered by a crow bar, hit Lord Kraven in the chest. The Savior of the Empire bent in two, breathlessly, but also instinctively, to prevent further blows from landing. Even children, their nails black with filth, tore at his cheeks. He felt a woman's hand, wearing a copper wedding ring, claw at his face. Dozens of fists hit his face and pummeled his body. This was no chivalrous battle with a well-manicured villain, but a blood-thirsty mob eager to do away with the Lords, the Bosses and the Fairy Folk and all those who had trampled on them all their lives.

With a superhuman effort, Lord Kraven managed to push back the human tide that threatened to tear him apart. He grabbed a mallet from someone's grasp and used it to force his attackers back. Then, turning towards the line of soldiers who had been waiting for his orders, he shouted:

"Fire!"

The men pointed their guns at the crowd and fired off a rapid volley. Throughout the night, the young soldiers–mere lads of 19–had been brought to the city; they had no idea of where they were or why they were there. They had only followed orders.

At once, Kraven felt liberated, both physically and spiritually. The mob fell out in disarray as the men advanced. Later, one journalist wrote: "The charge of the soldiers and the rushes of the mob could be seen as a turmoil so strange and exotic in contrast to the ordinary atmosphere of the Square that the impression conveyed to the eyewitness was, at times, that of an artificial production, a cinematograph picture which he was viewing with conscious detachment from the scenes it portrayed."

Lord Kraven looked around him; he saw bodies riddled with bullets, body parts being scraped up by survivors, and even a string of half-eaten sausages spread over a woman's corpse, like a pile of oddly shaped guts.

He turned towards English Bob.

"Bring the car. We're leaving."

But his assistant was curled up against the vehicle, crying. He had taken off his mask.

"Milord, if I had known that, this day, we would be shooting at women and children, I would never have agreed to come here. As far as I'm concerned, I'm through."

The man who had been a boy got up, gave the black mask to his mentor and walked away. Lord Kraven stood still and silent, his boots stuck in a growing pool of blood, which now mirrored the stain on his honor.

Prussian Chief of Staff Paul von Hindenburg
on the Victory of Verdun,
(September 1916)

Soon after I took over my new post, I found myself compelled by the general situation to ask His Majesty the Emperor to order a new offensive at Verdun.

The battles there had exhausted the French forces like an open wound. Moreover, it was obvious that our goal was well within our grasp, and that for us to persevere would eventually result in an overwhelming victory over the enemy.

We can only hope that, in the coming year, we will repeat the experiment on a greater scale and with equal success.

Excerpt from Trench Warfare (1917), *from The General Staff at the War Office*

The present type of warfare in the trenches has involved the training of a proportion of men in infantry units in duties of a special nature, e. g., grenade throwing, pioneer work, sniping, etc. A word of warning is necessary as regards the training of these men. They must be made to realize that their training in these special duties is in addition to their ordinary training as infantry soldiers and must not be allowed to interfere with their performance of the ordinary duties of infantry soldiers, except when they are required for the special duties in which they have been trained: to defend Albion with their very lives.

The Hammer of Portsmouth
(July 1917)

Corporal Robert Hammerstone was waiting patiently with his men when a Prussian shell hit the trench.

The conflagration tore through the air, projecting an enormous amount of debris and mud, temporarily drowning the shouts and cries of pain. The blast sent everyone scrambling to the ground. The stench of death was atrocious and filled every soldier's nose, mouth and eyes.

Corporal Hammerstone also found himself lying flat on the ground, his face full of bloodied mud, unable to stop his body from trembling. A few feet away from him, the cook's horse lay on its flank, its guts exposed to the open air.

The soldiers who, only a few minutes earlier, had been telling jokes and chewing tobacco, had been turned into a heap of mangled flesh and bones. Hammerstone dropped his gun, opened his shirt and realized that he had been wounded: a spoon handle had perforated his abdomen. *How ironic*, he thought, *to be killed by a spoon!*

He crawled to the edge of a huge crater and let himself drop to its bottom. The shock of his fall was absorbed by the body of a Royal Welsh fusilier who had preceded him there. He recognized the man because of his red hair; he had been a giant before he had been cut in half by a shell.

Hammerstone sank into the mud and cold water and waited for the shelling to stop. The Prussians were using the new Big Bertha artillery that they had painstakingly transported through Belgica and shipped across the Channel.

During his last leave–he couldn't remember when that had been–Hammerstone had read in *Punch* that the Invasion of Albion was a "mad enterprise" and that it wasn't enough to be called William (or Wilhelm) to be a Conqueror. The Corporal wished that the journalist who had written that article was there with him right that minute.

He stayed as he was for a few minutes that felt as long as a few hours, listening to the dreadful noise of shrapnel, trying to stay calm in order to still the pain that was beginning to spread through his gut. Then, there was silence, a heavy and doom-laden silence, announcing an even greater threat–that of the deadly gas.

The red picric acid cloud spread slowly over the no man's land that, before the war, had been the fields south of Portsmouth. The Corporal dug into the mud, turned the fusilier's body over and grabbed his gas mask. He managed to put it on, after three tries, and got up, repressing a sharp cry of pain.

He climbed the slippery sides of the crater and, as fast as he could, ran towards the rear of the lines. The smell of rubber and death inside the mask made him want to vomit; the goggles were fogging up. He moved like a blind man, avoiding stray bullets from the Prussian troops that were moving forward, slowly but decisively, in the deadly fog.

Finally, Hammerstone managed to find a shelter behind a pile of sandbags. He fired a round of shots with the Vickers gun that was there, shooting blindly at the enemy, without any particular conviction, out of a sense of duty, perhaps in memory of his previous life.

The *Stosstruppen* fell, one after the other, like a row of cut-out soldiers. But for each man that dropped, another took his place. They were assisted by a battalion of lancers, armored and masked, both men and their horses. Several Prussian were "cleaning" the trenches with flame-throwers. Supervising them was an officer who smoked a cigarette nonchalantly.

Hammerstone had emptied his clip and was prepared to die, when suddenly, he heard the familiar noise of an Allied airplane. A de Havilland, fragile and graceful as a dragonfly.

The aircraft nose dived directly over the enemy lines and crashed in a burst of flames. At that moment, Corporal Hammerstone realized that he would live.

The tall silhouette of a MechaMan appeared with a whistling of steam amidst the smoke and debris of the plane.

He casually pushed aside the wreckage, started the pistons that allowed his legs to move and faced the enemy. The bullets bounced off his armor, barely managing to chip the paint from the proud Union Jack emblazoned on his chest.

The MechaMan was, of course, Lord Kraven.

The Savior of the Empire extended his arm towards the Prussians holding the flame-throwers. With a slight pressure of his palm, he released tiny, exploding darts from his gauntlet. They hit the fuel tanks, transforming the soldiers into so many screaming torches.

Kraven powered up his jets, flew over the riders, decapitating them with blades that jutted out of his armored wrists. After he had either killed the enemy, or forced them to run away in panic, the Savior of the Empire kneeled on the ground and thanked Almighty God.

Hammerstone approached his former mentor and, with once familiar gestures, pressed the valve that released the MechaMan's helmet.

Kraven turned towards the Corporal. His hair was slick and shiny from a combination of sweat and the cooling fluid inside the suit.

"I know you disapproved of the way I handled that strike in Glasgow, my boy, but as you can see, I would never let you down."

English Bob burst into tears.

Vladimir Lenin on Russia's Withdrawal from the Brest-Litovsk Peace Negotiations, (February 10, 1918)

The peace negotiations are at an end. The Prussian capitalists, bankers and landlords, supported by the silent cooperation of the Albion and French bourgeoisie, submitted to our comrades, members of the peace delegations at Brest-Litovsk, conditions such as could not be subscribed to by the Russian Revolution.

The Government of Prussia possesses lands and peoples vanquished by force of arms. To this authority the Russian people, workmen and peasants, could not give its acquiescence. We could not sign a peace which would bring with it sadness, oppression and suffering to millions of workmen and peasants.

Prussian Chief of Staff Paul von Hindenburg on the Prussian Spring Retreat (March 21, 1918)

The hopes and wishes which had soared beyond Portsmouth had to be abandoned. Facts must be treated as facts.

Human achievements are never more than patchwork. Favor-
able opportunities had been neglected or were not always
exploited with the same energy, even when a splendid goal
beckoned.

We ought to have shouted into the ear of every single
man: "Press on to London. Put in your last ounce."

It was in vain; our strength was exhausted.

The Eagle Has Crashed
(April 1918)

On the morning of April 21, 1918, Lord Kraven was
flying over the Somme river aboard his Sopwith Camel, feeling cramped under three layers of cardigans all covered by a
leather flight suit.

He had requested that Sir Phileas transfer him to the
209th Squadron in order to have one last chance to face–and,
God willing, defeat–Rittmeister Baron von Tod, the greatest
Prussian hero.

It had not been easy to convince Sir Phileas, as the Head
of Intelligence, believed that Kraven's presence would be
more useful on the Homefront, now that, thanks to the
MechaMen Steam Guard, the Prussians had been driven back
to the Continent. With the collapse of the Brest-Litovsk peace
negotiations with Russia, Prussia was on the ropes.

However, Dr. Pavlov, a Russian *émigré* who headed Sir
Phileas' newly-created Office of Behavior Management, had
recommended that he grant Lord Kraven's request. After all,
the recent traumatic events, from the death of Lord Greystoke
to the resignation of English Bob, had taken a toll on the Savior of the Empire, a fact which, if it became known by the
public, would have adverse propaganda value. Sir Phileas had
finally concluded that, if Kraven was going to self-destruct, it
was better that he did so in a glorious death on the frontlines.

Pressing slightly on the broomstick, Lord Kraven stabi-
lized the aircraft, hoping that he would soon get out of the

layer of clouds that was obstructing his view. If the Prussian Fokkers had heard him, they would not take long to arrive, but he still hoped to surprise them.

Some time before the War, Lord Kraven had had the opportunity of meeting Baron von Tod. He came from a noble family in Silesia, with military and farming traditions. He did not care for the Prussian aristocracy's decadent pastimes, did not show off the scars he had gotten during his years as a student in Heidelberg, and lived almost a monastic lifestyle. He was always unfailingly polite, exhibiting a cool and flawless determination. Baron Manfred von Tod was interested in one thing and one thing only: hunting. That made him an implacable killer of the skies.

Sensing that he was not too far from the Allied lines, Lord Kraven began to pull the plane down. Although the Camel was not easy to steer, it was a very good plane, easily a match for the Prussian's scarlet triplane.

Baron von Tod was the final adversary left in Europe who was worthy of Lord Kraven. As the leader of what had become known as the "Flying Circus" or the "Circus of Death," he had acquired the status of legend. It was said that even the Fairy Folk feared him. No one could tell what part of Baron von Tod's life was real and what was sheer fiction. The French Sixième Bureau—the counterpart of the Office of Information Management—had even spread the rumor that the famous scarlet triplane was not piloted by the Baron, but by his even more mysterious sister. He was the last living legend from times that were already passing in the memories of men.

The age of Prince Spada and Doctor Fatal was long gone; the Great War had killed most of the European Heroes. Judex had vanished somewhere in the slaughter fields of the Marne. Miss Mousqueterr had disappeared in the night and fog of war. On the other side, the once-proud Siegfried Legion had been decimated. Lord Greystoke had defeated the infamous Loki in the sands of Syria. The Hammer of Thor, a robust, blond Bavarian, was missing on the Western front. At sea, it was rumored that Kapitan Mors and Capitaine Triplex had fought their final battle, the issue of which was still unknown.

A deciding duel in the air, that was what Lord Kraven sought. He had made the offer in a radio bulletin transmitted by TSF to the Jagdstaffel Jasta-2, von Tod's own, deadly flying squadron. A last showdown before the curtain fell definitely on the Flying Circus.

Suddenly, three Fokker DR-1 triplanes appeared between the clouds, flying in formation, their backs to the Sun. Kraven immediately pulled up his plane and started to climb. He saw the Prussians break their line. Two of the Fokkers made a big loop to give him some space. Kraven noticed that one of the them flapped its wings, as if ironically wishing him good luck. It was Lothar von Tod, the Baron's own brother, in his red and gold plane.

The center plane was being piloted by Manfred von Tod, known variedly as *der Rote Kampfflieger*, *le Diable Rouge* and the Red Baron.

Kraven armed his guns and spun his plane into a nose dive but, at the last minute, the Baron reduced his own speed and shot the exposed flank of Kraven's Camel. The bullets tore the fabric along the sides of the plane and Kraven only managed to escape death by doing a sudden loop that sent him flying upside down. The Savior of the Empire then quickly turned his plane upright and began chasing the Baron's Fokker.

The Prussian was avoiding the bullets by zigzagging through the sky. Suddenly, he reduced his speed and made a somersault that left him right behind Lord Kraven. The Rittmeister fired his two Spandau machine guns, aiming at Kraven's tail. However, the Hero, who had anticipated the maneuver, dove sharply. The two opponents then circled around each other, in ever tighter circles. The Savior of the Empire looked at the damage. Some cables had been severed, the side fabric was ripping in the air but the stabilizer had not been hit.

Suddenly, Lord Kraven felt a blow to his head. A bullet had ricocheted on the reinforced windshield and grazed his helmet.

Immediately, he pulled another somersault that brought him up on the left side of the Prussian triplane. Von Tod seemed amused and in no hurry to finish the fight. He was now using only a single gun, shooting sporadically through the propeller.

The wind had carried the unwary duelists towards the Albion lines, west of Sailly-le-Sec. They were now flying over the 53rd regiment of Australian artillery. Lord Kraven saw some woods down below and reduced his altitude, hoping that his foe would follow him. He did.

After skimming the tops of the trees, the two planes suddenly found themselves just above the Australian gunners. Exactly what Kraven had been hoping for! As soon as the Fokker was heard on the ground, the 18-pound cannons fired.

Despite his amazing skills, it was only by pure luck that the Baron managed to escape. At least, he was no longer concerned by the Camel. That was the opportunity Lord Kraven had been waiting for. The Hero did another somersault, sending him yet again beneath the tail of his opponent's plane. He then fired at the Fokker. His bullets destroyed the landing gear and tore the bottom from the cockpit.

Lord Kraven then flew over the Fokker; he saw the Baron, his tunic covered in blood, struggling in the tiny cockpit. Suddenly, in a desperate effort, the Fokker climbed vertically and hit Kraven's aircraft. The Camel went into a spin. The Savior of the Empire felt his eardrums burst. The wind tearing at his face was smeared with engine oil. He barely had time to see Baron von Tod's plane crash near the front lines before jumping for his life.

His white, silk parachute opened and gently lowered him towards his destiny.

Abdication Proclamation of Wilhelm II
(November 28, 1918)

I herewith renounce for all time, claims to the throne of the Holy Prussian Empire. At the same time I release all officials of the Empire, as well as all officers, noncommissioned officers and men of the navy and of the Prussian army, as well as the troops of the federated states of Alemania, from the oath of fidelity which they tendered to me as their Emperor, King and Commander-in-Chief. I expect of them that until the re-establishment of order in the Prussian Empire they shall render assistance to those in actual power in Prussia, in protecting the Prussian people from the threatening dangers of anarchy, famine and foreign rule.

Proclaimed under our own hand and with the imperial seal attached.

Coming Home
(December 1918)

As newly-appointed Secretary of State to His Majesty's Government, Winston Churchill had the huge task of demobilizing three-and-a-half million exhausted soldiers. This posed great problems. An army of a million men was required to occupy the Rhine and 14,000 soldiers were still engaged in fighting in Russia.

The Office of Information Management had proposed that the first troops to be repatriated should be paraded before the flashes of the Press photographers in order to keep hope alive among the families of those who would not be returning as soon.

The soldiers were rediscovering the faces of family and loved ones almost half-forgotten; it was all very moving and would sell millions of copies. The reporters were sniffing like a pack of hounds for the perfect story. They found it.

He was standing there, all alone, dirty and emaciated like all the others, possibly still suffering from some war wound, which would only make the photo more successful. Even the man from *The Times*, who had met him several times in the past, had a hard time recognizing him.

No matter what he would do with the rest of his life, he thought, when he saw the journalist approach, *he belonged to them for one more hour, time enough to tell them of his fear and his disgust of war. He owed them that much. They had so often put him in the spotlight before, that he could now do something for them in return. Besides, they had already written his obituary. Later, they would leave him in peace, they would find someone else to turn into a hero, but today, he owed them the truth.*

The journalists dashed towards the man, even pushing aside several Salvation Army volunteers. His earlier innocence had vanished, washed away by blood, left behind somewhere in a trench. His prematurely balding forehead made him look older.

"Corporal Hammerstone!"

"English Bob!"

The soldier looked at them in a way that no photographer present felt able to fully capture, and simply said:

"You must be mistaken, sir. My name is Rupert Hammerstein. I am a Citizen of the World."

Excerpt from Punch, or the London Charivari
(January 9, 1919)

"Peace is only a matter of time," says Lord Kraven.
The ex-Kaiser is said to be of the opinion that Lord Kraven might have been more explicit as to who is going to get that "time."
Meanwhile, the ex-Kaiser is growing a beard. He evidently has no desire to share the fate of "Wilhelmshaven."

Dinner at the Reform Club
(January 10, 1919)

A fine, cold rain had been falling on London for several days. The city tasted of ashes, from St. John's Wood to Peckham Rye. Nothing would be the same ever again, and yet it did not seem to matter. The past was lying buried under the ruins of the Crystal Palace and in the memories of those mourning it. The word of the day was to look forward towards the future, a future with food and shelter for all.

Lord Kraven politely rejected the umbrella that the servant at the Reform Club was handing him and climbed up the steps four at a time.

He signed the register at the reception's desk, then walked up the grand marble staircase, then down a long corridor, barely looking at the classical paintings on the walls. There was no room for modern art there. He presented himself to the officer on duty; the man was typical of the place: timeless and indifferent. The Reform Club had miraculously escaped the Prussian firebombing and had continued to serve the interests of the Empire.

After having checked the roster, the officer stepped aside to allow Lord Kraven to enter. It was not the first time that he had stepped inside Sir Phileas Fogg's notorious Blue Room.

Its walls held so many secrets that some said that they seeped out at night, like rising damp.

Sir Phileas showed him to a seat. He was probably the only man in the country who had managed to put on weight during the War. To see him like that, so fat and ponderous, one could hardly imagine that, in his youth, he, too, had been a hero. On behalf of the Reform Club, of which he was one of the founders, he had once traveled around the world in 80 days. The Press had claimed that it was to win an eccentric bet, and they had reported his exploits in great detail. In reality, it was all for Her Majesty's Secret Service, he had once admitted to Lord Kraven, when he had been in a confiding mood. Sir Phileas was extremely proud to have inspired that French writer, who had dedicated his book to him. Today, he managed the League of Heroes and lives vicariously through their adventures.

"Please join me for supper; let's enjoy our evening together."

Sir Phileas signaled to his butler to start serving the food before falling silent once again.

Everyone knew the ritual, established since the creation of the League. After returning from a mission, the heroes were invited to dine with Sir Phileas, a luxurious, refined meal, with celebrated wines, that could last for hours, depending on his regard for his guest. Annoyed at Sir Phileas' manners, who usually asked for silence while eating, Lord Greystoke had once refused a plate of pheasant and asked instead for raw meat. He had never been invited again.

Liqueur followed the dessert and Kraven thought his cigar excellent.

"A present from the late Lord Hook, I'm afraid," remarked Sir Phileas, having guessed what Kraven was thinking. "Nothing on this Earth compares to Neverland tobacco. Unfortunately, I'm on my last box. Now, on to business."

Sir Phileas pressed a button on his chair that activated a hidden door.

A man in his forties appeared. He had a long, sad face, prominent side whiskers and wore the clothes of a proper Edwardian gentleman. He appeared fumbling, and slow, and spoke with an interrupted speech pattern and a hesitant manner. Kraven recognized him: he was John Reeder, the best of Sir Phileas' "Mnemonics." Sir Phileas loved these men with total recall and photographic memory who could keep entire volumes of information in their heads. Weeks, even months after an interview, they could effortlessly recall everything that had been said, using the same words, the same intonations. The system was remarkable because it left no written records. The Mnemonic signaled to his superior that he was ready to begin recording.

"Report from January 10 regarding Agent K's stay in France," announced Sir Phileas. "Go ahead, Lord Kraven, I'm listening."

Kraven settled comfortably in the thick leather armchair and, ignoring Reeder who was mentally recording what he would be saying, began reporting on his mission:

"Further to your orders, I went to No. 28 Rue Monceau in Paris, where I was welcomed by the President of the United States of America, Mr. Woodrow Wilson. Mr. Henry White, the former American ambassador to France, was also present during our meetings. He was recently appointed commissioner to the Peace Conference by President Wilson."

"Any members of Congress present?" asked Sir Phileas.

"None, as far as I could tell."

"That's very tactless. The Federalists won't like it. Senator Henry Cabot Lodge must be furious. That augurs poorly for any eventual Treaty's ratification... How would you describe the President's health?"

"Not good. His wife appears quite worried about it."

"But he won't let that hamper his determination..."

Sir Phileas puffed thoughtfully on his cigar, his eyes lost in space. Then, with a gesture, he indicated that Kraven should continue his report.

"I told the President we were concerned about giving free access to the Channel to the Prussian fleet. He said it could be put on the table as part of the overall negotiations. "

Sir Phileas let out an exasperated sigh:

"That's Lloyd George's concern, not mine. Would you please address the main issue?"

"Of course. The President doesn't understand why we think that Points 5 and 14 of his 14 Points Program for World Peace could constitute a threat to the Empire."

"He doesn't understand? It's not difficult to grasp. Mr. Reeder, recite the aforementioned Points, please," ordered Sir Phileas.

The Mnemonic straigthened up and, in a monotonous voice, recited:

"Point 5: A free, open-minded and absolutely impartial adjustment of all colonial claims, based upon a strict obser-vance of the principle that in determining all such questions of sovereignty the interests of the populations concerned must have equal weight with the equitable claims of the government whose title is to be determined."

The sad-looking man coughed in his hand before carry-ing on:

"Point 14: A general association of nations must be formed under specific covenants for the purpose of affording mutual guarantees of political independence and territorial integrity to great and small states alike."

A long silence followed that recitation. Sir Phileas crushed his cigar in a large onyx ashtray and grumbled for himself:

"That's just what our colonies have been waiting for! And I'm not even talking about Neverland. You can be sure that Peter Pan and the Indians will use the 14 Points to chal-lenge our control of Neverland. Just as we're doing our best to rebuild the foundations of the Empire!"

"There's something else," added Lord Kraven.

He took a folded paper from his pocket.

"This is a note from the President himself asking that the League of Heroes endorses his 14 Points."

Sir Phileas stayed silent for a while before showing his disdain:

"Of course. He's facing harsh opposition in Congress. Senator Lodge dreams of humiliating him. An endorsement from the League might swing the undecided Members. What did you reply?"

"That I approved of his project for a World Government, and that I agreed to make a speech to that effect at the opening of the Peace Conference in Paris the day after tomorrow."

Kraven thought that his superior was about to faint after hearing this. The founder of the League of Heroes poured himself a glass of brandy, swallowed it in one gulp and suddenly ordered the Mnemonic to leave.

"You certainly know that I don't share your point of view," said Sir Phileas after Reeder had gone. "The League belongs to Albion, not the Americans."

Sir Phileas was referring to Kid Colt, the American hero whose behavior at the Bertram's at the start of the War had left an indelibly negative impression.

Colt had been President Theodore Roosevelt's personal friend; he had been at his side when the Rough Riders led a daring charge up San Juan Hill during the Spanish-American War. Politically faithful to his old companion-at-arms, Colt hated Wilson, whom he called a "gutless traitor," and his ideals for a Society of Nations. But Colt had been deeply affected by Roosevelt's death only four days before and had vanished from the public scene.

Kraven replied:

"Technically, Colt was never a member of the League. Besides, he won't be sitting at the Conference."

Another reason for Colt's reported absence was that he adamantly refused to sit next to the Steel Comrade, the new Russian hero sent by Vladimir Lenin himself to be the new Bolshevik Republic's representative in Paris.

Since the Bolsheviks had refused to sign the humiliating Treaty of Brest-Litovsk in 1918 and opened an Eastern Front that had further weakened Prussia, the Allies had refrained from intervening to support the Whites in the brewing Russian Civil War. As a result, the Bolsheviks had been formally invited to the Peace Conference by President Wilson.

"Very well, Milord Kraven," said Sir Phileas through gritted teeth. "Might I be apprised of the contents of the speech that you plan to give before the assembled leaders of the world?"

"I haven't decided on it yet. I'll improvise as usual."

After Lord Kraven's Speech
at the Paris Peace Conference
(January 12, 1919)

The speech was received with only a smattering of applause.

Lord Kraven looked at the audience of heads of state, ambassadors, diplomats and plenipotentiaries, leaders of 32 countries, representing approximately 75% of the world's population. A few were markedly unfriendly. Most were a study in neutrality.

The Savior of the Empire stepped off the dais and rejoined Sherlock Holmes, the French hero dubbed the Nyctalope, Baron Stromboli, the mysterious Zenith the Albino, the Steel Comrade and Kio Hako, who had come all the way from Tokyo.

He was still convinced of the validity of his project, a world government, a Society of Nations supported by an International League of Heroes. However, the American delegation and the representatives of Albion had purposefully left the grand salon before the end of his speech. And Georges Clemenceau remained obstinately deaf to his calls for leniency towards Prussia, even if the Nyctalope seemed more sympathetic to his plea.

When he left the room, Lord Kraven noticed many Albion and French officers, their noses stuck to the immense glass doors. As he walked by, many turned their backs on him. It was a sign that, in their minds, the Hero who had fought the Boche had now become a turncoat who was trying to buy peace at any price.

Sir Phileas' agents let them walk into the room that had been set aside for the Head of Albion Intelligence. There, Fogg attacked him without even giving him enough time to sit down:

"What's wrong with you? Have you gone mad?"

The fat man was almost suffocating with rage. Kraven replied:

"Isn't my mission to guarantee peace? Doesn't that serve the best the interests of the Empire?"

"The best interests? That's what you call 'the removal of all economic barriers and the establishment of an equality of trade conditions among all nations?' 'The impartial adjustment of all colonial claims, based upon a strict observance of the principle that in determining all such questions of sovereignty, the interests of the populations concerned must have equal weight with the equitable claims of their colonial masters?' Why didn't you invite Peter Pan on stage while you were at it? If any part of your insane scheme were to be enforced, it would spell the end of Albion!"

"And ya can kiss my ass 'fore America turns commie, ya Limey bastard."

Kraven turned around. Kid Colt was sitting on the sofa, playing with a huge revolver.

"Such a big gun for such a little man," said another voice.

It belonged to Aleksander Dovzhenko, the Steel Comrade himself. The hero of the Russian people stood well above eight feet. He was dressed in workers' overalls and his face was hidden beneath a welder's mask. He was holding a hammer and a sickle in his hands. A broken chain, symbol of the shattered yoke of capitalism, was wounded around his thick, right arm. Kid Colt hesitated for a second, then put the gun back in its holster.

"Ah see," he said, finally. "High an' mighty Lord Kraven's true color is showin' at last–red! Remember what I said, Sir Phileas. You can do what you like with yer fairies, put 'em in reservations or give them their independence, for all we care. But America won't stand for it if you ally yerselves with the Commies. You used ta be called 'Savior of the Empire,' Milord, but from where I stand, yer its gravedigger."

The American hero picked up his famous fringed leather jacket and left the room.

"He's got a point, Kraven," said Fogg, gravely. "I'm afraid we can't let you, or the new League of Heroes, do what you suggest. You must turn back before it's too late. There is more at stake here than even you can suspect."

"Is that a threat, Sir Phileas?"

"No, Lord Kraven. Not a threat. Merely some advice."

Excerpt from The New York Times
(March 14, 1919)

Responding to the assassination of Vladimir Ilyich Lenin in Petrograd yesterday, Lev Davidovich Bronstein, People's Commissar for Military and Naval Affairs and Commander-in-Chief of the Red Army, has passed a decree that, some say, has become the legal foundation for a new wave of massive repression. The decree states that, in cases involving those accused of terrorist acts, judicial authorities are not to allow appeals for clemency or other delays and the NKVD is ordered to execute all found guilty immediately. Today, amid the stirred emotions over the assassination, the first to be arrested were Vyacheslav Mikhailovich Molotov and Aleksander Petrovych Dovzhenko, better known in the West as the Steel Comrade.

Excerpt from The Daily Telegraph
(January 10, 1920)

Lord Kraven Missing In Action! South Pole Expedition Ends In Tragedy!

News reached London today of the untimely death of the Savior of the Empire in the explosion of his airship, HMS Albion Ascendant II, *near McMurdo Sound in the American Antarctic.*

The South Pole Expedition was a joint American-Albion-French Mission set up to investigate reports of a landing by mysterious three-eyed aliens from Venus, following interplanetary broadcasts intercepted by a French scientist last year.

Tragically, the explosion occurred the very day the newly-formed League of Nations held its first meeting to ratify the Treaty of Paris effectively ending the Great War, during which Lord Kraven performed numerous heroic actions.

Lord Kraven was deemed to be an influential figure in the One World Government Party and some believe his passing may spell the end of the Movement.

Upon hearing the news, His Majesty proclaimed a National Day of Mourning throughout the Empire. "Albion had no stronger, nor more faithful champion than Lord Kraven," the King declared. "He will be missed by all."

Lord Kraven's former assistant, Robert Hammerstone, a.k.a. English Bob, refused all requests for interviews.

The two had split up soon after the beginning of the War. Some claimed it was because of Hammerstone's Prussian origins; others, because of Lord Kraven's part in the so-called Bloody Friday in Glasgow in May 1916.

The death of Lord Kraven, following that of Lord Greystoke during the bombing of London four years ago marks the passing of the last of the original members of the League of Heroes—the end of an era by everyone's reckoning.

Richard, Lord Kraven, Baron of Glen Bogle...

Hollywood, CA. Producer David O. Selznick announced today that he optioned Arthur Pyke's best-selling novel Enter the Lion: The Tumultuous Life And Times Of Lord Kraven, *for the sum of $50,000. Selznick further announced that the role of the Albion War Hero would be played by Cary Grant. "I will have to let my moustache grow," the dapper actor confided to Louella Parson. A reliable studio source stated that W.C. Fields would be playing the role of Sir Phileas Fogg.*

PART TWO

The Old Man

If there was only one truth in this life, it was this: George loathed his father-in-law.

It had been that way since the first time he saw him, standing in the doorway of his home between two government bureaucrats.

The taller one had handed him a pile of official-looking papers and asked him to sign at the bottom, then left him with the copies and disappeared with his smaller colleague, without taking the Old Man with them.

At first, George thought it was a ghastly mistake, a delivery error like those that sometimes happen with mail order parcels or Chinese food takeaway. But even if he was always ready to denounce the incompetence and the negligence of the Civil Service, in this instance, he had to admit that they had been right.

The Old Man's name and his wife's maiden name were the same. He was indeed her father. At least, that was what the documents said.

George rubbed his hands on his work pants and leaned over to see if, behind the Old Man standing in the doorway, the neighbors had cleaned their yard. They hadn't, of course. That type of neglect would surely cause the property values in the area to go down. He endlessly repeated this philosophy to his wife, hoping that she would spread it around her at work and the supermarket. It was clear, however, that the message hadn't gotten through to his neighbors.

George straightened back up and stared at the Old Man again. His chin was a few inches above his. He looked scruffy.

A closer look revealed that the man he thought of as *"Him"* (since there was no way he could think of him as *"Dad"*) was about 60 and looked rather muscular. He had a large face, an impressive moustache and long white hair making him look a little like an aging hippie.

George was thoroughly unimpressed with his new father-in-law.

"What do you want?" he asked *Him*.

The Old Man was tempted to reply that all he really wanted was to see Peace on Earth for all of Mankind, but thought better of it. Instead, he said:

"A home. I believe I'll be living with you now."

George felt that he had no other choice and stepped aside to let the Old Man in.

His wife was unable to throw any further light on the situation. Indeed, she appeared equally surprised when, returning home from work, she found the man George now referred to as *"Your Father"* sitting on the dark-red leather sofa in the living room, listening to music.

The only thing she knew about him came from the times her mother had talked about their ruined lives, complaining that he had abandoned them years before and had never been in touch again, not even sending so much as a postcard.

George made sure that she had not signed for anything at the Post Office or the Town Hall, and then told the boys that it was time for dinner.

The Old Man got up and walked into the kitchenette where he immediately chose a place at the table, near the door looking into the garden. The meal was silent, except for the sounds of chewing, although to be honest, that wasn't particularly different from most of their meals.

As soon as dinner was over, the eldest boy led the Old Man to his room, but explained that it was not going to be a permanent arrangement.

"It's only until we get the attic fixed up, Dad says, so don't go moving anything," he ordered.

The Old Man sent the boy away, put his bag down near a chair full of dirty clothes, stared at the model planes hanging from the ceiling, then looked for something he could use as an ashtray. He chose a white steel box that had once contained cream-filled chocolates. He didn't bother to remove the bed-spread before lying down, smoking as he waited to fall asleep in the soothing blackness of the night.

The next morning, George's wife seemed to have emp-tied all the contents of the cupboard for breakfast. Bacon, eggs, tea, bread and cereal covered the table. It was not as much that she wanted to make a good impression, but simply that she did not know what he would want.

It turned out that the Old Man merely wanted a cup of coffee and two pieces of toast with marmalade and no butter.

Nothing further happened until George got back from work. He went straight to the boys' room, complained about the noise they were making, slapped the oldest and told the youngest that he couldn't watch his favorite program, a sci-ence fiction series about an alien doctor with a Beatles-like haircut who saved the world in a blue police box. Conscious of having done his fatherly duty, George went to sit in his fa-vorite armchair, which gave him a comfortable view of the living room and the stairs. He put a can of beer on the glass tabletop, stared at his father-in-law and grumbled:

"So, what are we going to do with you?"

The Old Man puffed slowly on his cigarette before re-plying:

"I don't even know what to do with myself."

Great, a philosopher, thought George, as he grabbed a creased copy of *News of the World*, read a bit, then closed his eyes and began to snore.

In the mid-1950s, George had been offered a temporary job as foreman on a building site in London. Calling it "temporary" was a matter of semantics. There was more than enough work to go around at the time, so a permanent position seemed a certainty, but George had hesitated to commit himself more fully to the job. Not out of fear of moving to the big city–George was not a fearful man–but out of sheer laziness. The idea of getting up early every morning, taking the train and looking for a new home (especially since he already had one) irritated him. But his young wife had managed to convince him that it was the right thing to do. On a grey Wednesday morning, the couple had left their home in Wolverhampton, never to return.

Since then, they had been living in an unremarkable house, in an unremarkable suburb in the East End. Over the years, they had reached a certain state of tranquillity. The first few years had been difficult, as both of them had strong tempers, but those problems had disappeared after the birth of their first child. His wife had transferred all her attention to the baby and, soon after, George had finished repaying their mortgage.

He was able to fix his car, loved his sons in his own way and, once in a while, liked to get involved in some dodgy scheme that didn't make him very much money, but gave him the sense that he was somehow getting away with something, or "screwing the system," to quote his older son.

In short, George was no longer worried about what surprises life might put in his path. That was, until the Old Man showed up.

Sheer coincidence–luck had nothing to do with it–caused George to glance through one of his older boy's textbooks a few days later. There, he learned that men were not naturally social creatures and that, instead, they had been forced to live together by some sort of cataclysm or natural catastrophe. At least, that was what that crazy Frenchman, Rousseau, had written.

George knew the name because he had seen it on some paintings, and even if those had not made much of an impression on him, he thought the man was a terrific thinker. George's natural unsociability had finally found a theoretical underpinning!

He had decided that he would force himself to tolerate *Your Father*'s presence, but that didn't mean that he had to make life easy for the old bugger.

The first weeks of their cohabitation reminded him of a television program he had watched one night. It was a report about Japan. Two sumo wrestlers had been sizing each other up by waddling around in circles, before finally attacking. Even if the Old Man and his son-in-law were neither fat, nor even big, the comparison was not inappropriate.

When George was not working, which was happening far more often these days, the two men divided up the house equally. One sat in the living room, while the other stayed in his bedroom, waiting for the battle to resume. When the Old Man would head down to the kitchen, George immediately jumped up to make himself a sandwich or to get a beer. He would push aside his father-in-law, grumbling while looking at what was on his plate, until the Old Man would go back upstairs. To avoid going up to the bathroom, which was on the first floor, and which would have given the Old Man free access to the ground floor, George would recap his bottle of brown ale and try to suppress any urge to pee until his wife got home.

One thing, above all, irritated him: the Old Man did not share information.

They could ask him any question about his past, any friends he might have made, his travels, anything at all, and he would not answer; he simply waited for the conversation to change subjects. That usually took a while, because George, egged on by his family or his pub mates, knew better than most how to stretch a tiny anecdote into a never-ending story. The Old Man, on the other hand, said nothing. He told no stories, made no lies about drinking, or women, spun no yarns to liven up an evening.

It was almost as if he had not had a life until he arrived. Or maybe, he no longer remembered it. That is what his daughter thought: that he had lost his memory, that he was an amnesiac who had been sent to live with them by Social Services in the hope that he might, someday, regain his memory.

Amnesia made things simpler.

Unable to remember the past, and thus compare it to the present, the Old Man was impervious to his daughter's criticisms and his son-in-law's resentment. He was even beyond feeling any fondness for his two grandsons, who in any event, showed him little respect.

The days slipped by, unnoticed. The Old Man was indifferent to others because he was a stranger to himself. Sometimes, he was bored, but for no particular reason, simply because boredom comes with age, and not with life.

Until the Crystal Palace.

George was a Crystal Palace football club man. Always had been, always would be.

The Old Man began following the matches on the radio, but not because he loved the sport–he did not understand anything about it despite the lengthy explanations provided by George and his sons–but simply because he liked the name.

The Crystal Palace.

It sounded like an invitation to a magic ball, a relic from a half-forgotten, wonderful past, one that his imagination could shape. A word in the newspaper, a glimpse of an image on the telly, was all that was required to stir long-gone echoes in his memory.

Of course, he did not mention any of this to his family. How could he admit he preferred a fantasy life of his own making to the one he was being offered? At least, that was how they would interpret it.

He started to glimpse more frequent clues about his shrouded past on a daily basis, and began jotting them down in a small notebook.

The first of these was Astra's bosom.

Astra was Garth's true love.

Garth was a comic book that reprinted strips from *The Daily Mirror* about a mysterious, super-strong hero who traveled through time to a variety of eras and encountered a wide range of opponents, such as the evil mad scientist Madame Voss.

Garth had two companions: the kindly Professor Lumière ("Mon Dieu! Sacrebleu!") and the incredibly beautiful Astra, she of the remarkable bosom. She was pictured in all her glory on the comic book cover.

He had found the magazine stuck between the mesh springs and the mattress while looking under the bed for his lighter. Thinking that his grandson had lost it, he had put it on the nightstand. But George had been in a particularly foul mood that day and had kept him from going downstairs at all. With nothing better to do, the Old Man had ended up reading the comic.

He forgot to eat dinner that night.

The story was a tale dedicated to courage and loyalty, containing the exploits of a man of mystery, who had washed ashore as a baby in the Shetlands in a tiny coracle, then had been pulled out of the sea by an old couple who had adopted him and brought him up. As to Astra, Garth's romantic interest, she had been known to the Romans as Venus; she was the last of a race of ancient god-like entities dating back to ancient civilizations, who had conquered the natural world and were virtually eternal.

The Old Man stopped reading several times to copy entire passages into his notebook.

"I won't say a word to your father about the comic," said the Old Man to his grandson.

The teenager looked at his grandfather suspiciously. During the last five minutes, the Old Man had talked to him more than he had in the last two months. It was strange talk, too. And somehow, that bothered him and just felt weird.

"I can understand why you kept it hidden." the Old Man continued. "It's not the kind of stuff he'd like to catch you reading. I'm proud of you, son, but you've got to do me a favor..."

So, here it was. Without looking at the Old Man, who was sitting on the bed, the boy moved closer to the door. Someone at school had told him how old people were all perverts.

"I want more of these comics!"

To illustrate his point, the Old Man waved the comic under his grandson's nose. The boy took a deep breath, scratched his nose and said in a voice that sounded eerily just like his father's:

"Then, I guess you'll have to talk to Syd."

Syd lived in a converted van parked at the entrance of an abandoned lot. He had not always lived like this, but he had been thrown out of his last flat the year before after refusing to share his record collection with his landlord.

Since then, he had gotten used to his awkward nomadic lifestyle. He even realized that it had certain advantages. Exploiting the laws of supply and demand, he thrived on a barter economy on the fringes of society. People showed up at Syd's place at all times of day and night to swap a bottle of gin for a carton of cigarettes, or spicy books for engine parts.

When the Old Man and his grandson knocked on the door, Syd had just traded two copies of *Dan Dare* and a 1966 *Doctor Who Annual* for the latest Who single, "*I'm free / Tommy can you hear me,*" the Polydor German pressing to boot. That, he was going to keep for himself.

"So, Grandpa, what do you want?"

The Old Man immediately liked Syd. Somehow, he trusted him right away. He also liked the bold way he dressed, with long hair that fell below his shoulders and red silk briefs. You had to be self-confident to get away with that look.

"My grandson told me that you've got some more copies of this comic."

The young man took a quick glance at the issue of *Garth* the Old Man was still holding and mumbled something that sounded like approval, then made a flourish with his hand, as if doffing his hat like a musketeer would have done.

"Let's talk about this inside. Come on, climb aboard!"

The van's interior was a perfect model of tidiness, with the exception of the kitchen, which was a helter-skelter mess of soup cans and Milky Way candy bars. Syd scratched his crotch and told them to make themselves comfortable. The Old Man sat in a deck chair, opposite the shelves that covered the entire wall. Besides the pulps and the bagged comics were at least a thousand records, all ranked according to the year and artist.

When they were settled, Syd asked:

"Tell me, mate, why do you fancy *Garth*?"

The Old Man gathered that he was being asked the reason he sought more comics. He lit up a cigarette, put his lighter on the table next to a dog-eared paperback edition of Hobbes' *Leviathan* and blurted out:

"It impressed me deeply. Its art style, its vivid imagery. Astra's beauty. Professor Lumière's wisdom. The villains, the action. But above all, I was struck by Garth himself. The simple nobility of his soul, devoid of any ulterior motive, his sense of duty, his virtue..."

Syd nodded his unreserved approval.

"Good old Garth, the original Man of Mystery himself, eh? A Superman who appeared out of nowhere. No fancy schmancy Planet Krypton or Wizard Shazam. Just a pure hero who fights despots and tyrants..."

Syd reached towards the nearest shelf, and pulled down a comic.

"*When Venus was Born*, from 1962... The Origins of Astra.... It's a classic. Have a go at this one, I'm sure you'll love it!"

Like a monk who had just been handed the Shroud of Turin, the Old Man grasped the comic with shaky hands. Suddenly, he realized that he had no means of paying for it and felt a deep shame. Syd immediately realized the Old Man's problem and made a contemptuous snort:

"Don't worry, Gramps, we can talk about payment later."

George was waiting for them in the garden. He had spent a good part of the afternoon pulling out vegetable seedlings that his wife had planted only a week earlier. There would be consequences to his actions, of course, but he did not really care. He stood there, drunk and violent, looking like a feudal lord betrayed by one of his vassals.

He had prepared a volley of insults and petty retributions to punish what he felt was disloyalty within the ranks of his own family His reasoning was simple. His father-in-law was an outsider. To take his side was an act of betrayal. He felt that the contamination was spreading. His own flesh and blood had shared something with the Old Man, communicated with him, in a way that he, George, the *pater familias*, had been unable to achieve. Such misbehavior could only be forgiven after a proper thrashing.

Of course, he couldn't actually beat the Old Man, as much as he wished to, because of Social Services. The same two men who had delivered him in the first place had stopped by that morning with a series of questions. Nothing about George himself (adding insult to injury), but all about his father-in-law. Was he starting to fit in? Did he talk to his daughter? Did he play with the boys? Did he tell them anything interesting?

George had answered yes to all the questions, without giving out any details. When they left, one of the two Civil Servants had given him a card stating the date of their next visit.

George told his son to go and help his brother. Then, when they were alone, he asked the Old Man what he thought he was doing.

"Getting my education, for starters," he replied.

That night, the Old Man could not sleep.

Images from *Garth* danced in the remotest corners of his mind, Professor Lumière's laboratory, Garth's heroic actions, the incredible flying machines, the fancy foreign lands, the megalomaniacal villains... None of this connected with any conscious memories, but managed to weave a tapestry of strange, hybrid images, like a word association game where saying one word leads the mind to think of another word. Most of these visual associations were bright and ephemeral, barely memorable. However, one image dominated all others: that of a faceless hero, a man of mystery with longish hair, endowed with strength, courage and daring, wearing a colorful uniform.

George looked at his wife as if she had just gone mad. She had served him his eggs and told him that she believed that her father was someone important.

She thought that he might have been connected to the Mafia, the KGB, MI6, or possibly the CIA, and been brainwashed before being released, because of the information that was in his head, like in that television series with Patrick McGoohan. She said that there were plenty of things being hidden from them by the Americans. It said so in *The Daily Mail*. For instance, between 1958 and 1962, the CIA had taken a Harvard student named Theodore John Kaczynski to be the subject of "psychological experiments." If it worked that way, why wouldn't it work the other way around? If they could take a young man to play with his mind, they could surely return an Old Man with scrambled memories to his family.

"Maybe," replied George, "but in that case, how can you be sure he's really your Dad?"

Overwhelmed by the ramifications of her husband's question, George's wife leaned on the sink, her eyes fixated on the vortex created by the water running down the drain. It sucked down her final certainties along with the leftover tomato sauce.

It made for a miserable life, she reflected, beginning with no father and ending up with possibly a fake father, or an amnesiac one.

George threw a bunch of odds and ends into his lunchbox and declared that, today, he would take the bus.

The only thing that made Syd take the bus was his desire to observe his fellow men like an ornithologist observes the migratory pattern of birds. Every Tuesday morning, Syd took the bus going to St. Pancras and stared at the crowds from its upper deck.

He had no particular reasons for doing so, other than the desire to stay in touch with what was going on in the world around him. Syd did realize that he needed the occasional normalcy of that trip to clear his head between the different kinds of trips brought on by his ingestion of LSD.

He also needed to think clearly to fill some of the unusual orders he had been receiving recently. That very morning, someone had asked him to find a rare *Captain Marvel* lunchbox, from before the character had been renamed *Marvelman* by Mike Anglo. The image was that of the Big Red Cheese giving a message of peace at the United Nations. It was for the birthday of a disabled child the following day.

Syd cursed under his breath. He was not Albert Steptoe, he could not just snap his fingers and conjure up the stuff! That is why he enjoyed the bus rides. It gave him time to think, to plan.

Syd looked at the passengers, evaluating at a glance their simple joys and their quiet sorrow, taking measure of their everyday's life. Suddenly, he nearly fainted when he saw what the man next to him was holding. A lunchbox that had clearly seen better days, but which was the answer to his problem, for

Captain Marvel's face, pockmarked with rust, stared up at him from its emblazoned side!

Syd pulled the cord to get off, pretended to lose his balance when the bus lurched to a halt, then as fast as he could, grabbed the lunchbox and ran away. It was worth trekking home on foot.

That day, George bought a bag of chips for lunch from a street vendor.

Needless to say, he was in a foul mood when he got home that night.

The Old Man enjoyed his meetings with Syd, and in fact, so did the young man. They somehow completed each other, each appreciating the other's tastes.

Syd envied the Old Man his spaced-out mind, which was better than anything he had been, so far, able to achieve with drugs. He hoped to be just like him when he got to be that age.

For his part, during each of his visits, the Old Man discovered another side of his life that he thought had been permanently buried–not the life that everybody else wished him to have, but the life that was really his, a life of adventure, courage and dignity.

The Old Man had become transfixed by *Good Times, Bad Times*, the first song on Led Zeppelin's debut album, the cover of which featured a photo of the *Hindenburg* disaster in New York.

The song's words expressed his present situation:

> *In the days of my youth*
> *I was told what it means to be a man...*
> *I know what it means to be alone,*
> *I sure do wish I was at home.*
> *I don't care what the neighbors say...*

Yes, thought the Old Man. *I sure do wish I was at home...* But where was home?

(1970)

"I can't even shit right anymore. It's because of my age, and I don't like the way things are either. Hell, I'd never have said 'shit' before. I'd never even have thought about 'shit.' It's a matter of education, of breeding..."

The Old Man kept grumbling to himself.

He emptied the kettle, put a scoop of tea leaves into it, filled it with water and put it back on the fire. He was not even consciously aware of making the repetitive gestures, as he did them.

He lit a cigarette, his first that day, and went out to sit on the steps. He had decided to go to the school with his grandson and talk to the Headmaster, before George got involved in the boy's business and made things worse. A gull was perched on one of the bars of the rusty swing in the playground across the street. Like him, it looked confused.

His daughter came out, looking for him, he guessed. He threw away his cigarette and went back inside. She shuffled her feet when she walked and her slippers made a scratching sound on the dirty linoleum that drove him crazy. But what could he do? Tell her, "I know that I'm a daily intrusion into your bone-crushingly dull and dreary life, but for God's sake, get yourself a new pair of slippers–or a new pair of feet?" It was really too late for that and, besides, he felt sorry for his daughter.

The tea was ready. The Old Man poured out two cups and offered one to his daughter.

"Dad, why don't you go and get a haircut today?" she said. "You look like a hippie."

"Why don't you stop shuffling your feet, dear."

His grandson joined them and grabbed a piece of toast. It was time to leave.

The Old Man and his grandson walked side-by-side along the road. They were both lost in their memories, one had too few of them and the other had too many.

The boy knew what lay ahead: talk of homework not handed in and badly forged parents' signatures, detention and punishment. He would have to feign contrition, remorse and redemption. But, inside, he found that he could not bring himself to actually care.

The Old Man was dressed in the leather jacket that the insufferable George had given him at Christmas, after watching, with vague unease, the TV broadcast of *Carry on Christmas,* starring Sid James as Scrooge. He was still trying to find his way back to somewhere, like a sailor who has not seen the sea for a long time but keeps looking for it.

The school was typical of the sixties, an invitation to truancy–or arson. The very path that his grandson seemed to be following, in fact. They were supposed to meet the Headmaster to discuss the boy's future for ten minutes of routine, programmed compassion.

After informing a janitor of the purpose of their visit, they went looking for the Headmaster's office, crossing dreary hallways that connected a depressing row of spiritless classrooms to the administration wing. Outside, several red-cheeked students, wheezing and panting, were slovenly kicking a ball in an unconvincing parody of football.

Once they reached the Headmaster's office, a secretary told them to wait in the corridor, under a poster that bleated: LIFE IS BETTER WITH EDUCATION.

Headmaster Putnam was a small, middle-aged, rotund man, who tried to hide his premature baldness by combing a lock over his rather large forehead. A Mongol warrior might have been proud of that forelock, but on him it looked really stupid. After asking them to sit down, he shuffled a batch of papers, then addressed the Old Man.

"I'm pleased to meet you, but I was expecting…"

"I'm the boy's grandfather."

"Ah! I see."

The Head looked at the file in front of him before continuing:

"Of course, I'm quite happy to see you. I've had some, er, communication problems with this young man's parents. With him, too, to tell the truth. Which is why we're all here, isn't it?"

The main guilty party pretended not to hear and grabbed a snow globe from the desk. He then went on to inflict the worst storm ever on the miniature Big Ben inside.

"Please put that back on the desk and listen to me, young man," said the Head. "Thank you. You see, that's precisely our problem. The boy has no respect for authority, no regards for the belongings of others. He does what he wants, takes anything that grabs his fancy and completely refuses to obey the school's regulations. That antisocial behavior, if it's allowed to continue unchecked, will only result in far more serious problems in the future."

"I see," said the Old Man, with a poker face.

"We're running out of time. Your grandson is 14 and still in the sixth grade; in other words, he's two years behind."

The Old Man took a pack of cigarettes out but stopped as the Head pointed an accusing finger towards a poster that said: *HEALTHY FOOD, PHYSICAL ACTIVITY AND **NO SMOKING** FOR HEART HEALTH.*

"So, he's a little behind. So what? Not everyone can be as smart as you are."

Puffed up by what he took to be a sincere and heartfelt compliment, Headmaster Putnam, who had the air of a priest counseling a sinner on his deathbed, tented his fingers and began to pontificate.

"Let me make things clear. One of the central tenets of our school is that it is possible for each student to fully develop his true personality and abilities. Faculty members strive to encourage students' own self-realization as well as to foster the development of upstanding citizens who not only contribute to the advancement of the community, but also function as contributing members of society. But that doesn't mean that we encourage laxity. Personal expression must be for the benefit of the entire school, and not become a nuisance or an impediment to others. Do you understand me now?"

"No."

The Head sighed. *It must run in the family*, he thought. "Then I'll give you an example..." he continued, aloud. "Last week, your young man set the canteen's dustbins on fire, then ran off. We just barely avoided a major catastrophe. Several parents complained..."

"Why didn't you just spit it out?"

With a brusque gesture, the Old Man slapped the boy hard with the back of his hand. The boy fell off the chair, crying. The Old Man jumped up and began kicking him in the shins; the boy tried to crawl under the Dean's desk, bawling and screaming. The Old Man, cursing loudly and promising more kicks, tried to grab his grandson by the hair to pull him out from under the desk.

Horrified, the Head got up and grabbed the Old Man to restrain him.

"Sir! Sir! Stop! This behavior is completely unacceptable!"

"But you just told me he's a good-for-nothing troublemaker. Well, I'm gonna teach him a lesson so he won't bother you again."

"Please, sir, you must stop! That's no the way to treat a child." He called out. "Miss Wentworth, show our visitors out. As far as I'm concerned, this conversation is over. I regret having asked you to come see me and I don't want to ever hear from you, or any of your family again!"

"Fine," said the Old Man. "With all due respect, Headmaster, you oughta stick your precious upstanding citizen community program up your ass and buy yourself a goddamn toupee instead. I think that would do more to improve discipline around here. Good day, sir!"

Outside, sheltered by the porch, the Old Man and his grandson each lit a cigarette and waited for the drizzle to stop.

"You all right? I didn't hit you too hard?" asked the Old Man.

"Nah! Nothing compared to what Dad would have done. But you didn't warn me about the kicks."

"A little bit of improvisation makes a scene more convincing. OK, I think we can go home now."

While they were trudging along Macklin Street, a sickly-looking passerby bumped into the Old Man and immediately apologized.

Suddenly, a name sprang, unbidden, into the Old Man's mind: *English Bob*. But he had no idea what it meant.

The other man must have felt something too. He turned to watch the Old Man and his grandson walking away, dropping a bottle of milk in the process.

When he finally noticed the white puddle spreading over the sidewalk, the Old Man had disappeared around the corner.

The other man reflected that some memories are the same color as milk.

That night, the Old Man's daughter had bought fish and chips for dinner. They were still wrapped in newspaper and smelled of vinegar. He barely ate and paid little attention to George's unusual good mood.

"So he told that faggot Headmaster off?" asked George.

"You should have been there to see it, Dad! It was wicked," said his son.

"Yeah, why wasn't I there? What did that ass Putnam want anyway?"

"Ah, er, it was just my gym shoes, Dad," said the boy, realizing his mistake. "We're supposed to take them off after practice and put them back in our locker, but I forgot and Putnam said…"

"Well, no point in having gym shoes if the boys can't walk in them, I say," remarked George's wife, coming to her son's support.

The Old Man had stopped listening.

He was in another world, all his own. The myriad noises of the dinner table had transmuted into a series of sounds and names, evocative of memories that still escaped him, were just beyond his grasp.

The Crystal Palace. And now, English Bob.

He had to find out. Put all the pieces together. Confront whatever picture would ultimately emerge.

"I'm going to the pub," he said.

The local pub was a place to drink beer and occasionally play darts. The usual customers were there: the two Llewelyn-Davies brothers, two old men with child-like eyes, always dressed in tweed jackets and brown corduroy trousers, playing darts to pass time, the local lothario, Ken Barlow, and the ever-acerbic Ena Sharples.

The Old Man ignored their comments and sat off in a corner.

English Bob.

He was holding on to that name like a life preserver in a storm. He knew that it was the key that would unlock the mystery, the thread that would unravel the veil that had been obscuring his vision.

The name of a friend, and yet one that evoked a sense of shame, embarrassment.

"A game of darts?" asked one of the Llewelyn-Davies.

"Loser buys a round of drinks," added his brother.

"Not tonight, thanks."

"You've got a chance tonight. Nibs' quite drunk already."

"Speak for yourself, Tootle. I'll teach you a lesson that'll make you cry!"

The Old Man ignored them and finished his drink, watching a report on the telly about the next *Apollo XIII* mission scheduled to be launched the following month.

When he returned home, his daughter was still waiting for him in the kitchen. She was sitting on a stool, wearing white sandals instead of her usual slippers. He almost cried when he noticed that detail. In her own, simple way, without resentment, she had been responsive to the needs of a father who had too often ignored her.

"You don't look well tonight, Dad. You barely touched your food."

The Old Man sat opposite his daughter, under the kitchen's bright neon light.

"I'm sorry. I know you're making an effort, and believe me, I am, too. But I'm not feeling comfortable here; with your husband and sons."

The young woman laughed bitterly.

"Feeling uncomfortable is the story of my life, Dad. Sometimes, I envy you. You don't know what it is to have a life cluttered with thousands of insignificant, ordinary little things. I wish I could go back to a simpler time, like when I was a small girl. Mommy used to say that parents are the guardians of their children's memories. Well, I'd gladly trade all of mine against that lost innocence of a blank state of mind. No past, no worries."

"Jeezus, so that's why they killed Paul McCartney!"

Syd was jumping up and down inside the trailer, like a frog on acid, an analogy that was not too far from reality.

"But Paul isn't dead," objected the Old Man's grandson. "I saw him yesterday on the Beeb. He was talking about the break-up of the Beatles."

"Listen, kid, there's some issues of *Vampirella* on that top shelf–go jerk off while I talk to your granddad. No, not that one, that's No. 1! Yeah, it's simple: until '66, Paul wrote mostly crap, stuff like 'yeah yeah yeah,' good enough to attract chicks, but suddenly, he turns into a fucking genius. So, Grandpa, do you know what I think?"

Since that the question was purely rhetorical, the Old Man let Syd rant on.

"I'll tell you what really happened. In '66, Paul died in a car accident in Scotland. Then, a look-alike took his place."

Pleased with his revelation, Syd let a long silence pass before brandishing some album covers.

"An accident, my ass," he continued. "A Government conspiracy! They had the Beatles by their short and curlies because if they told the world Paul was dead, the others could have kissed the money and the pussy good-bye! But John inserted some secret messages in their songs. Listen!"

Syd put *Magical Mystery Tour* on the turntable and went to the very end of *Strawberry Fields Forever*.

"I'll play it backward; pay attention."

The Old Man almost jumped out his chair when he heard a noise that sounded like the skinning of a cat ripping through his eardrums.

"Did you hear it?"

"Not clearly, no."

"Fuck you, Old Man! Make an effort!"

Thanks to Syd's prodding, the cat's mewlings finally produced something audible.

"There! Did you hear it: 'I've buried Paul. I've buried Paul.' If that's not a confession, I don't know what is! Luckily, John's got that Chinese chick to bring him down to Earth."

"She's not Chinese, she's Japanese," said the Old Man's grandson.

"Chinese, Japanese, who cares! It's an Asian bird who doesn't care about money and doesn't want to see her man reincarnated as a rabbit, just because he betrayed his friend for a lot of dough."

"That's not enough evidence," said the Old Man.

"Not enough? What about *Sgt. Pepper's Lonely Hearts Club Band*? Look at the cover–all the VIPs are attending a funeral. There is a flower display of yellow hyacinths, in the shape of a yellow left-handed guitar. Paul was left handed, the guitar represents him and it's got only three strings on, meaning that there's only three Beatles still alive. And the fake Paul is holding a black *cor anglais*–the only one with a black instrument–symbolizing death–and he's holding it with three fingers–again, three Beatles. Issy Bonn, a member of the crowd, has his right hand raised above Paul's head. That's a symbol of death in a lot of Asian cultures! And there's an Aston Martin on the right side of the cover; that's what he was driving."

"These are just coincidences..."

"Fuck, man, you retarded or what? If you hold a mirror horizontally through the middle of *Lonely Hearts*, the message 'I ONE IX HE ◇ DIE' appears. 'I ONE' is 11, 'IX' is 9, so it reads '11-9,' the date of the crash, 'HE DIE' and the diamond shape points straight up at Paul. And what about the facts that all the Beatles are looking straight at the camera, except the fake? What do you say to that, eh?"

"All right, but so what? Where's the conspiracy? Why would the Government care about the Beatles? And why should I care, for that matter?"

"*You* ask me that, Grandpa? Think! It's the same old story all over again. Louis XIV locked his twin brother inside an Iron Mask, doubles run rampant through Wilkie Collins' fiction, Chaplin impersonated Hitler, Doctor Doom switched bodies with Mister Fantastic and now, they replaced Paul with his double. But the music goes on, Grandpa, the music always go on."

"What music?"

"The military music, the John Philip Sousa marches, the flower in the rifle, marching to war in the pretty uniforms in step with the music. But inside, you're empty. Remember the Johnny Rivers song, Old Man: '*They've given you a number and taken away your name.*' It's not just your name they took away, but your life, your heart and your spirit. Just like Paul's. And they've left you with nothing but a lonely heart."

When they got back around 7 p.m., the family was watching television, playing the Ad Game.

George was slouched in his armchair, his pants undone, his stomach hanging out. The Ad Game was as simple as it was stupid. When a commercial break came on, each of them had to ape whatever the ad was airing, whether it was singing the merits of a new soap powder, pretending to drive a fancy sports car or delight in savoring the latest tomato soup. Needless to say, the experience was humiliating for the victim, but great fun for those watching.

If one of his boys had to pose as a housewife praising a detergent, George would insist that they talk in a high-pitched voice. The Old Man had always refused to participate in the game, and even left the room when his daughter had been forced to act the part of someone in love with a new brand of diapers.

For now, George was grumblingly muttering about a shaving cream. It could have been worse; he had managed to cheat and avoid his turn, which would have forced him to impersonate Raquel Welch.

"Oh, there you are," said George. "How much did he want for that spark plug?" he asked his son. "That much? That goddamn hippie's got a cheek! Go up to your room and do your homework. I'm sure Headmaster Putnam has more on you than that shoes business. Don't make me call him. You," he added, pointing at the Old Man, "stay here. I want to talk to you."

The Old Man settled at the other end of the sofa.

"The two Stooges from Social Services came back today. I don't care for all that crap. What do they want with you?"

"I don't have a clue."

"Really? Well, I've got news for you. I'm fed up with that constant harassment–after all, it's not like we force you to sleep in the attic or feed you garbage–so I went to the Department of Health and the City Mental Health Trust and the Social Services Department–I must have been sent to at least a dozen different departments. And no one knows anything about you. All I've got was that you must be part of some new Government aid program being tested and I should do exactly what I'm told. What to do you say about that?"

"That you should do exactly what you're told."

"Smart guy, huh? Well, I'll find out more at the end of the month. Because that's when they're coming back, and this time, they told me they want to talk to you."

"Do you remember the young fellow we ran into the other day?"

His grandson was listening to him carefully. Since the meeting with the Head, the Old Man had gained his trust.

"Yeah. The one who bumped into you?"

"Yes. He was holding a bottle of milk and carrying a bag of groceries. So he must live somewhere in the neighborhood. I want you to find him, and tell me where he lives and what he does. It shouldn't be too hard, he's the only one with short hair. Also, don't say anything to your Dad or your brother. If he's who I suspect, I want to be alone when I talk to him."

"Who is he?"

"He might be someone who was once called English Bob."

The monthly comics convention took up the whole hall. There were around 50 dealers, crammed into a space too small for them, with boxes and boxes of (mostly) American and (some) British comics. Syd–who had a table there–had told the Old Man that he might enjoy it. So he had gone, unfortunately accompanied at the last minute by George, who had decided to sell a complete collection of *Jeff Hawke* confiscated from his son.

"Serves the bugger right for not mowing the lawn properly."

They now stood in front of Syd's table, which was manned by the hippie and a friend of his nicknamed "Bolo," a true Marxist-Leninist Revolutionary. The Old Man had met him a few times when he visited Syd and had taken an instant dislike to him.

Bolo was a scruffy, pot-bellied man who wore a military jacket above a dirty Che Guevara sweater. He never listened to anyone but himself, always interrupted the conversation and filtered everything through a Marxist prism. Taxes? A capitalist ploy denounced by Marx. The neighbors' son had gone into the Army? A traitor to his class. Rock music? Marx. Cunnilingus? Also Marx. Marx, Marx, Marx. For Bolo, any topic led to Marx. Bolo, who lived with his mother (a decent woman who earned her living as a housecleaner), was impressed by George, whom he took to be an authentic representative of the exploited proletariat. George, on the other hand, pretty much ignored him.

"So, you're Syd?" asked George. "We've already done some business together, through my older son. How much for this run of *Jeff Hawkes*?"

Syd felt ill at ease, because due to a series of unforeseen circumstances, he had not yet managed to unload the *Captain Marvel* lunchbox, which now sat on top of a box behind him, next to a G.I. Joe doll still in its original box. And, of course, he had recognized George instantly as the box's previous owner.

The Old Man had caught his game, which consisted of trying to hide the lunchbox behind his skinny body, while performing a series of intricate dancing steps, left-right-left, to match George's shuffling on the other side of the table. Finally, George got tired of Syd's wiggling and asked:

"What's wrong with you, you got the runs? Stop fidgeting and give me a price."

Wishing to close the deal quickly and avoid any unpleasantness over the box, Syd offered George a goodly sum.

"That much?" whistled George. "If I'd known, I would have taken the rest of his collection. It sounds like you've got a hell of a good business there. Show me what else you have."

"Nothing that you would be interested in, sir," said Syd, wishing George would go away.

"Only comics and pulps. The opium of the people," said Bolo.

"Did I ask for your opinion, fatso?" said George. "Let me have a look."

As he perused the goods before him with an acquisitive eye, he suddenly froze when he spied the *Captain Marvel* lunchbox, despite Syd's attempts to hide it.

"Hey! I've seen that box before. I had one just like it."

"Really?" said Syd, who started to sweat. "If you want to sell it, I'll be happy to make you an offer."

"Didn't you hear what I said? *Had.* As in, someone stole it from me."

"I'm sorry to hear that. It's quite a collector's item."

"I'd like to have a look at it."

Displaying unexpected swiftness for a man of his bulk, George reached over the table and grabbed the box, which he proceeded to examine carefully.

"It looks just like mine..."

"Of course. They were mass-produced. Must be thousands of them still around," said Syd, hopefully.

George pointed at the rust spots that made Captain Marvel look like an actor in a Kabuki play.

"And these rust spots, they were mass-produced, too?"

"What do you mean?"

"It's simple. My lunchbox was stolen on the bus and I think I'm looking at the thief."

"It can't be, sir. I swear to you, I just bought this lunchbox yesterday from a crippled boy who needed the money to take a holiday. It was his most treasured possession."

"Well, I can tell you where you're going, and it's not on holiday, mate. I'm going to call Old Bill..."

The Old Man suddenly jumped in and handed Syd a couple of pounds.

"Give me the box, and these comics too," he said, grabbing a few books off the table.

"What? You're going to let that thief get away with it?" said George. "That's not right! I want to teach the bastard a lesson..."

The Old Man pointed at a number of onlookers who had begun to gather around.

"First, you don't know he's not telling the truth. Two, if you call the police, you'll be the one who'll look like a fool on Monday morning when your mates find out that you got into a fight over a stolen comic book lunchbox."

"Something I had nothing to do with," said Syd. "But if the gentleman says the box is his, I'm more than happy to let it go at that price–a very good deal, I might add."

George was fuming and getting increasingly red in the face, but he dimly saw the wisdom of the Old Man's words. Grabbing the box, he turned round and dashed towards the exit.

"Thanks, Grandpa, I owe you one," said Syd. "And enjoy the comics. You picked a good run."

Back home, the Old Man started to read the comics. They were indeed quite spectacular.

It was a run of *Captain America*s by Stan Lee and Jack Kirby, starting with No. 100, the April 1968 issue when Marvel had given Cap his own title.

The first issue told the story of Steve Rogers, a puny non-entity who volunteered to become the guinea pig in an experiment that turned him into a super-soldier. Then, at the end of the War, just as the Nazis were on the rope, Cap had been frozen in a glacier, only to be thawed out 20 years later by the Mighty Avengers.

The Old Man did not remember the War, but the vision of young Steve Rogers being experimented upon by the kindly Professor "Reinstein" and of his subsequent reawakening, his Captain America costume under his shredded soldier's uniform and still carrying his famed shield, caused him to experience a pounding pressure in his ears.

Long-suppressed memories were trying to smash their way into his conscious mind.

The Old Man was thirsty. He put the comic books back on his nightstand, got up, walked towards the door and collapsed.

The Old Man did not know how long he had been wearing his son-in-law's pajamas.

He felt the scratchy beard on his face and guessed that it must have been several days.

He was in a white room, probably in a hospital, separated from his neighbor by a white, opaque curtain. Someone had left flowers and a box of chocolate on a bedside table.

The wall clock read six, but he did not know if it was a.m. or p.m.

The Old Man moved his toes, then his arms and his legs. Obviously, he had no major wounds, but he knew he still needed more rest.

And more importantly, for the first time in years, *he knew who he was.*

Lord Kraven fell sleep, the quickest and safest way to reach a four-color world of make-believe, which had suddenly become very real.

But he also knew that, soon, he would have to return to this world, George's world, because there were still too many unanswered questions.

"How do you feel, Grandpa?" asked his grandson.

"You gave us quite a fright, Dad. The doctors said you had a stroke," said his daughter.

"I loaned you my best pajamas so that we wouldn't be embarrassed," said George. "Make sure you don't pee on them."

The entire family stood by his bed, dressed in their best Sunday clothes.

A family that SOMEONE pretended was his. But who was that SOMEONE? Certainly not that young woman who had never known her father, and who had welcomed him as such, by default. Not George and his children, who had been presented with a *fait accompli*. Why had he been delivered to the doorstep of their house, an old and nearly decrepit man, like a useless boat good only to be moored on the beach, never to go at sea again...

"The doctors said you could come home at the end of the week," said the woman who thought she was his daughter. "And good news, the Social Services people put off their visit. Time you need to get better, they said."

Now he remembered everything.

The beginning and the end.

It had all begun in the spring of 1897 in Cambridge, on a rainy afternoon, while he was studying in his little bedroom under the College's rooftops.

A prefect had come to fetch him, telling him to hurry, because someone important wanted to see him. He had put down his book and put on his jacket, not knowing that he would never return.

Outside, it was pouring; the rain was flooding both St. Andrew's Street and the courtyard of Christ's College. He had climbed the worn-out steps leading to the Library and, after a shy knock on the heavy oak door, had been admitted into the Special Studies Office, where no student ever went.

Three men were waiting for him. One was his House Master. Another was Sir Reginald Plumdritch, a well-known biologist and physiologist. The third man was hugely fat and was busily toasting a muffin in the fire place, beneath a plaque commemorating Darwin's stay at the College. The young man briefly wondered what the father of the Theory of Evolution would have thought of the Fairy Folk who had just appeared through a hole in the "aether" three months earlier.

His House Master gestured to him to sit down.

"These two gentlemen have expressed the wish to meet you, Richard. I'll let them tell you why."

Having finished his muffin, the fat man walked away from the fireplace and poured some tea.

"There is no need for you to know my name at this stage. But I'm sure a bright lad such as yourself must have recognized Sir Reginald here. All you do need to know is that we're in charge of a research program to identify and recruit a certain number of, let's say, exceptional people throughout the

Empire. The appearance of the Fairy Folk from Neverland last year has shaken the very foundations of our society. Some in the highest echelons of Her Majesty's Government fear the threat they may represent. Right now, we want people to believe that the situation is under control–but 'under control' doesn't mean 'in control,' does it? No one knows what tomorrow might bring... Do you know what 'ethology' is, young man?"

"It's the study of animal behavior, relative to their environment. It can be traced back to Darwin and his work on the expressive movements of man and animals, I believe."

Sir Reginald sputtered with enthusiasm.

"Excellent, boy, excellent! That is precisely my field of research. Since the Fairy Folk have arrived on Earth, I've dedicated myself to their study–the diversity of their species, the transmission of their racial characteristics, what makes them tick... I call it *evilution*. Did you realize that they are superior to us in many ways?"

"I've heard that, sir, yes."

"Therefore it's quite lucky that they seem to have spontaneously adapted to our way of life."

"With a few exceptions," said the fat man who was now watching the downpour through the window.

"Certainly, certainly," continued Sir Reginald. "And that is precisely why we're here. But let's not jump ahead of ourselves. You see, my young friend, we may not be so lucky forever. Yes, for the most part, the Fairy Folk have assimilated into our society, playing by our rules as we abide by the rules of, say, cricket when we choose to play it. But what if they suddenly get tired of the game? We must think ahead. The Empire needs to be protected. Our regular guardians–the police, the army, the navy–might not prove adequate. That is where Science comes in. We must create a new breed of protectors, a new kind of guardian... In short, *a League of Heroes*!"

The imposing stranger returned from the window and took over:

"We want the best Albion has to offer–a team able to intervene successfully whenever, wherever the need arises. A last rampart to protect us from the creatures of Neverland and the forces that they have–perhaps unwittingly?–released on Earth. And you, my friend, have been chosen to become part of such an elite."

"Me? Why me?"

The House Master gave a thick file to Sir Reginald, who began to leaf through it.

"Why, that should be obvious. Eton, Cambridge, good grades, an exceptionally fine mind, outstanding physical condition. Boxing, cricket. *Mens sana in corpore sano*. Good breeding. And you're an orphan, too. It's all exactly perfect for our purposes, even though there's still a long way to go. I have developed what I have dubbed a *metaconditioning program...*"

Sir Reginald was becoming visibly excited as he began spelling out the details:

"Actualization of life potential, comprehensive training in all weapons and hand-to-hand fighting techniques, intensive psycho-physiological reconditioning..."

"And a new identity," added the fat man. "Yours is far too common and wouldn't impress people at all. Totally unsuitable for the man who will soon become the Savior of the Empire. There's a small barony in Scotland that hasn't had any heirs for a couple of centuries. Would you like to become its Lord? What do you think of becoming–Lord Kraven?"

That very night, they took him to a secret military camp in Northumberland where Sir Reginald began implementing the metaconditioning program that would remake him into the nearly superhuman Lord Kraven.

There, he was made to go through an exhausting schedule of lessons, drills and exercises; he learned fencing, riding, gymnastics and a thousand ways of disabling or killing an opponent; he was taught how to survive in the jungle, the desert and the icy wastes of the Poles; he was shown how to hone his instincts, to develop his senses beyond the range of normal men; and finally, he was trained to be the very incarnation of Albion, equally at ease in the ballrooms of Washington and the gambling dens of Shanghai, a symbol and a role model– Lord Kraven!

Only when he would share the occasional meal with others in the mess hall, wearing a non-descript uniform, did he again mingle with ordinary men.

Twice a week, he was subjected to the most humiliating medical examinations and forced to go through unusual, experimental procedures devised by Sir Reginald and his medical team, led by an eccentric doctor named Armand Moreau. As his former persona was erased and reshaped into that of Lord Kraven, his physical prowesses continued to reach new peaks. He would run for hours on end inside a giant training wheel, not unlike a hamster's, tubes connected to every orifice of his body. Sometimes, the wheel itself was submerged in a tank full of one of Moreau's pseudo-amniotic liquids and he had to keep running while letting his lungs be filled with the green, almost fluorescent solution. At other times, they injected him with toxic substances that would have killed an army of lesser men, and exposed him to mysterious rays that bleached his hair but only made him stronger.

Finally, one November morning, Sir Reginald declared that he was ready. Albion was at last ready to meet Lord Kraven.

He was given a not inconsiderable amount of money, a first-class train ticket to London and told to present himself at the Reform Club.

There, he met the fat man from Cambridge again, only now he had a name: Sir Phileas Fogg. He was given a mission: to gather other exceptional people, worthy of joining the League.

Lord Kraven looked for such people from the rocky coast of Cornwall to the Orkneys of Scotland. But John Bull and Lady Guernsey, who had in their times defeated Spring-Heeled Jack and Sweeney Todd, were too old, and Charles

O'Malley, the Irish Dragoon, was, well, Irish, and therefore could not be relied upon. As for Challenger, he wanted nothing to do with Fogg, for whom he bore a mysterious, relentless enmity.

Finally, Lord Kraven recommended the personal shaman of Tiger Lily, who had chosen to take up the mantle–and the identity–of Albion's Greatest Detective, the late Sherlock Holmes, who had perished in locked battle with his deadliest enemy, Professor Moriarty, at Reichenbach in 1891. Tired of the ritual songs of his people, his Moon worship shaken by the crossing from Neverland to Earth, the Indian had decided to embrace rationality and dedicated himself to serve the Empire on which the Sun never set.

Sir Phileas, at first, refused to consider this new Holmes' application, even feeling offended by his impersonation of one of Albion's shiniest stars, until Sir Reginald showed him the advantages that they could derive from the Neverland Indian's assistance.

"First, the creature *is* very good. You should have seen him solve the *Bruce-Partington* affair. The true Holmes couldn't have done it better. Second, announcing the return of Sherlock Holmes to the League of Heroes will be a major publicity boost. The Office of Information Management will have a field day with the news. Consider also that, by recruiting him into the League, I'll be able to study him at close range. Finally, his joining us will be a propaganda blow to Peter Pan. One of his precious Indians becoming a trusted servant of Albion will considerably weaken his cause among the Fairy Folk."

Sir Phileas had agreed and the shamanic Sherlock Holmes had been added to the League.

Together, he and Kraven had then traveled to the equatorial jungles of the Congo, following rumors that a man–a peer of the Empire, no less!–had been raised by apes. The simians, a species of Bonobos dubbed *Mangani*, had managed, beyond belief, to achieve the same results as Sir Reginald with all his scientific techniques: John Clayton, Lord Greystoke, was a living god, the Lord of the Trees. But His Grace had a bad temper and had, at first, refused to leave his jungle to join the League. He had, however, changed his mind upon making the acquaintance of the lovely Jane Porter, one of Sir Phileas' agents.

"After the savage, the primate," had ironically commented Fogg when Lord Kraven had returned from mission. But, all things considered, the Master of the League of Heroes preferred to be forced to associate with an Ape-Man rather than any of the inhuman creatures that had crossed over from Neverland. In fact, because of such feelings, Sir Phileas never truly warmed up to Sherlock Holmes and the spirit of the League was tainted.

That had been the beginning.

And now, the end.

In January 1920, Lord Kraven had chosen to undertake one last mission for the new League.

After his speech in Paris, Lord Kraven had had much hope for the new League of Nations–and the new International League of Heroes.

But soon, fractures had appeared. None of the western powers trusted the Steel Comrade, with whom Kraven had forged a powerful bond of friendship in the days following the Conference.

Then, after Lenin's assassination, Bronstein had taken over the young Bolshevik Republic and the Steel Comrade had disappeared.

Denied access to the Blue Room and Sir Phileas, at the Americans' request, Lord Kraven had found himself increasingly isolated. The French Hero, the Nyctalope, did not trust him because he had pleaded in favor of lesser reparations for Prussia. He had accompanied Holmes and Baron Stromboli on one mission, his presence tolerated mostly because of his prior knowledge of the Shangri-La Electric Company, but it had felt like a last hurrah.

The new, International League of Heroes was dead before even the first official meeting of its sponsoring organization, the League of Nations.

It had then been suggested that he join a new expedition to the American Antarctic, sponsored by the major western powers, to look for mysterious three-eyed aliens, whose signals had been intercepted by a French scientist the year before. He had agreed to do so, but only because Lars Christensen, the man theoretically in charge of the expedition, was an old friend.

Lord Kraven had been welcomed by Christensen and his team, not like a hero preceded by his reputation, but as a great aeronaut. Kraven wanted to be just another member of the team. The airship *HMS Albion Ascendant II* was a pure marvel of aeronautical engineering. Kraven had been flying it above McMurdo Sound towards Mount Erebus for a few days when the mechanic reported that the envelope had developed a tear. They had to land to mend it. But they never did.

An explosion put an end to the mission. The powerful hydrogen blast set fire to the entire airship, melting its hull and causing the gondola to crash. Three Norwegians died on the ice field; Kraven fell into the black, icy ocean.

The water hardened his irises and seeped into his lungs while he was still struggling, until he finally gave in to the icy repose of death.

The wall of his new bedroom was now almost entirely covered with pictures.

After leaving the hospital and returning to George's home, Kraven had forbidden the others to enter the new room that had been set up for him in the attic.

He had begun to decorate it with images of his past life. Ignoring his family (if that is what they were?) and their entreaties, surviving mostly on sandwiches and nicotine, he had begun to take apart and cut out images and photos from the pile of comic books and magazines Syd had given him.

First, images of Garth, with his aviator's jacket, defying death from castle tops, struggling against Asian hordes, rushing to rescue Astra, a reasonable surrogate of Lord Kraven himself, filled the left side of the wall.

Then, next to him was Sherlock Holmes, a collection of photos of Basil Rathbone and Geronimo. Lord Greystoke had been easier to cast; the American swimmer Johnny Weissmuller made an acceptable double.

Below were photos of Queen Victoria, Kaiser Wilhelm, King Edward-Albert VII (curiously known here only as Edward VII), George V, Winston Churchill, Georges Clemenceau, Theodore Roosevelt and Woodrow Wilson.

He had not found any satisfactory pictures of Sir Phileas, Sir Reginald and Cavor, so he had had to resort to a bit of trickery. He had stuck a photo of Charles Laughton's head over the body of Sydney Greenstreet for the Master of the League, and had drawn glasses over a photo of a young Vincent Price for Sir Reginald. For Cavor, he was still toying with a photo of Billy Bunter, played by Gerald Campion, except that it was missing the signs of genius and occasional maliciousness of the inventor of Cavorite.

Entirely absent altogether were Peter Pan and the Fairy Folk. Kraven had rejected the nauseatingly sweet images of the Disney version–the real Peter Pan would have laughed had he seen them! The closest image he had found was that of a particularly evil-looking Pan in an encyclopaedia of Greek Mythology.

Every day, he added new photos: Errol Flynn as Prince Spada (except Spada had never had such beautiful teeth), Joe Kubert's *Enemy Ace* as von Tod (recolored with a red crayon), Kerwin Mathews as Sinbad (which had necessitated drawing a new mustache and beard all over his face), a villain from the *Fantastic Four* comics, the Puppet Master, as Baron Samedi, portraits of well-known actors or panels cut out of comic books, which reminded him of their far more vivid real models who now lived forever in his memory.

At night, Kraven pressed his face against the window. A storm had just broken. The dark, empty void outside exactly mirrored what he felt inside.

Rationally, he should have been in his mid-90s, yet his body did not look a day older than 60. Had he been frozen in ice, like Captain America, only to be mysteriously recovered 30 years ago? But if so, by whom? And where had he been in the interval? Or was his delayed aging the result of some experiment performed on him by Moreau during Sir Reginald's metaconditioning program?

So many questions, so few answers.

Outside, the wind continued to blow away the fragments of truth he had so painfully gathered, like so many bits of rain-soaked garbage, until nothing was left but the promise of a brighter tomorrow.

His grandson–was he?–had succeeded in tracking down English Bob. Every evening, after working at the local plant, he shopped for groceries in a Pakistani-owned store, where he bought a pint of milk and some biscuits. Kraven had approached him outside the shop and asked if he wanted to join him for a drink. The other man agreed.

"English Bob, yes, that's my nickname," he said, after having taken a sip of beer. "They call me that at the plant because my folks were supposed to have come from Germany. They all think it's funny."

He was–should have been–a good ten years younger than Kraven, but didn't look it. He was skinny, balding, with a waxy complexion; he stooped and frequently rubbed his stomach.

"Yes, your birth name was Rupert Hammerstein," said Kraven. "Which was changed to Robert Hammerstone, before you became English Bob. Then, you went back to using your original name after the war."

Kraven was careful to not specify which war he was talking about. It was clear that whatever fate had befallen him and slowed down his aging had also affected English Bob. But rushing his companion before he was ready would only risk driving him away.

"Do you remember any of that?" he added, to confirm his guess.

"Honestly, I can't tell you," replied the other. "Because of the accident. I was caught in an oven explosion at work ten years ago. I was on a lunch break and a spoon perforated my stomach. Apparently, I developed some kind of traumatic amnesia. I forgot most of my past. They told me later that my parents were dead, that I had no immediate family and that I was all alone. I don't remember anything from before the explosion. In fact, seeing you is the first time that I ever felt as if I was on the verge of remembering something from my past."

Kraven smiled inwardly and let the other finish his beer. He was starting to like him. Exactly as he had felt the first time he had met him–so long ago.

"What do you remember about me?"

"It's still confusing. Affection and respect, mixed with some fear and concern. I'm positive we've met before."

"Don't tell him too much, Your Lordship. He's not ready yet."

The two Llewelyn-Davies brothers had suddenly stopped their regular game of darts and joined them. Nibs was whispering in his ear, while Tootle looked like he was standing guard.

"You can talk in relative safety here. They might think you're just a senile old fool, like my brother, Tootle, who pretends he suffers from seizures. Take your time, there's no rush, especially considering how much time they stole from you. But, above all, don't say the names of the people you never want to see again out loud. *The Fairies have very sharp ears.*"

They rushed away before he could question them further.

Kraven walked English Bob home. The younger man was renting a room from an old retired couple. They were simple folk who had found in their lodger the ideal listener.

The room that was perfectly clean and smelled of furniture polish. The walls were sparsely decorated with faded watercolors and there were no books on the single shelf. The only luxury was a small transistor radio next to the sink.

Kraven suggested that they meet again. Bob agreed, but not that week, for he was expecting a visit from two men—from Social Services.

In the halcyon days of the League of Heroes, Kraven would have merely had to cable Sir Phileas to obtain all the information he needed within the hour. He would have known who the men from—allegedly—Social Services were; he would have been told their names, their rank, their addresses and even if they had some kind of secret in case he needed to blackmail them.

Now he had only Syd.

It turned out that his "family" was being compensated for their accommodation. Every month, when the two men from Social Services came calling, they gave George money—always in cash.

When Kraven had remarked on the oddity of alleged civil servants giving away cash instead of issuing a proper Government check, his son-in-law had replied that he was quite happy with the arrangement.

"You'd rather get a medal than some honest cash," he had said. He might not have been wrong.

Kraven had searched the family's archives—a shoebox containing stacks of old photos—for clues, without any luck. There had been no letter announcing his arrival, only the carbon of the "receipt" signed by George when he had been delivered on their doorstep. For all he knew, the document was a fake. It did say "Social Services" and was printed on Her Majesty's Stationery, but the address was a postal box somewhere in Central London.

Then, there were the interviews.

During each of their visits, the two men had insisted on talking to George in private. Kraven had tried to question his son-in-law about the contents of their conversations, but either because he had been sworn to secrecy, or more likely just to irritate the Old Man, George had remained obdurately discreet.

Only once, after several stiff drinks, to make himself appear important or to torture him further, George had dropped a hint:

"They want to know if you read any papers or borrow books from the library. When I said you didn't, they looked disappointed. But I told them about the comics you get from that little thief. That did seem to interest them, so I gave them his address."

He knew George was a fool, but he had underestimated his pettiness. If it had not been for the rest of the family, and the need to not raise any red flags, he would have taught him a valuable lesson. But instead, he meekly finished drying the dishes.

His collection of mementos in the attic had grown rapidly, expanding to cover a second wall.

There were now pictures of an airship, a castle in Bavaria, the Great Pyramid of Gizeh, the Eiffel Tower, the *Lusitania*, the Antarctic, the trenches at Ypres, San Francisco, Bela Lugosi in *White Zombie*, a labor strike... In an issue of *Marvel Collector's Item's Classics*, he had found a picture of the original Iron Man in his clunky grey armor, which he had stuck next to an image of Robot Archie from *Lion* magazine. And in the center of it all was the panel from *Avengers* No. 4, when the Wasp cries out: "Wait! Don't you recognize it? It's the famous red, white and blue garb of–Captain America!" The return of a hero, decades out of time

He was hoping to find more answers next month when he would finally meet the men from Social Services for his own interview. Until then, there was only Syd.

"So you were an agent for something called the 'Albion' Empire? And back in the days of Queen Victoria? Boy, someone sure owes you a lot of dough in back wages, Gramps!"

Syd had listened to the Old Man carefully, interrupting his story only to change a record or roll a joint.

"I'm supposed to be dead. I fell into McMurdo Sound in the Antarctic."

"It's not that I don't believe you–I do, really!–but that's a lot to swallow at one go."

"There are other clues. For instance, when I was at the hospital, the doctor told me that I have an old scar on my head. As if there had been a hole drilled through my skull. And one was, in 1911, when I fought the Sons of the Pharaoh!"

"Let me have a look. Wow! That's quite a hole!"

"Yeah. I've often wondered if it had anything to do with my amnesia," said Kraven.

"*I'm fixing a hole where the rain gets in and stops my mind from wandering where it will go,*" sang Syd. "It's a door you've got to open, my friend. And, don't worry about George giving my address to those Government guys. If they come round, I'll try to sell them a new set of tires. I'll always be there for you–and for this English Bob of yours, once you tell him the whole story. Mind you, I still think 'English Bob' sounds kind of like a brand of sausage!"

"Fairy Folk? Why not the goddamn seven dwarfs while you're at it? Are you pulling my leg or have you finally gone totally ga-ga?"

George had first spat out his beer, then laughed in his face. For the first time since the Old Man had moved in with them, he looked seriously worried.

"All I did was ask you if you'd ever heard of the Fairy Folk of Neverland."

George didn't bother replying; instead, he got up and went into the kitchen. The evening had started OK. The Old Man's daughter had gone up to bed early, leaving the two men to watch television. The BBC had been broadcasting a documentary on the battle of Stalingrad.

"It's weird, but back then, I never thought they'd make it," Kraven said. "Everyone hated the Bolsheviks."

George, who had been busy munching his way through a box of cookies, raised a quizzical eyebrow but didn't reply.

That's when Kraven had dropped his bombshell.

"You see, where I come from, England was called Albion. I find it hard to imagine the fragile Bolshevik Republic I knew as one of the world's two superpowers. I've gotten used to the idea of World War II and the end of the Empire and that Franco-Prussian alliance you call the Common Market, but what I don't understand is, whatever happened to the Fairy Folk? To Neverland?"

George finally returned from the kitchen with a beer.

"I've heard of Neverland," he said.

Kraven had looked at him, suddenly puzzled.

"You have?"

"Sure, like everybody else. It's in that movie and that book, *Peter Pan*, isn't it?"

Kraven's heart sank. He had come across various mentions and pictures of Peter Pan, which had first appeared in print in a 1902 book called *The Little White Bird* by Sir James Matthew Barrie. But the Barrie he remembered had not written that book; instead, a distinguished scholar and author, he had been appointed by Queen Victoria as her personal ambassador to Neverland and later made into a baronet by her son.

The mystery remained intact.

"Why are you asking me about *Peter Pan*? Have you seen any, er, Fairies lately?" asked George, suspicious.

While in the kitchen, he had wondered what they would do if his father-in-law began to lose his marbles. He had heard once that common delusions, like hearing voices or talking to invisible people, were the first signs of senility. If the Old Man began to see Fairies, soon they would have to spoon-feed him and change his nappies. Not a pleasant prospect.

Kraven was so intrigued by the mystery of what seemed to be divergent histories, that he entirely missed the cause of the concern in his son-in-law's voice.

"No, of course not." (George sighed with relief.) "That's why I'm wondering where they all went." (George's relief disappeared as fast as it had come.) "Maybe they all left after the Paris Peace Conference," continued Kraven, oblivious of his son-in-law's sputterings. "I tried to use it to broker a peace for a better, more unified world with the help of the Steel Comrade, hero of the Russian people, Baron Stromboli and my friend, the Great Detective, who used to be Tiger Lily's shaman. But we failed. Maybe that's why they left?"

It was all too much for George to digest.

"Who left?" he was almost afraid to ask.

"The Fairy Folk. The Indians. The Lost Boys. The Pirates. Didn't anyone tell you about them? Your parents? They weren't just characters in a book, you know!"

George began to panic. For probably the first time in his life, he was virtually speechless. He had no idea what to say. He sputtered a hasty good-night and quickly retreated to the safety of his bedroom, his mind filled with images of bedpans, nurses' bills and stained pajamas.

Kraven remained alone, staring at the television screen, not paying attention to the shaving cream commercial leading into that night's episode of *Callan*.

Suddenly, his daughter walked in the room.

"I don't know what you've been telling George, Dad, but he's really upset. I know you don't think much of him, but he isn't a bad sort; he worries a lot about you, you know. He said something about you believing in Fairies and *Peter Pan*. I don't really know what he was talking about, but my Mum used to read me *Peter Pan* every night before bed. She used to say that he was a mean little child... Anyway, I kept that book. I thought, maybe it was a gift from you to her... I don't know... I haven't opened it in years, but here it is..."

And she gave him a beautiful first edition of the 1911 *Peter and Wendy* by J.M.Barrie.

The book was a masterpiece of clever disinformation.

Remarkably written and well-documented. In it, one could find an accurate description of Neverland, its topography, a description of the people who lived there, and a study of their customs. It was all there: the names of the Lost Boys, the *Jolly Roger*'s crew, even the secret of the crocodile, which had generally been kept quiet at Lord Hook's request.

There was so much information in the book that had been kept secret in the days of the League of Heroes, even information that would never have been disclosed to Barrie himself. And yet, the book was real, not fake. There were, however, certain subtle shadings that only someone with Kraven's experience would have noticed. Peter Pan was described in a fashion that made him appear more human. The arrogance was there, but mixed with enough innocence that the Boy Who Would Not Grow Up seemed friendly, almost endearing. Even Arthur Rackham's drawings lacked the sheer ferocity of the real Peter Pan. He was a monster of pride and willfulness who fought the Indians with the Lost Boys and the Lost Boys with the Indians, a tyrant who ruled his troops with an iron will, brooking no disobedience, and most of all, a criminal who snatched young children away from their mothers' breasts.

Kraven had met James Barrie before he had received his appointment from Her Majesty. He had played cricket with him. He remembered him as a small man with fine features, a straight nose and a magnificent moustache. He often wore a hat with a large brim that made him look like a mushroom. But he could not be the author of this book!

Soon after the Fairy Folk had arrived on Earth, Peter Pan had met Barrie during one of his rare visits to our world. For some reason, he had almost fallen in love with the man. Their shared obsession with the fantasmic universe of children was undoubtedly the source of their mutual admiration. Barrie had written some stories that greatly appealed to Peter, who henceforth had selected him to be his confident and biographer.

When the Resistance had begun to coalesce around Peter and Tiger Lily, Sir Phileas Fogg had forcefully reminded Barrie that his duty lie with Albion (or else...) and the writer had been appointed Her Majesty's Secret Ambassador to Neverland–another word for spy and double agent. Barrie, still sympathetic to Peter Pan, had nevertheless used all his skills and cunning to avoid the worst between the Empire and the Boy Who Would Not Grow Up. The real Barrie would no more have been tempted to write a book like the one Kraven held in his hands–especially one that recast Peter Pan in such a favorable a light–than Sir Hudson Lowe would a kind memoir about Napoleon.

Barrie had written a book, in fact, *A Young Child's Guide to History,* penned at Sir Phileas' suggestion in order to warn the children of Albion about Peter Pan. The first draft, judged too positive towards the Fairy Folk, had been sent back to Barrie for a rewrite. It had taken the author several tries before "getting it right." The writer had never forgiven Sir Phileas. Despite being made a baronet, he had become very bitter. In 1917, he had written *Dear Brutus,* which contained a fierce satire of Fogg.

When Kraven left the public library, the next day, it was with the certainty that *Peter Pan* was indeed a real book, and that J.M. Barrie's *A Young Child's Guide to History* was not.

He sat on a bench in a small park adjacent to the building. He was still grappling with the notion of finding himself in a world that differed so much from the one he now remembered.

On the one hand, there was his life spent in the service of the Empire of Albion, which seemed to be a fiction; on the other hand, there was this new reality full of disinformation and false clues. And here he was, an old man split between the two, trying to reconcile his past with his present.

Kraven lit a cigarette, looking idly at a non-descript piece of modern art erected in the middle of the park. He pondered over his age, English Bob's age (had he, too, been ex-

136

perimented upon?), their missing years, their amnesia, reviewing all that had happened to him since he had left the hospital. But the disconnect between the two worlds seemed total. Except...

And suddenly, he remembered the Llewelyn-Davies brothers, the only ones who, like a Greek chorus, seemed to have knowledge of both worlds and who had spoken a message of warning to him, as if it came from the gods.

"Nibs and Tootle? Funny that you should bring them up today. Bolo here was almost snatched by them when he was but a baby, weren't you, Bolo?"

Syd was delicately replacing damaged parts in an amplifier with all the dexterity of a Doctor Barnard of hi-fi.

"Oh, crud, Syd, you shouldn't say a word about that; it's personal," whined his associate.

"C'mon, Bolo, it's no secret. Your Mum told everyone on the street; Gramps would have found out sooner or later."

The fat teenager wiped his hands on his greasy T-shirt that was imprinted with a red star.

"The old crock's potty," he complained. "For all I know she might have imagined the whole thing. She's batty enough for that."

"You shouldn't talk about your mother like that, young man," said Kraven.

"I don't need any morality lessons from you, you imperialist pig. I know what you lackeys of the bourgeoisie are all about!"

"What do you mean?"

Looking as if he was the only one to know something confidential, Bolo tapped his nose.

"I know about Prince Eddy and the brothel on Cleveland Street and Annie Crooke and Lord Arthur Somerset who used to bugger boys. They tried to suppress the truth like always, Queen Victoria and Lord Salisbury and Sir Robert Anderson, but it all came out; it always does. It's sickening what those fat

137

pigs did with small boys and whores. That's why I became a Marxist."

Kraven felt so angry that his face went red. He would have heartily punched the young Marxist in the face, had he not restrained himself. Information was more important than avenging the honor of his beloved Royal family.

"You're lying. No member of the Royal family would have dared molest a child. Only Peter Pan committed such crimes."

Bolo looked at him, surprised.

"Peter Pan? That's some trip you're on, man. OK! Come and meet my Mum–you'll get along great with her, I bet. Birds of a feather and all that."

Syd had followed the conversation without interrupting. He wiped his hands on a Petula Clark poster, put on his denim jacket and pushed the two men towards the door.

"Let's go. It'll be an opportunity to taste her biscuits."

Olga Lovinsky–Bolo's mother–received them in her humble kitchen, which smelled of roastbeef and mashed potatoes. A sweet woman with a pale complexion, she dedicated all of her time to her son. Bolo–his first name was actually Boleslaw, after his grandfather–had been conceived by accident after a chance encounter with a handsome Russian émigré and Olga mothered him like a female bird when she found a cuckoo in her nest.

"It's a blessing that you have come, sir. I've been waiting for this moment for years."

Syd and Bolo had gone upstairs to look at Bolo's comics collection, their stomach full of pastry. Kraven had stayed behind, alone with the old woman. He told her about his past–not his entire life story, not the most extravagant or hard to believe elements, but just enough to create a sense of complicity, of intimacy with a person who was about the same age as he. Soon, she began to confide in him as he had confided in her.

"The doctors had told me I couldn't have any children. My Boleslaw was a gift from God."

Outside, one could hear the laughter of children playing in the street. The children. *It was all about the children*, thought Kraven. *"Every time a child says 'I don't believe in fairies,' there is a little fairy somewhere that falls down dead,"* Peter Pan had said. That's why he hunted children and brought them to Neverland. To keep the Fairy Folk alive.

"It was in the early '50s," Olga continued. Kraven realized that he had missed a portion of her story but did not interrupt her. "I was hanging my clothes in the garden. My baby was by my side, when someone knocked at the door. Nothing important, but I can still remember it as if it were yesterday. Someone from the Salvation Army. Calling on me, who had barely a penny to my name! Well, when I returned to the garden, Bolo was gone! I thought he might have crawled to the shed, but then I noticed that his crib was gone, too. Have you ever seen a female wolf whose pups were taken away? Well, me neither, but I know how she must feel. I went crazy, ran across the main road without paying any attention to the traffic. That when I saw them, with my own eyes, right in front of me. They were running in their best Sunday suits carrying my little darling."

"Who? The Llewelyn-Davies?"

"Yes. Whatever their name was. They were young then, but so was I. I caught up with them. I grabbed my baby back then I hit them and scratched them and slapped them as hard as I could. They ran away like the cowards they were."

"Did you call the police?"

The woman smiled through her tears.

"Times were rough, sir, even more for a single mother, the daughter of communist immigrants. It's from his granddad that my Boleslaw got his political beliefs. No, there were no witnesses to support my story, so I didn't say anything."

Olga took a small, perfectly ironed handkerchief from her sleeve and rubbed her eyes.

"You look like a good man, sir. I'll tell you something I never told another soul. A few years later, I saw the two of them again, at the opening of the local supermarket. And you know what struck me as strange? They looked really old, much older than their age, considering how many years had gone by. A horrible idea occurred to me then. In the old country, there were legends about creatures that stole children to feed on their lifeforce. It was as if their failure to suck the life out of my poor Bolo had left them drained. Yes, that's what I believe... We called them *vourdulaks*... Vampires..."

In his attic, Kraven was looking at the latest additions to his wall of memories. A third wall was now devoted to the missing chunks of his life. He had bought a *Time-Life* encyclopaedia and cut out photos from a past that was as alien to him as the surface of the Moon that now bore the American flag. Under the color photo of Neil Armstrong saluting the Stars & Stripes was a black-and-white image of the 1929 stock market crash in Wall Street. Next to it was Hitler giving the Nazi salute over the heads of his soldiers. There were photos of the atomic bomb mushroom cloud and of the Berlin Wall, of the Korean War and Viet Nam, of Chuck Yeager and Yuri Gagarin, of Lenin and Joseph Stalin, of Charles Lindbergh and Howard Hughes, of Max Schreck as Count Orloff in *Nosferatu* and Sean Connery as James Bond in *Goldfinger*, of General de Gaulle and Konrad Adenauer, of Elvis Presley and the Beatles, of Clark Gable and Vivien Leigh, of Werner Heisenberg and Albert Einstein, of Mao and Fu-Manchu.

According to his grandson's history books, in this world, the Great War had also ended with Prussia's–Germany's–defeat, but with no landing in Portsmouth. Even though the actors on the world stage were the same–Woodrow Wilson, Lloyd George, Georges Clemenceau, the Treaty of Paris was the Treaty of Versailles, and the Society of Nations, the League of Nations. But Lenin had not been assassinated, Sir Phileas Fogg had not pulled the strings of British (pardon, Albion!) Intelligence–and the League of Heroes was nowhere to be found. Bloody Friday had occurred on the same Glasgow square, but three years later, in pretty much the same way that had cost him English Bob's friendship and respect, but he, Lord Kraven, was conspicuously absent.

At that point, Kraven thought that he could either give up his mad quest and hope that senility would soon obliterate all his questions, or he could persevere and try to fathom what had happened to him. It would have been easy to accept the notion of a parallel universe, an alternative reality, like in the comics, when Barry Allen, the Flash of Earth-1, had met Jay Garrick, the so-called Golden Age Flash of Earth-2. But somehow, he could not accept it. All his instincts rebelled against it. Deep in his soul, he *knew* that the English Bob he had met was *the same* English Bob who had been with him in Ingolstadt and aboard the *Lusitania*.

And then, there were the Llewelyn-Davies brothers. The Lost Boys. The Vampires. Kraven had taken four jacks from a deck of cards and stuck them to the wall. There were meant to represent not only the two brothers but also the two mysterious Social Services employees who pulled the strings of his life.

He took James Barrie's book and read out loud:

I don't know whether you have ever seen a map of a person's mind. Doctors sometimes draw maps of other parts of you, and your own map can become intensely interesting, but catch them trying to draw a map of a child's mind, which is not only confused, but keeps going round all the time. There are zigzag lines on it, just like your temperature on a card, and these are probably roads in the island, for the Neverland is always more or less an island, with astonishing splashes of color here and there, and coral reefs and rakish-looking craft in the offing, and savages and lonely lairs, and gnomes who are mostly tailors, and caves through which a river runs, and princes with six elder brothers, and a hut fast going to decay, and one very small old lady with a hooked nose. It would be an easy map if that were all, but there is also first day at school, religion, fathers, the round pond, needle-work, mur-

ders, hangings, verbs that take the dative, chocolate pudding day, getting into braces, say ninety-nine, three-pence for pulling out your tooth yourself, and so on, and either these are part of the island or they are another map showing through, and it is all rather confusing, especially as nothing will stand still.

"I don't understand a word of what you're saying!"

Kraven gestured to English Bob to speak in a lower voice. His landlady had not appreciated his late visit and he did not want to attract more attention.

"It's quite simple. I found you in the streets when you were just a little thief with a grimy face. But you were skilled and it didn't take long to bring your full potential to light. Young Rupert Hammerstein became Robert Hammerstone, then English Bob of the League of Heroes."

The other man had a far away look, as if the walls of his modest bedsitter had suddenly opened to reveal a new, exhilarating vista. But his mind was still struggling with these revelations.

"But what about the Fairy Folk? I never heard they were real. I've never seen any."

Kraven thought of what George would have said. "You've never seen my ass either, but it's still there." But English Bob deserved better.

"I understand your skepticism. Frankly, I don't have all the answers myself. In the past, that same skepticism of yours saved me from many perils. Well, you're right to be skeptical. I can recognize the same mistrust that once saved us from many dangers. Think of it this way: what if you met a traveler from China who told you about places and creatures you never heard of? Would you doubt his word just on that basis—if he really came from China? Just think of me as that traveler, who has returned from a place that is closer and yet, in some respects, much farther away." Kraven crushed his cigarette in the sink and added: "And you, too, come from that same place; you just don't remember it yet."

Bob threw a spoonful of bicarbonate in a glass of water and swallowed it with a twitch.

"I don't remember anything from before my industrial accident. All those adventures, me piloting an airship, the Crystal Palace..."

"The Queen herself decorated you that day. To reward you for stopping Doctor Fatal–and saving my life."

The young man smiled shyly.

"How do you explain my amnesia then?"

"It's clear that both of us were the victims of some kind of plot. I fell to my death after the explosion of the *Albion Ascendant* in Antarctica. You were severely wounded in the stomach during the War in a fashion similar to that of your 'industrial accident.' "

"You mean, the explosion of that oven at the factory?"

"Yes. I suspect this was a conveniently made-up explanation, used to provide a cover for your memory loss. The unarguable result, however, is that we ended up here, in 1970, eking out a miserable existence in the suburbs of a London whose history has changed. There is also the matter of our respective ages..."

"What do you mean?"

"I should be in my mid-90s, yet at the hospital, they said I was 64. How old are you?"

"52."

"You were a teenager when you joined the League. You should be in your 80s. Both of us are 30 years younger than what we should be. Something–I don't know what–has slowed down our aging process. Or maybe, we were somehow frozen, or brought here out of time. I don't know what really happened to us, but I intend to find out."

"So you think it's the two of us against the rest of the world?" asked English Bob.

"Yes. A righteous man will not allow himself to be swayed by a gaggle of liars. I have a task in mind that may give us the answers to the questions we ask. It may be a bit risky, but the way I see it, we haven't got a choice."

Since he had nothing to lose, his mind remaining steadfastly blank, English Bob listened to Lord Kraven late into the night.

When he returned home, it was 4 a.m. The entire family was up, waiting for him in the living room. They were not alone.

The two men from Social Services were with them.

"Please sit down," said the taller of the two.

Kraven knew immediately that something was wrong. The late hour of the visit, of course, but also the fact that George was steadfastly silent. Normally, his son-in-law would never have let a stranger order anyone around in his own home.

Kraven sat on the sofa between his daughter and his grandson.

"Some time ago, we left you in the good care of this family in order to ensure you a peaceful life. Our regular visits have shown us that you were adapting rather well to your new existence. All this is very good. So this may well be our last visit."

"Great news," grunted George. "But couldn't it have waited for tomorrow?"

"There's one last check we have to make," said the Government agent. "Listen to this." He gestured to his colleague. The other man pulled out a portable tape player and pressed a button.

"*That's just what our colonies have been waiting for! And I'm not even talking about Neverland. You can be sure that Peter Pan and the Indians will use the 14 Points to challenge our control of Neverland. Just as we're doing our best to rebuild the foundations of the Empire!*"

Kraven shuddered with his entire being. He had recognized Sir Phileas Fogg's voice.

He also remembered its context: that evening at the Reform Club, the project of a League of Nations and the reluctance of his superior.

How had they obtained such a recording? Had Sir Phileas not trusted his Mnemonics and installed secret wire recorders? And then had the recordings later transferred to magnetic tapes, a device perfected during World War II?

The reel-to-reel tape ended, making a whirly paper noise.

"We're going to ask you one last question and if we like your answer, this will be our last visit."

The family leaned forward, as if they were listening to a game show on the radio.

"What does 'Neverland' mean to you?"

The younger boy raised his hand up in the air, wiggling on his chair as if he was at school. But a stern look from the agent was enough to calm him down.

Kraven instinctively knew that, one way or another, the next moment would determine the rest of his existence. So he decided to waffle a little to buy himself some time.

"That's the place where Peter Pan lives," he said finally.

Obviously, the two agents were not satisfied with his answer. They looked at each other.

"Yes, Peter Pan, Tinker Bell, Tiger Lily, we all know the novel," continued the agent. "But what does it mean *to you*?"

Fortunately, before Kraven had time to answer, George, who had endured enough, sprang from his chair and began yelling at the two men:

"No! Not *Peter Pan* again! What's wrong with you lot? Why not ask if we've seen Dorothy and the Tin Woodsman in the living room while you're at it!"

"Please, sir. This doesn't concern you. Sit down," said the agent.

"This is *my* home!"

"That's right, sir. You should reflect on that and not endanger it by making our task more difficult."

"Is that a threat? That's it! You two wankers are going to get out right now or I'll smack you both!"

"Please calm down, sir. That's your last warning."

Since George looked like he was not going to be complying, the taller agent seized him by the collar of his shirt and threw him to the floor. His wife, screaming like a mad woman, jumped up and scratched the man in his face. Without losing his composure, the Social Services man pushed her away, took out a gun from his pocket and pointed it at the children.

"I think it'd be better if we continued our conversation elsewhere," he said to Kraven. "Get up and follow us, sir."

They had been driving for a good hour. Blindfolded, Kraven was focusing on the sounds of traffic, trying to guess their destination. Either the driver did not know his way around London, or he was doing it purposefully to confuse him, but it seemed to him that they had been driving in circles.

Finally, the car stopped and his blindfold was removed.

The *White Hart* had once been a posh, secluded hotel where a minister or a businessman looking for a discrete tryst would be guaranteed he wouldn't find his name splashed on the pages of the tabloids, or where a pop music star could take his latest paramour without worrying about the prying lenses of the paparazzi. But those halcyon days were gone; the hotel had fallen on hard times, victim of the changing fashions of the '60s and of the completion of the M2. Today, it was only a shadow of its former self. Only transients, junkies and runaway teenagers used the place. And the men from the non-existent Office of Social Services.

Ignoring the agent's offered hand, Lord Kraven got out of the car by himself. The lobby of the *White Hart* reeked of urine and damp. The wallpaper was pockmarked and torn in places. They took the stairs to the first floor, the elevator having long since surrendered to lack of maintenance, stepping over the scruffy body of a snoring bum.

The room into which they walked was clean and even smelled of disinfectant. A king-size mattress had been pushed up against a wall to make room for what looked like a dentist's chair, surrounded by several tables and trays containing various surgical instruments and appliances, the uses of which Kraven could not even guess.

With the same, unfailing civility they had displayed so far, the two agents had him sit in the chair. Then, they bound his arms and legs with Velcro straps. The taller man pulled up Kraven's sleeve, took a syringe and injected him with a solution.

"Can you tell me what that is?" asked Kraven.

"Ketamine. A drug that's not yet on the market. It's a dissociative anaesthetic that separates perception from sensation. The proper dosage should be enough to facilitate our conversation."

"I've been immunized against all drugs."

"Not this one."

The second agent put an oxygen mask on the headrest.

"Noninvasive nasal mask-assisted ventilation in the event of respiratory failure," he explained. "I think we can begin."

"What do you know about the League?"

"The football league? The Southern League Division. Crystal Palace is having a good season."

Already, Kraven could hardly feel his body. The drug was altering the way he saw things, amplifying voices, reducing the sizes of objects. The face of the man questioning him became like a hole, a tunnel drilled through the very hotel itself.

"What about the Crystal Palace? Does that name remind you of anything?"

The words were melting like honey on the pores of his skin. It made a noisy layer that covered his flesh and forced him to talk to breathe.

"It was the Queen's palace."

Like the day of his arrival at George's house, the first day of his new life, he was inside a body he could not control.

"Tell us more about the Queen."

"She's... our sovereign."

The two agents stepped out of his field of vision. His answers did not seem to satisfy them. There was no certainty, one way or another. Kraven took advantage of this pause to regain control his breathing, slowly, until more oxygen could get to his brain. Step by step, he was regaining awareness of his surroundings, reducing each illusionary sensation to a tangible perception. Then, he heard:

"*Maybe Fogg is wrong*. It doesn't look as if he remembers anything."

So Sir Phileas Fogg was, somehow, behind this after all. It would have been surprising if that had not been the case.

"Yes, but then, why did he go to see English Bob? And why has he been checking out all those books about Barrie and Peter Pan and the Fairy Folk at the library?"

"What are you saying?"

"I think we should increase the dosage."

Kraven felt the cold sting of another injection in his arm.

"I'm going to ask you to be more specific. Did you or did you not work for the Empire during the first two decades of the century?"

Kraven struggled to find an answer that was truthful–the drug would not allowed him to lie–but evasive enough to not reveal the extent of his regained memory. To work for the Empire was to work for Albion. Didn't anyone serve his country in one fashion or another?

"I've served my country like everyone else."

"Did you know a Doctor Fatal?"

"My doctor's a *good* doctor." He was getting the hang of this.

"A Baron von Tod?"

"I don't speak German."

"Prince Spada?"

"I don't know any Princes."

"The Steel Comrade?"

"Bolo is a Marxist."

Inwardly, he smiled. He was winning. Whoever his enemy was, he was not getting the information he sought. But the pressure in his chest increased with the stress caused by the efforts it took to thwart the drug.

Suddenly, Kraven felt a heavy weight crushing his legs and a spear tearing at his heart.

"He's having a heart attack!"

Then, there was fighting in the room.

George was hitting the agent who had been interrogating him with a fire extinguisher. The man was screaming, his face distorted like one of Francis Bacon's painting. Kraven was unable to know if it was an effect of the drug or a nightmarish reaction to his son-in-law's attack.

The pain was spreading through his chest and reaching his arm.

There was total confusion in the room. There were actually two fights going on at once. The other battle pitted the second agent against Syd. The man from Social Services was pointing his gun at the comic-book dealer who, in turn, held a can of hair spray and a zippo lighter. The flame sprang, burning the agent's clothes and face, until George smothered it by throwing the mattress on him.

Syd dashed towards the tray with the surgical instruments. He nervously filled another syringe.

"What the hell are you doing?"

"Atropine," replied the hippie. "It'll get his heart starting again."

"You're sure about that?"

"Don't worry. He won't be the first man whose life I've saved this way."

Kraven felt a violent shock, immediately followed by a sensation of well-being. When Syd strapped the oxygen mask on his face, his life flowed back into him.

They gathered around the table for an improvised breakfast.

They were four, like in the heydays of the League, because English Bob had agreed to join them when they had stopped by his flat on their way back.

"Since I haven't got any memories, I might as well make myself some," he had said. Since he had spoken with Kraven, he no longer suffered from stomach pains.

They laughed out loud about the events of the night which were still fresh in their minds.

Lord Kraven let them.

"It was child's play to follow their car," said George. "And since it was on the way, I stopped to pick up Syd."

He cut a sausage in half with his knife and ate it with good appetite.

"You must be kidding," said Syd, dipping his toast into his eggs. "Listening to you it's as if we went to the corner shop to buy a pack of ciggies."

George washed down the other half of his banger with some milk.

"Well, if we're going to be heroes, we should be modest about it. Like the caped crusaders in those comics you keep peddling."

Kraven was observing his companions. George, who despite his frailties had not hesitated to set aside his resentment in order to come to his rescue, even allying himself with the man who had stolen his lunchbox. Syd, the hippie drug dealer, junk peddler and petty thief who saw in his story the confirmation of all his paranoid fantasies.

And English Bob, the faithful companion and assistant.

If Kraven let them split up again and each go their own ways, they would return to their dreary, ordinary lives. Watching football on the telly, stealing and peddling junk, clocking in at the plant.

But together, they had shown that they could accomplish great things. Together, they could save an Empire.

Lord Kraven raised his glass and began to speak.

From this day onward, George's kitchen became the headquarters of the New League of Heroes.

PART THREE

The Theater of Crime

Excerpt from
Freedom Is Slavery:
Considerations on the Rise and Fall
of a Totalitarian State,
by Eric Arthur Blair,
Secker and Warburg, London, 1948.

The year 1920 saw the beginning of a series of events that ultimately led to the abolition of the monarchy in Albion and the establishment of the Second Republic of the Commonwealth, under the iron rule of its modern-day Cromwell, Sir Phileas Fogg.

The sudden death of Lord Kraven was a blow to the One World Government party which he had been spearheading. The new League of Nations was further crippled by Bronstein's decision in April 1921 to have the Bolshevik Republic withdraw from the League. The subsequent territorial dispute between the Bolsheviks and the United States of America was further worsened by President Harding's decision to annex Alaska in June of that same year. His opponent, James Cox, declared: "From Seattle to Vladivostok, an iron curtain has descended across the North Pacific."

The International League of Heroes, now led by its sole surviving founding member, Sherlock Holmes, also floundered. The Steel Comrade had vanished inside the Siberian gulag in 1919. Baron Stromboli repeatedly clashed with the Great Detective. Without a strong leader, lacking real governmental support, the International League quietly disbanded in the Spring of 1922, its newly-born hopes, already dead.

Sir Phileas had already abandoned the League, no longer trusting it to be his tool, and replaced it with a corps of "Double-0" agents whose bodies had been enhanced with artificial organs and cybernetic prostheses designed by Dr. Moreau.

Meanwhile, the representatives of the Fairy Folk had become disillusioned with the lack of progress towards recognition of their independence and began a strategic rapprochement with the Resistance, led by Peter Pan and Tiger Lily. That, in turn, led to their joining forces with other anti-imperialistic organizations, such as Sinn Féin and the Irish Republican Army in Ireland, as well as the CPA (Communist Party of Albion), set up in July 1920.

The "Great Jest," as Peter Pan and his fellow travelers called it, was a plan to sow chaos throughout the Empire during the next decade.

It was to succeed beyond even his expectations.

On November 11, 1920, Ireland's first "Bloody Sunday" signaled a further escalation in the struggle when an IRA bomb in Dublin killed 14 police officers. The violence continued despite an attempt to negotiate a first Anglo-Irish Treaty in July 1921 that would have created an Irish Free State. Instead, the battle spread to Albion proper. In 1922, Sir Phileas Fogg ordered one of his Double-0 agents to assassinate the Irish revolutionary leader, Michael Collins. The deed itself was to take place on August 22 in an ambush near Cork, but it failed. By the following year, the whole of Ireland was ablaze. In 1925, however, a new, charismatic Irish leader, The Dullahan, arose among the Fairy Folk and managed to bring together the warring Irish factions of the Sinn Féin and the Leprechauns. On December 6, a Second Anglo-Irish Treaty was drafted and, this time, signed.

Immediately, Sir Phileas Fogg rammed the Third Transportation Act of 1926 through Parliament ("An Act for Effectual Transportation of Fairy Folk and other Non-Human Offenders; and to authorize the Removal of Same to Ireland in certain Cases; and for other Purposes therein mentioned").

Under it, the Fairy Folk were massively deported to the new Free Irish Republic. Fogg also proposed the Preference Act, which gave priority to Humans over Fairy Folk for civil service and private industry jobs.

These Acts were enthusiastically received in Albion by a population which generally blamed the Fairy Folk for its problems; it helped Fogg become Prime Minister in April 1926, replacing Stanley Baldwin who had fought against the passing of the Transportation Act.

Over three million people were now unemployed in Albion. Peter Pan and the CPA stoked the fires of anarchy. A general strike was called, lasting for nine days, from May 3 to May 12, 1926. But Sir Phileas' Conservative Government had prepared for it, creating organizations, such as the Office for the Maintenance of Supplies, to keep the country moving. It rallied support by emphasizing the revolutionary nature of the strikers and vilifying their non-human allies. The armed forces were enlisted to help maintain basic services, and to crush the Neverland Pirates who had seized control of the dockyards. Finally, Sir Phileas was able to convince King George V to place the Empire under Martial Law in June 1926.

Then, the Consumption struck. A new disease affecting mostly the Fairy Folk spread through the ghettos of London's East End where Neverlanders still resided. Some theorized that it might have been manufactured by the Government's newly-established Office of Bacteriological Research, headed by the notorious Dr. Moreau, but that was strongly denied by the Office of Information Management which labeled the suppositions "offensive" and "outrageous." In any event, the Consumption spread uncontrollably and further destabilized the Empire.

On the international front, Vice-President Blaine "Kid" Colt had assumed the Presidency of the United States after the untimely death of Warren G. Harding in August 1923. He was easily reelected the following November, and again, in 1928, leading America on an increasingly ultranationalist and isolationist path.

In Europe, Mathematician Henri Poincaré had been summoned out of retirement to assume the Premiership of France in March 1924. His first decision was to create the ambitious Douzième Bureau to develop extra-dimensional ("ED") travel and thus open new colonial opportunities for France. Despite some early failures, such as the doomed ED flight of Nungesser and Coli in May 1927, France turned its back on Europe to focus on ED research. Poincaré was succeeded in 1929 by Paul Langevin, nicknamed "Miraculas" or the "Man of a Thousand and One Marvels."

In Prussia, Sir Phileas sought to prevent the rise of Socialism by sponsoring a new party, the National Socialist German Workers Party (Nationalsozialistische Deutsche Arbeiterpartei, unusually known as NSDAP). However, its leader, an Austrian watercolor artist named Adolf Hitler, was deemed too reckless and unstable. Sir Phileas dispatched one of his Double-0 agents to cause the projected "Beer Hall Putsch" of November 1923 to fail. Hitler was arrested and replaced by the far more suitable Alfred Rosenberg, editor of the Völkischer Beobachter *(*National Observer*), the NSDAP newspaper. On April 24 of the following year, Hitler was found guilty of High Treason and executed.*

Rosenberg went on to publish a book on racial theory The Myth of the Twentieth Century *(*Der Mythus des 20 Jahrhunderts*) on July 18, 1925. In it, Rosenberg announced his hatred toward what he believed to be the twin evils of the world: Communism and Judaism, and he stated that his aim was to eradicate both from the face of the Earth. He also announced that Prussia needed to obtain new territory to the East: Lebensraum, all of which served Sir Phileas' designs.*

In Italy, after winning two-thirds of the popular vote, the popular Cesare Stromboli, "Il Barone," announced that he was taking dictatorial powers in 1925.

When the London Stock Market crashed on October 24, 1927 ("Black Thursday"), King George V, who had been ailing since the proclamation of Martial Law the preceding year, sunk into a deep depression, and shot himself the following Tuesday.

Sir Phileas realized that this was the opportunity he had been waiting for: the King's heir, Edward VIII, had been spending a lot of time at his estate, Fort Belvedere, near Sunningdale in Berkshire, conducting affairs with a series of married women, including Anglo-American textile heiress Freda Dudley Ward and the Viscountess Furness née Thelma Morgan, an American beauty of partly Chilean ancestry.

Sir Phileas cunningly used this information to persuade the King to abdicate. Edward VIII signed the instrument of abdication on December 10, 1927. The Parliament passed His Majesty's Declaration of Abdication Act the next day and, on December 13, the Second Republic of the Commonwealth of Albion was established with Sir Phileas Fogg as its new Lord Protector.

During this transition, Sir Phileas had relied on the unconditional support of the army and of the captains of industry. By making empty promises to the population about the abolition of social inequality and the need to eliminate magic, the former master of the League of Heroes secured domestic peace and kept the socialist "menace" at bay.

Despite the appeal of a new charismatic Bolshevik leader, Joseph Vissarionovich Jughashvili. a.k.a. "Starshego Brata" (Big Brother), who had taken power in Moscow after Bronstein's assassination on January 17, 1928, the CPA of Albion was on its last legs.

The Second Republic moved quickly to eradicate all of its opposition. At the notorious Bristol show trials of March 1928, dozens of Labor Leaders were convicted of High Treason and hung, among them, Labor Party Secretary Ramsay McDonald, Robert Williams, the Secretary of the Transport Workers Federation, Hamilton Fyfe, the editor of The Albion Worker and Thomas Bell, the head of the CPA. Even the notorious Professor Cavor, who had been found complicit of helping the Unions by refusing to allow his MechaMen to break strikes, was placed under house arrest. In December

1928, after Mohandas Gandhi called on the Albion Govern-
ment to grant India dominion status or face a campaign of
non-violence, he was arrested and summarily executed.

Thus, Albion embarked on a new path, one of interna-
tional isolation, of science and technology, of mass produc-
tion, discarding the trappings of the Empire and its quaint
reliance on magic and the "dark arts." Historians still argue
today over whether this watershed transformation had been, in
effect, Peter Pan's true plan all along–his "Great Jest."

And that is why it is necessary for all of the Second Re-
public's children, before they go to bed, to be utterly con-
vinced that Peter Pan is truly evil.

The Murder of Roger Shamwell
(September 1930)

"I now know how Lord Shamwell was murdered!" announced Sherlock Holmes, twirling his waxed moustache,
with just the right *soupçon* of a French accent. "And I have
never seen such a devilish scheme in my entire career. Indeed,
the murderer might have gotten away with it entirely, if it
wasn't for my little grey cells," he added tapping his long,
aquiline nose knowingly.

The Great Detective enjoyed the reaction of his audience.
At his request, they had all gathered in the library: Lady
Shamwell, the wife of the deceased, the Rt. Hon. Ronald Partridge, the renowned explorer, Señor Miranda and his wife,
Pilar, the famous exotic tango dancers, Mrs. Latimer, sister of
the deceased and, finally, Evans, the butler, who stood by the
door.

After marking an appropriate pause, the Detective carried on:

"I admit for a long time I was puzzled by the presence of
the Mirandas at Lord Shamwell's birthday party. His last
birthday party, as it happens. Why had he invited them? Or

had he? It was only a seemingly trivial comment by the deceased himself, innocently repeated to me by our brave Evans, that provided me with the final clue I sought: 'I don't like those damn dagoes one bit. *Never have.*' Precisely. This meant that Lord Shamwell must have had some acquaintance in the past with people of foreign extraction. We shall return to this later.

"You will note that the type of tango performed by Mrs. Miranda–*Tango Milonga*, if I'm not mistaken–requires a good 45 minutes, a period of time which would have given anyone in this room enough time to slip the poison into Lord Shamwell's curry. This provides us with the opportunity.

"Now, let us note that Indian curry from Rajasthan was Lord Shamwell's favorite dish. But knowing that it is too hot and spicy and frankly, not to everyone's taste–I can't stand it myself!–Lady Shamwell, ever the good hostess, had ordered the cook to prepare and serve a much milder form of curry–a Chittagong curry–to all the other guests. But only Rajasthan Curry could hide the taste of the poison! So the murderer had to know in advance what kind of curry Lord Shamwell would be eating that day!"

Holmes was holding them all spellbound. They were staring at him in fascination as he sprang towards Lady Shamwell, shouting:

"And that means you, Lady Shamwell!"

The woman burst into tears.

"Yes, I hated him; he had ruined my brother. If I could have killed him, I would have. But I didn't do it, I swear it."

"*Naturellement*, you did not, Lady Shamwell," continued Holmes, twirling his moustache. "Because that very day, *the cook had run out of Rajasthan curry!*"

There was an audible gasp from the audience *out there*. *It's all in the timing*, thought Holmes.

"Yes! Without Rajasthan curry, at the last minute, the cook had to find a suitable replacement. The mysterious visitor who spoke to Lord Shamwell in the gazebo at 5:03 p.m. was none other than the Chef asking what Lord Shamwell would prefer instead. And he chose Dhall Curry from Bombay—a city the culinary practices of which are well-known to one of you..."

His face red as a tomato, Donald Partridge stood up and shouted at the Detective:

"What are you implying, you vile French Iroquois! Yes, it's true that our company, the Shamwell & Partridge Spices & Curry Blend, is experiencing some temporary cash flow problems, and that Shamwell could have rescued it by selling his collection of Chipewayan Bilboquets, which he steadfastly refused to do, but that's no reason to murder a man!"

"I beg to differ, *Monsieur*," replied the Shaman Detective. "Many have been murdered for far less. But in this case, the real reason might have been not a sordid business transaction but *l'amour*."

At once, Lady Shamwell turned quite pale. Partridge took a quick look at her and offered his wrists to Holmes.

"It's a fair cop. You've got me bang to rights. I confess. I did the old bastard in."

"Your courage does you honor, *Monsieur*," said Holmes. "But in this case, there's no need to lie. Neither you, nor your lover, Lady Shamwell, could have murdered Lord Shamwell, because in the end, *it was not the curry that killed him!*"

There was another gasp *out there*. This was turning out to be a successful night.

"What I didn't know until I saw the *small marigold blue bottle* was that Lord Shamwell suffered from a rare disease of the liver called Antitrypsin Deficiency. Unbeknownst to all, he had to take a most unique drug, one with strong emetic properties that could have easily obliterated the taste of poison. As Evans testified, the bottle, which had been on his nightstand the night before, was found in the library the next day. So. I asked myself, who would have known about Lord Shamwell's affliction? Who—*but his own sister!*"

Mrs. Latimer looked contemptuously at Holmes.

"That's ridiculous. I had no motive to kill my own brother."

"But you did, *Madame!*" interjected Holmes. He pulled a sheath of papers from his pocket. "This is your brother's missing will, which I found in the remarkably ugly blue-and-pink Chipewayan Bilboquet where you'd hidden it. It clearly establishes that your brother intended to disinherit you!"

Mrs. Latimer went pale, then she straightened up in her chair and snapped her fingers. At once, Evans brought her a full glass of whisky which she drank in one large gulp.

"The swine was going to ruin my life, just because he'd found out I was the one who'd stolen his teddy bear as a child. I couldn't let that happen."

"You mean, the old bat killed Roger?" exclaimed Partridge. "I never thought she had it in her."

"No, the 'old bat,' as you so colorfully put it, *Monsieur* Partridge, did not poison Lord Shamwell. Yes, she saw an opportunity to steal his will, planning to return later to destroy it, but she is not the one who administered the fatal poison."

"But if it's not her, then who?" moaned Lady Shamwell. "Oh, I can't stand it."

"All will be revealed, Lady Shamwell, I give you my word," said Holmes. "Now, we return to the question I asked earlier. Why did Lord Shamwell say: 'I don't like those damn dagoes one bit. *Never have.*' This cable from Buenos Aires, which I received only an hour ago," continued the Detective, pulling a blue telegram from his pocket, "gave me the answer."

There was an audible sigh *out there*, followed by a "high time, too." Holmes ignored it.

"Stay where you are, Professor Miranda! And you too, Señora!" he exclaimed, pointing his finger at the Argentinean couple who had gotten up.

"Thirty years ago, Lord Shamwell made a stop in Argentina and there visited the most notorious brothel of Buenos Aires, *El Conventillo*, famous for its *Tango Milonga*, I note. And there, well, men will be men, won't they?... Need I say more, *Señor* Miranda?"

"No, *Monsieur* Holmes. You are indeed correct. There is no need for me to hide the truth any longer. That *puerco*–Lord Shamwell–was my father!"

A faint *boo* and a few yawns were heard *out there.*

"Except that my mother knew him under the name of Billy Goat. It took me 15 years to track him down. But when we finally made contact, he refused to recognize me! I had no choice but to kill him! I will say no more!"

Miranda sat down, crossed his arms on his chest and remained steadfastly silent.

The sleuth avoided a piece of rotten fruit that suddenly splashed onto the carpet. *I must wrap this up quickly*, he thought.

"I will then explain how Lord Shamwell was killed," said the Detective. "*Tango Milonga*, as you must have noticed, requires the female dancer to wear stiletto heels. The crime was simplicity itself. When *la Señora* Miranda here invited Lord Shamwell to lead in the first dance, she cunningly scratched his leg with her heel, which had been previously dipped in the deadly poison. *Voila!*"

The police entered to take the Mirandas away.

Then the curtain fell on the stage, to scattered applause, mixed with a few cries of "Goddamn Indian fairy" coming from the audience.

It had not been such a successful night after all.

So it went, three nights a week at the Theater of Crime, for the Great Detective who had once been the shaman of Tiger Lily and a founding member of the League of Heroes.

Backstage at the Theater of Crime

The Detective ate his supper with the other actors in the Theater's cantina. Ironically, the real-life Shamwell residence had been confiscated by the Second Republic in December 1928 and had been converted into the cantina, for the benefit of the Theater of Crime players.

The Theater of Crime itself was located in the former Adelphi Theater. There, three times a week, Holmes was condemned to relive watered-down dramatizations of some of his most famous cases, written by Agatha Christie, a young woman whom he had met in December 1926. For him, she would always remain *The* Woman.

The official purpose of the plays was to pacify the masses with easy-to-digest, entertaining *pablum* while at the same time teaching them about the vileness of the former ruling classes during the days of the Empire.

The popularity of the exploits of real-life French detective Jules Poiret, had meant that Holmes' character had been rewritten by Christie with the most atrociously fake French accent and a ridiculous mustache. Anything to please the public. The show must go on.

Holmes occasionally wondered if it was not Sir Phileas–pardon, Lord Fogg's way of teaching him a lesson as well, by forcing him to relive his best cases.

"If you're not going to finish that, I wouldn't say no to seconds," said Paddy McKenzie, a ruddy-faced Irishman who was playing the part of Partridge, this time.

Corned beef with boiled potatoes. A far cry from Sir Phileas' dinners. But these days, Holmes' throat hurt all the time and he could barely swallow anything. Besides, he wasn't hungry.

The shaman pushed his plate towards Paddy. The last actor who had played Partridge had been replaced at the last minute, without anyone knowing the reason why. That happened frequently these days.

The Great Detective took a small quantity of tobacco from his pouch–he was trying to make it last–and began to fill his pipe. Willy Masterson, a former ballet dancer who played Professor Miranda, asked the cook for another serving of meat.

"If you put on weight by stuffing yourself like a pig, you won't be able to play the part anymore," the man rebuffed him. "Be happy with what you have. Think about our Welsh brothers who don't have enough to eat. They're doing a real work, too, in the mines!"

The door suddenly opened and a Double-0 agent appeared. The young man was lean and fit as a wolf. He ordered them to board the bus that would take them home.

The open-roof Guy Motors double-decker dropped him in front of the Baker Street community center. In the glorious days of the League, the Detective used to own his own house not far from the legendary 221B. But in accordance with the latest urbanization plan, confiscated properties had been divided up to house new apartments.

All his trophies–the twin mouths of Demonia,[13] the framed page of the *Necronomicon*,[14] the medallion of Hurlemort,[15] the mask of the Red Tiger [16] and even the Cartel's symbiotes [17] had been vacuum-packed, crated and stored in the basement.

The Great Detective inserted a coin into the central heater–it was his turn today–and walked into the common kitchen where he stayed, sitting on a chair, staring into space, not doing anything.

Excerpt from President Blaine "Kid" Colt's
Inauguration Speech
(March 4, 1929)

My Fellow Countrymen:
This occasion is not just the administration of the most sacred oath which can be assumed by an American citizen. It

---

[13] See *The Mouths of Demonia.*

[14] See *The Strange Case of the Living Dead of Caldwell.*

[15] See *Shadow of the Horla.*

[16] See *The Red Tiger.*

[17] See *The Strange Case of the Symbiotic Cartel.*

is a dedication and consecration under God to the highest office in service of our people. I assume this trust with humility and the knowledge that only through the guidance of the Almighty can I hope to discharge its ever-increasing burdens.

It is in keeping with tradition throughout our history that I wish to express simply and directly the choices I have made concerning a matter of the gravest importance. We shall go to the Moon in this decade.

We shall choose to do so not because it is easy, but because it is hard, because that goal will serve to organize and measure the best of our energies and skills, because that challenge is one that we are willing to accept, one we are unwilling to postpone, and one which we intend to win.

A Hole Full of Water

The Double-0 agents came for Holmes just after 9 a.m. It was too late for an arrest, which generally took place at dawn, and too early for the afternoon rehearsal.

"Was I that bad last night?" asked the shaman with a smile.

"Stop joking and be ready in five minutes," said one of the agents.

The Great Detective took the time to knot his hair and to cover his face with ritual paintings.

Mrs. Smith was waiting by the door, with several half-naked, mewling brats hanging onto her skirts. The dignified woman pushed aside the children and declared emphatically:

"It's about time you arrested him. We've already sent you four anonymous letters. He keeps us awake at night with his heathen singing, too."

The senior agent ignored her ranting and pushed Holmes into a waiting van.

The van drove down Baker Street, then veered East until it reached Buckingham Place, where it entered an underground car park located beneath the new Ministry of Central Services.

The Hellenistic-styled facade of the new building was covered with flags bearing the symbol of the New Albion: a black cog wheel inscribed inside a white circle, superimposed over the Union Jack.

The Detective was escorted up the service stairs to the first floor. There, the agents handed him over to a young Ministry officer. The man, who had a rash above his collar, ordered him to sit on a bench in a long corridor with a tiled floor. On the yellow wall behind him were propaganda posters: *IF YOU WANT TO BE A GOOD SON TO THE SECOND REPUBLIC, BE A GOOD FATHER FIRST.*

Two Lost Boys were there, arguing. Obviously brothers, they wore the same autumn clothes. The argument was about a darts game.

"If Peter had been there, he'd have put you in your place, Nibs!"

"Not so loud, Tootle. Look at that Indian over there, pretending to look at the floor. Why, he might be a Republican snitch who's come here to rat on his neighbors."

They were waiting patiently at the Office of Racial Services (Fairy Folk Only). Humans were sent to another floor. The Preference Act made it compulsory for Fairy Folk allowed to remain in the Commonwealth to obtain renewable Residency Certificates, which entitled them to second-rate jobs and healthcare vouchers. Some believed that the Second Republic sent agents disguised as Pirates or Lost Boys to spy on them, even there. Humans suspected of being Fairy Sympathizers or "Furries" were also subjected to State scrutiny. It was not uncommon for a malicious child who had been sent to bed without dessert to turn on his parents and rat them out the next day at the local police station. The parents would then be taken away–no one knew where, although rumors circulated about labor camps built in the Scottish Orkneys–and the brat would be sent to join the Commonwealth Young Republican Legion.

After a half-hour, the young civil servant returned and ushered the Detective into a large office. The man sitting behind the desk introduced himself as Francis Hawkins, Director of Central Services Administration. Three other people were already present in the room. One, Holmes recognized immediately: Sir Oswald Mosley, First Deputy of the Lord Protector himself. He was accompanied by a non-descript, meek-looking man in a brown suit and a young woman wearing the black uniform of the Second Republic. Mosley immediately addressed Holmes:

"I wanted us to meet here in order to not attract undue attention. This is Mr. Bedford, who is our liaison with Professor Cavor, and Chief Commissioner Zyd of Party Headquarters. I must insist on the greatest secrecy. If we ever find out that even the tiniest bit of our conversation has been leaked, I wouldn't hesitate to ship you to the Orkneys, or to shoot you in the back of the head like a dog myself, understood?"

"Not too different from my current lifestyle. I'm reassured, then," said Holmes, not bothering to hide his sarcasm. "Now would you mind telling me what the First Deputy of our Lord Protector could want with an old Indian from Neverland who is the very incarnation of a decadent race which has out-lived its usefulness–at least, that's what it says in your newspapers."

Mosley swept away the mockery.

"If you want to carry on being a second-rate actor, please continue. But we have something better to offer you. A most puzzling and serious case, that only you may be able to solve. I'll let Mr. Bedford tell you all about it."

The meek man in the brown suit smiled gratefully at Mosley and began to speak:

"As you might know, in the last year or so, our Republic, in partnership with the United States of America, has embarked on a joint Outer Space Exploration Program. We aim to send a man to the Moon before the end of the decade. So far, everything has proceeded quite smoothly, despite a few, not unexpected problems, which have all been solved. Until last week."

Bedford turned towards Sir Oswald, who nodded at him to go on.

"A terrible tragedy occurred at our Outer Space Research facility in Cambridge. Let me show you the file."

CC Zyd handed a thick file to the Detective. Holmes took it and first focused on a stack of photographs clipped to the inside front cover. One showed a young man dressed in a white lab coat. Another the same man (likely) lying face down on the floor, in a room which looked like a laboratory.

There was a pool of blood under his head.

"Who was he?" asked the Detective.

"Alan Turing. One of our most brilliant minds."

"What was he working on?"

"You don't need to know that right now."

Holmes examined the crime photos carefully. One showed a swelling at the base of the victim's neck.

"What did he die from?"

"He was found dead in his lab in Cambridge. There was a small hole on his neck near the first cervical. It was found to be full of water."

"An ice needle?"

Sir Oswald reacted diffidently:

"Come on, let's not jump to conclusions. I thought you might say that, but there may be other explanations–ones that would not involve them."

"You mean the Fairy Folk?"

"Yes."

"I'd be curious to hear these 'other explanations.' In any event, the manufacture of Fairy Daggers has been strictly pro-hibited for many years, so there must be more to it than that... What else am I allowed to know about your Mr. Turing?"

"He was a remarkable man, but unfortunately one with deviant sexual proclivities. He was part of a strict reeducation program which, we know, he found painful and humiliating. One of our theories is that he might have committed suicide."

"By drilling a hole in his own neck with a water pick?"

"That's why we decided to call you out of retirement, Detective."

"By 'we,' I presume you mean Lord Fogg?"

"Indeed. Our Lord Protector thought you might enjoy the challenge. I will add that, for the duration of the investigation, you will be made a temporary Deputy Commissioner, reporting directly to Chief Commissioner Zyd here, with concomitant salary and benefits. That is all. You may leave now."

Before Holmes could walk out of the door, he heard the metallic voice of CC Zyd say:

"I'll pick you up tomorrow at 8 a.m. sharp. Don't keep me waiting."

Excerpt from Sir Oswald Mosley's Speech before The House of Commons (May 21, 1930)

My admiration for the Civil Service has vastly increased since I have been in office. But to achieve our policies, it is absolutely necessary that the whole initiative and drive should rest in the hands of the Government itself. The machine which I suggested is a vast, central organization armed with an adequate research and economic advisory department on the one hand, linked to an executive machine composed of some ten higher officials on the other, operating under the direct control of the Lord Protector and the head of the Civil Service.

By Royal Appointment

An abomination, the Detective concluded after reading the file cover to cover.

What the murderer had done to Alan Turing was, to Holmes, less horrible and barbaric than what his own country had inflicted upon the scientist. Convicted of being a homosexual, he had been forced to endure regular hormonal injections, or face castration.

Tears of rage and shame blurred the Detective's eyes. He had seen Fogg rise in power, the League of Heroes disband and the Second Republic emerge like a black beast slowly crawling out of a dark tunnel–and yet, he had done nothing.

Even today, he was still Fogg's bloodhound, secured on a tight leash.

He had been shunned by his brothers, Peter Pan and Tiger Lily, because he had given up the child-like existence of Neverland to grow up and join the world of the adults. But *this* world, he loathed and rejected.

He coughed, spitting into his handkerchief, as if his body was expelling the toxins contained in the report, and unclipped the smiling portrait of Alan Turing.

He put it on his nightstand, as a reminder of what could lie in store if he failed. And then he fell asleep, a final curtain falling on the horrible drama of reality.

The next morning, when he walked downstairs at five minutes to eight, he found Chief Commissioner Zyd waiting for him in the corridor. She was listening to the complaints of Mrs. Smith, who was surprised to not yet be rid of her irksome neighbor.

"You should smell what comes out of his room sometimes," wailed Mrs. Smith. "Not honest English tobacco, for sure. It stinks up the whole place, there's no other word for it."

"I'm ready, Chief Commissioner," said Holmes. "Would you like a cup of herbal tea before we go?"

"No, thank you, Deputy Commissioner. We've got work to do."

"Deputy Commissioner?" said Mrs. Smith whose face suddenly turned very pale.

"Yes, Madam, since this morning," said Holmes. "I might have earned this promotion by telling them about your black market racket, who knows?"

"Please, forgive me, Sir. You've got the wrong family. It must be them Scots on the third floor!"

"I don't think so, at least not if I believe what your husband said. He's the one who confided in me the other night."

The Detective walked out of the building, chuckling at the thought of the impending family clash at the Smith's.

He settled in the passenger seat beside Zyd inside a black Bentley.

"Where are we going first?" asked the young woman.

"Limehouse, Chief Commissioner."

The Bentley traveled smoothly throughout London and, due to lack of traffic, the trip took less than half-an-hour.

They parked the car near what looked like an abandoned warehouse. They could smell the docks from where they were.

"We'll have to walk the rest of the way," said Holmes. "Aren't you worried about leaving your vehicle here unattended?"

"The people cannot steal what already belongs to them," replied Zyd.

They walked down a large, winding road, which was bordered on either side by brick buildings in an advanced state of disrepair. No one had effected any repairs to the area since the firebombing of London by the Prussian airfleet in 1916.

Here and there, between the rusty steel doors, he caught brief glimpses of fairies, their faces and arms wrapped in rags stiffened by oozing pus. The few who had been spared by the Consumption were forced to flee from the Sun. They eked out a miserable existence in the dark, peddling mostly ineffectual spells to gullible citizens.

"We've arrived."

The shop was located in an old brick building that still stood, mostly intact. Just as in the great, old days, no one could see from the outside what made it so special. It had one sign, and one sign only, on its door: *By Royal Appointment.*

It was still there.

The Detective walked down three steps and knocked twice, then three times, then once more, on the ancient oaken door, which had once been pristine but was now covered with soot and grime.

The door opened, revealing the shop's owner: Aloysius Keys, a small, roundish man with marble blue eyes and a wisp of white hair.

"By all that's holy! If it isn't the great shaman himself! Oh, what a surprise this is!"

"For me too, old man. May we come in?"

Keys looked at Zyd with suspicion.

"This is Chief Commissioner Zyd," said Holmes. "You've got nothing to fear from her. Isn't that so, Chief Commissioner?"

"All right. But don't push your luck," replied the young woman.

The inside of the shop was deep in grey dust. Covers protected a few uniforms that were still hanging on racks. Various paraphernalia were locked inside a display case.

"Business isn't quite as brisk as it used to be," said Keys. "But I'm not complaining. Besides, I started saving my money for a rainy day when Kraven died."

"If he did. They never found his body," said Holmes.

"Well, maybe, maybe not. But surely, you haven't come here to reminisce about the past?"

"You're quite correct. But first, let me explain something to the Chief Commissioner." Holmes turned towards Zyd. "Madam, this man was the official costumier of the League of Heroes by Royal Appointment of Her Majesty Queen Victoria herself."

The small man who looked like an imp made a modest, little laugh:

"Perfectly right, Miss. I was indeed the exclusive supplier of the League–and quite a few villains as well. I had to juggle appointments sometimes, so that they wouldn't all come in at the same time. Do you remember the time when my clerk gave the same uniform to Spada and Kraven? My word, I thought they would never fight again so ashamed they were at the thought of being seen together. Those were the good old days..."

"Days which are no more; we've seen to that," said Zyd.

Keys sniffed and spat on the ground.

"With all respect due, my little miss, it's not you who've 'seen to that.' It's the goddamn Second Republic who killed the Fairies when they decided their destruction would bring about political victory and enrich Sir Phileas Fogg and his cronies."

"Watch out, old man. You're dangerously close to being labeled antisocial."

"What are you going to do? Murder me in my own shop?"

The Detective took the photo of Turing's body out of his pocket and showed it to the costumier.

"Enough of that. I've come for information. Can you tell me what might have done that?"

The old man put on his glasses and examined the document carefully.

"I might have an idea, but I'm not sure I should tell you."

"No charges will be brought against you," said Zyd. "You may speak without risk."

"I'd rather hear it from the Detective, if you don't mind."

"I give you my word you'll be kept out of it. Tell me about it," said Holmes.

"It's a Fairy Dagger, an ice needle, circa 1898, I'd say. A beauty. Look at the wound: perfectly neat. A weapon like that can remain solid for years, but once it's been used, it'll melt in less than 10 minutes."

"Who do you think might have used it?" asked the Detective.

"Hard to tell. You can't find that kind of stuff anymore, at least not easily. 'Obsolete, decadent, perverted, blah, blah, blah,' as your new friends put it. But there's always a way... Not more than a week ago, two men came to see me. They showed me a card stating that they were working for the Government, but it might just as easily have been a forgery. They requisitioned my entire inventory of Fairy weapons, including three Daggers–enough weapons for a small massacre. They said they needed props–for the Theater of Crime."

Outside, four Lost Boys, armed with penknives and slingshots, were gathered around the Bentley. The younger one stepped forward and spoke to Holmes:

"So, you're not play-acting anymore. You're back on the real stage." With his hand, he wiped his boils as if they were snot. "Peter and Lily have their eyes on you. Be sure you choose the right side this time."

Reviews for
The Mysterious Affair at Canterbury
(January 1929)

"The cleverest murder mystery of the London theater." The Weekly Telegraph.

"A truly entertaining thriller." The Republican Times.

"It is the absolute right of the Second Republic to supervise the formation of public opinion." A. K. Chesterton, Minister of Performing Arts.

Backstage at the Theater of Crime (cont'd)

The Detective and Chief Commissioner Zyd crossed the stage and proceeded directly to the glass office of the Theater of Crime's stage manager, Joris Lodge. The thin, lanky man was emptying a bottle of brandy while looking at the mug shots of actors spread across his desk.

"Oh, my lead star's back," he said when he saw Holmes enter. "But it's a bit early in the month for your tobacco rationing tickets."

"I haven't come for that. Do you know if you acquired a new set of props, Fairy weapons, about a week ago?"

"I don't have to answer your questions. You're not even in the show anymore. You're fired."

"I seem to lack the power of persuasion, Chief Commissioner," said Holmes, turning toward Zyd. "Will you try your own, unique brand of charm?"

The young woman walked around the desk, grabbed Lodge by his tie and shoved her Party card in front of his nose.

"State security. I want to see your books. Now."

The manager straightened up, smoothed his hair with his hand, and replied in an obedient tone:

"No problem at all. Forgive me if I spoke out of turn. Bonnie, bring the ledgers. Right now," he shouted.

His assistant, a fat woman with nicotine yellow fingers, brought several ledgers and began turning the pages one by one in a frustratingly slow way.

"No weapon props, unless you consider underskirts and mascara to be dangerous," she gave a bawdy wink.

"Have you signed for any engagements outside London?" asked the Detective.

"Let me see," said Lodge, looking through another ledger. "You know that we report to the Ministry of Performing Arts. Normally, I'm not supposed to share that information, but since your friend here insists... Yes, we have a private performance booked next week for Lympne Castle in Kent. Hey, Redskin, forget what I said about you being fired. I'm counting on you for that one!"

"Sorry, it will have to be without me."

The manager's face turned beet red.

"You can't do this to me! Your understudy is drunk half of the time." He turned towards Zyd. "Please, Chief Commissioner, tell him to stay. The other guy may be a real Apache from America, but he can't remember his lines..."

They left Lodge's office while the stage manager was feverishly looking through an old players' directory for a suitable replacement.

"Lympne Castle," said Holmes. "That rings a bell..."

"It's Professor Cavor's current assigned residence," said Zyd.

Excerpt from The Encyclopaedia Albianenses
1948 edition

In 1928, after his public confession during the Bristol show trials, Professor Cavor was placed under house arrest at Lympne Castle in Kent. The former holder of the Lucasian Chair of Mathematics was then set to work on the applications of Cavorite in the field of Outer Space Exploration. That fact, leaked to the Press by the Office of Information Management, contributed to promote the idea that, unlike its Imperial predecessor, the Second Republic of the Commonwealth was not mired in the superstitions and magic of the past.

Old Friends and Secret Meetings

Holmes was seated on a heap of cushions, all the documents he had collected gathered in a messy pile around him. He was smoking his calumet, having been given a ration of tobacco by the ever-helpful Chief Commissioner Zyd, and was evaluating what he knew so far.

Alan Turing, a member of the Outer Space Exploration team, had been killed with a Fairy Dagger. Some men, who might or might not have been Government employees, had removed a stack of forbidden weapons from Aloysius Keys' shop, claiming it was for the Theater of Crime. Said Theater of Crime was scheduled to perform the following week at Cavor's current place of residence, therefore closing the circle that returned them to Outer Space Exploration.

Holmes was shaken by a coughing fit, spitting blood into his handkerchief. As one of the Fairy Folk from Neverland, he, too, was suffering from the effect of the Consumption, a milder case than that which had decimated much of his people, but still extremely painful. He did not know which would kill him first: the dreadful disease or the throat cancer which he suspected was beginning to impair him.

The Detective calmed himself and thought about Chief Commissioner Zyd. The small, thin woman, with her carrot-red hair, cut in a boyish style, reminded him of English Bob. They shared the same seriousness, inherited from their harsh childhoods as well as irrepressible energy. If only she could purge her mind of the Republican propaganda, she might make a very acceptable partner.

The shaman then pulled out a stack of papers documenting the American Outer Space Exploration effort. It was a report signed by President Colt, whose photo could be seen smiling on the cover. Still handsome, his hair now an elegant silver, the President was shown shaking hands with the first American spacenaut, Major Julian James, whom the Press had dubbed the "Moon Man."

Under the soothing effect of the smoke, perhaps his memories triggered by seeing Colt's photo, Holmes began to reminisce about the League of Heroes–not the exploits that were recorded, but his secret encounter with Comrade Steel a year earlier...

It had been a secret meeting. He was near the end of the run of *The Murder in the Cemetery*, and had begun rehearsing *The Big Five* with that poseur, Laurence Olivier.

A stagehand had slipped him a note purporting to be from the great Bolshevik hero, giving him an appointment for that same night on the Isle of Dogs.

He had been on time (as usual). His old partner and friend was waiting for him, standing tall under the full moonlight, in a long black leather coat. Aleksander Dovzhenko had lifted him with powerful arms, hugging him like a maudlin bear. Luckily, he wasn't wearing the chains he usually wrapped around them.

"It's been too long, my friend. But you haven't changed," he said.

The Detective wished he could say the same as he watched his friend take a long drink of vodka from a silver flask. Dovzhenko had been sent to the Siberian *gulag* by Bronstein in March 1919 after the assassination of his protector, Lenin. He had only been brought back when Bronstein, in turn, had been assassinated by Jughashvili two years before. Some said the burly Georgian, who was nicknamed "Big Brother," had personally driven an ice pick through Bronstein's skull. But this might have been Republican propaganda.

Jughashvili had made the Steel Comrade his personal agent–and enforcer. Still, even if you could take the man out of the *gulag*, you could not take the *gulag* out of the man. Dovzhenko had a haunted look, an emptiness that Holmes had learned to recognize among those who had had the misfortune of falling into the hands of the Second Republic's security apparatus.

"I won't be able to stay too long," continued Dovzhenko. "My men are waiting for me underwater. A pocket submarine, undetectable by your own navy. Technology has never been your strong point, has it? Anyway, I'm here because we would like to find ways to get in touch with the Resistance."

The Shaman Detective was prepared for a request of that kind. He took time to think, filling his pipe and letting the wind blow out the match three times.

"I've always had tenuous contacts with them, even at the best of times. Tiger Lily doesn't speak to me anymore and I feel that Peter has become out of control."

"*Da*, I know all this, my friend, but we've got to try. Like you, I once shared Kraven's dream of a brotherly world at peace. Mankind cohabiting in harmony with the Fairy Folk. But that dream died with Kraven."

"They never found his body, you know..."

"*Nichevo*. We must still forge another future."

"Peter Pan and the Resistance have lost all the credibility they once had. They're in cahoots with murderers and terrorists. People are afraid of them these days. You should not consider them as reasonable partners."

The giant suddenly stood up, crushing a crab under his boots.

"We're not looking for 'reasonable partners,' but for weapons to be aimed at the Commonwealth. And circumstances being what they are, we don't have the luxury of choice. Trust me, sometimes, you just have to do what it takes..."

Long-buried feelings, repressed memories of a golden age of what-might-have-been, or perhaps simply the vodka, caused glistening tears to appear in the corners of his eyes.

"Last month, Big Brother told me to travel to Prussia. They gave me the address of a beer hall in Berlin where a meeting was to be held. I walked inside and ordered a beer, which I drank. There were a number of women and children, but mostly men in brown shirts, gathered round their leader, Alfred Rosenberg. He was a White Russian who had fled to France after we gained control of the country. Then, he moved to Munich after the Great War, where he became the leader of the National Socialist German Workers Party. He was built into a prominent German politician thanks to your Sir Phileas, who decided he needed someone reliable to counterbalance the Socialists. Rosenberg used the *lebensraum* theory to promote the notion of military expansion towards the East. He made attacking Poland, Ukraine and Russia his main platform. With German elections coming up soon, we could not afford the chance. So Big Brother sent me to Berlin.

"I listened to what he had to say and forged my own opinion. Then I left–after triggering the bomb I carried. Sixty people died. The men in the brown shirts, but also the women and the children, I'm sorry to say. I'm not proud of what I did, but it had to be done. So you see, we wouldn't be ashamed of Peter Pan's actions. As my own mentor, Vladimir Ilyich, said once: 'If the end does not justify the means, then in the name of sanity and justice, what does?' "

"What do you want from me, Aleksander?"

"Talk to the Resistance; tell them we want to help. Supply them with weapons, cash... Your Second Republic is a bigger threat to world peace today than Prussia. Sir Phileas is more dangerous than Rosenberg. And now he's building a new alliance with America, with that pig Colt, who took Alaska away from us... They not only want to rule the world but now they're reaching for the stars. They must be stopped. I beg you, join us in our efforts!"

Holmes did not have time to reply. Suddenly, there were two rapid shots, one right after the other. Comrade Steel straightened up, took a step back, then staggered and fell in the mud, shot twice in the chest.

Spotlights blanketed the area. Holmes thought he would be next to die and almost welcomed the end. But instead, a voice coming out of a loudspeaker instructed him not to move. A sniper and several Double-0 agents emerged from the darkness. The agents silently and efficiently removed the body of Comrade Steel. The sniper approached Holmes and pointed towards a black Rolls-Royce which had slowly driven out of the night. Holmes, shivering in the cold, walked towards the car. One of the windows rolled down.

"You've always been so predictable, Detective," said Sir Phileas Fogg, Lord Protector of the Second Republic of the Commonwealth. "I only have to follow your trail to keep the enemy at bay. Go on living, Indian, you're still of use to us."

Excerpt from The Shape of Things to Come
by H.G. Wells
Hutchinson, London, 1933

On June 15, 1896, Professor Joseph Cavor was still a young and mostly unknown geologist laboring in relative obscurity in his Kent laboratory.

The object of Cavor's search was a substance that should be opaque to all forms of radiant energy–including gravity.

Oddly enough, it was made at last by accident, when Cavor least expected it.

He had fused together a number of metals and certain other things and he intended to leave the mixture a week and then allow it to cool slowly. Unless he had miscalculated, the last stage in the combination would occur when the stuff sank to a temperature of 60 degrees Fahrenheit. But it chanced that, unknown to Cavor, dissension had arisen about the furnace tending. His assistant ceased to replenish the furnace, and no one else did so either, and the Professor was too much immersed in other problems to perceive that anything was wrong.

I remember the occasion with extreme vividness. Cavor's active little figure was black against the sunset, and to the right the chimneys of his house just rose above a gloriously tinted group of trees.

And then, the chimneys jerked heavenward, smashing into a string of bricks as they rose, and the roof and a miscellany of furniture followed. Then overtaking them came a huge white flame. The trees about the building swayed and whirled and tore themselves to pieces that sprang towards the flare.

My ears were smitten by a clap of thunder, and all about me windows smashed, unheeded. I took three steps forward, and even as I did so came the wind. Cavor was seized, whirled about, and flew through the screaming air, vanishing at last among the laboring, lashing trees that writhed about his house.

I saw one of my chimney pots hit the ground within six yards of me. A mass of smoke and ashes, and a square of bluish shining substance rushed up towards the zenith. A large fragment of fencing came sailing past me, dropped edgeways, hit the ground and fell flat, and then the worst was over.

In that instant the whole face of the world had changed. The tranquil sunset had vanished, the sky was dark with scurrying clouds, everything was flattened and swaying with the gale. I staggered forwards towards the trees amongst which Cavor had vanished, and through whose tall and leaf-denuded branches shone the flames of his burning house.

Associated Press Report
(June 15, 1896)

Sanriku, Japan. A tsunami (a seismic sea wave) caused by an undersea earthquake struck the coast of Sanriku, Japan, today, killing and injuring more than 20,000 people.

Excerpt from The Times
(June 15, 1896)

There is a surprise in store today for the children who planned to go to Kensington Gardens to feed the ducks in the Serpentine this morning, according to a report received from art nouveau sculptor George Frampton. Down by the little bay on the southwestern side of the tail of the Serpentine, they will find the figure of a boy who calls himself Peter Pan blowing his pipe on the stump of a tree, while he sits with fairies and mice and squirrels all around.

Excerpt from a speech by Henri Poincaré
(Paris, 1900)

One flap of a butterfly's wings in London might be enough to alter the course of the world forever.

An Evening in Lympne

"I can't tell you anymore."

Chief Commissioner Zyd had pulled down the top of the Bentley. Now, one hand on the wheel and the other on the gearshift, she raced through the narrow Kent country lanes.

"At least tell me if you believe Turing was killed because of his homosexuality," asked the Detective.

"As far as I know, he had no current lover, male or otherwise. Don't judge us too quickly, Deputy Commissioner. Many of us genuinely appreciated Professor Turing."

"So there's a heart beating under that strict Republican uniform? And don't call me Deputy Commissioner."

"As you wish, Deputy Commissioner. We've arrived."

Professor Cavor's house was a large building with tall, white chimneys that could be seen from the main road. There were two Double-0 agents standing guard at the door. Zyd stopped the car just in front of the threshold and ordered the men to bring the luggage inside.

The entire ground floor of the house was cluttered with scientific equipment. Cavor's team had also managed to cram as many of their supplies as possible into the rest of the house, from the basement to the attic.

Bedford joined them in the hall, dressed in a pale linen suit and pretending to be in a good mood.

"The Professor will join us at tea time," he said. "He's taking a walk near the Roman walls. It helps him think."

"Can we meet the rest of the team?" asked Zyd.

"They're waiting for you. Would you like a drink first?"

"No, we're not thirsty. Just show us the way."

The Detective followed his young superior. He could not help smiling while watching her. Yes, she definitely reminded him of English Bob.

Holmes was getting ready for dinner when Cavor walked into his room.

"It's strange seeing you again after all these years," said the scientist. "We're like two lost souls rescued from the storm."

He still wore his cricket cap and cycling knickerbockers and stockings, but he had lost a lot of weight. His twitching looked to be more intense now than at the time of the League. It seemed as if the last years had not been good to him.

"Don't look for the mark of the Orkneys, Detective. I've paid for my mistakes, but the Second Republic has treated me fairly overall. They trust me now. That's why I'm allowed to talk to you without being watched."

Cavor cleared his throat then sat–or rather, almost collapsed–on the bed.

"Let's skip the reminiscences over the League, the Danger Room, MechaMen and all that ancient history. I know you never liked me–none of you did. I've often asked myself why, but I'm not here to dwell on the past. At the time, no one would have dared interrogate me; I had complete freedom to carry on with my experiments as I pleased. Sadly, this is no longer the case. So, tell me what is it you want?"

Holmes looked at the small man for a long moment.

"Tell me what Alan Turing was working on," he finally asked.

"That's top secret, but since I've been informed you have clearance... In any event, I know you. You'd find out sooner or later. You see, there are differences of opinion between us and the Americans regarding the best way to reach the Moon. That ass Goddard will undoubtedly brag to you at dinner tonight about his newest design, OSEPM-1. Pah! His latest rocket missed the Moon by a mere 238,799-and-a-half miles! Anyway, Turing had been assigned to help Goddard calculate his trajectories. The man is useless with numerical integral calculus. What is he good for, I ask? So Turing designed a mechanical calculator, capable of working on hundreds of algorithms at the same time. A veritable thinking machine. He called it a *computer*."

Lindbergh's Transatlantic Flight: Timeline
(May 20-21, 1924)

4:52 a.m. - Flying in the fog. Lindbergh continually falls asleep with his eyes open, then awakens seconds, possibly minutes, later. The pilot also begins to hallucinate. Finally, after flying for hours in or above the fog, the skies begin to clear.

The Lindbergh Baby Case

After Cavor left, Holmes reminisced about his last two visits to America. He had visited Washington in 1913 and had nearly been framed for murder by the Red Tiger.[18] And then, there had been the Lindbergh Baby Case...

The 1928 kidnapping had marked the beginning of the fall of the World's Greatest Detective. It had been, perhaps, less dramatic than Cavor's public trial in Bristol, but was equally devastating.

Charles Augustus Lindbergh, Jr., 20-month-old son of the famous aviator and Anne Morrow Lindbergh, was kidnapped at about 9 p.m., on March 1, 1928, from the nursery on the second floor of the Lindbergh home near Hopewell, New Jersey. The child's absence was discovered and reported to his parents, who were then at home, at approximately 10 p.m. by the child's nurse, Betty Gow. A search of the premises was immediately made and a ransom note demanding $50,000 was found on the nursery window sill.

Written in a dodgy handwriting and with clumsy grammar, it said:

---

[18] See *The Red Tiger*.

Dear Sir,

Have 5000$ redy. 25000$ in 20$ bills 15000$ in 10$ bills and 10000$ in 5$ bills After 2-4 days we will inform you were to deliver the mony We warn you for making anyding public or for notify the police the child is in gut care.

Indication for all letters are singnature and three holes.

During the search at the kidnapping scene, traces of mud were found on the floor of the nursery. Footprints, impossible to measure, were found under the nursery window. Two sections of the ladder had been used to reach the window, one of the two sections was split or broken where it joined the other, indicating that the ladder had broken during the ascent or descent. There were no blood stains in or about the nursery, nor were there any fingerprints.

The next day, after a conference with the Attorney General, J. Edgar Hoover, Director of the Bureau of Investigation, had contacted the headquarters of the New Jersey State Police. He officially informed the organization that the U.S. Department of Justice would afford Colonel H. Norman Schwarzkopf, the Superintendent of the New Jersey State Police, the assistance and cooperation of the Bureau in bringing about the apprehension of the parties responsible for the kidnapping.

By March 3, all criminal-detection agencies of the U.S. government went into action to aid in the recovery of Lindbergh's son. From the White House to the halls of Congress, the kidnapping of the baby assumed major importance. Even the Governor of New York, Franklin D. Roosevelt, known for his personal dislike of Lindbergh, sprung into action.

The case was soon labeled the "crime of the century." In Albion, sensing an opportunity to gain easy popularity by coming to the rescue of the hero who had first flown solo across the Atlantic, Lord Protector Fogg had volunteered the services of their greatest sleuth, Sherlock Holmes.

The Detective had gone to America followed by massive press coverage. But he had been greeted at the small airport of

Newark rather coldly. J. Edgar Hoover himself was there to see him and made it clear that the Bureau had a file indicating he was a Bolshevik sympathizer.

Several Bureau agents, all dressed in similar dark suits, took him to the Lindbergh's residence. Mrs. Lindbergh greeted him warmly and offered him coffee. He liked the couple. They were beautiful and showed a dignified and discreet sadness, indifferent to anything not related to their missing child. Holmes spoke with Henry Breckinridge, the Lindberghs' lawyer and friend, who had advised them to pay the ransom. He also spoke with Betty Gow, the Scottish nurse. Tearfully, she went over her declaration, point by point. Before going to bed, she had looked in the baby's room; he was sleeping peacefully. He had been taken as he slept.

The muddy footprints that trailed across the floor from the crib to an open window bore mute testimony to how the baby had disappeared. Beneath the nursery window were marks where a ladder had stood and the footprints of one person. There were no shoe prints. The kidnapper, it seemed, had worn socks–or moccasins!

Sixty feet away in some rocky ground at the edge of the woods, the police had found a makeshift ladder. Its rungs were caked with mud. Holmes had no difficulty in following the footprints across the muddy ground. A second set of tracks joined them near the woods. These were much smaller. The Detective thought they might belong to a woman. The tracks were followed to the main highway, about half a mile from the house, where they finally disappeared. The police thought they had gotten into an automobile at that point. Holmes wondered if they had not merely flown away.

Holmes minutely examined the ransom notes sent by the kidnapper (several by then). Two spots in blue ink making a "P" at the bottom left of the first letter confirmed his worst fears and left him with no doubts as to the kidnapper's identity.

It was the work of Peter Pan and Tiger Lily.

In his report, Holmes stated that a combination of motives were at work: Pan was jealous of the man who had been nicknamed the "Eagle." He theorized that Lindbergh had actually run out of water during his solo flight and had secretly received Pan's help–but upon arrival in Paris, had broken his word to the boy who would not grow up and claimed all the credit. It turned out that two months earlier, Peter had tried to steal the Lindbergh baby. At the time, this had been put down as a cruel practical joke played by Lindbergh himself on his wife.

There was no doubt that the self-appointed leader of the Resistance was planning to use the case to discredit his opponents and wreck the new Albion-American alliance being forged by Fogg and Colt.

The Great Detective had joined the ranks of the many sleuths, participating in the nationwide search for the missing baby.

However, on May 12, the body of the Lindbergh child was stumbled over by accident, partly buried and already badly decomposed, about four and a half miles southeast of the aviator's home. The Coroner's examination showed that the child had been dead for about two months and that death was caused by a blow to the head.

The next day, President Colt himself directed that governmental investigative agencies should place themselves at the disposal of the State of New Jersey and that Hoover's Bureau of Investigation should serve as a clearinghouse and coordinating agency for all investigations into the case.

It was then that Holmes realized that his own investigation was being hijacked. He knew that Peter did not kill children. So was it a ghastly mistake by one of his local accomplices–or something far more sinister, such as a Bureau conspiracy?

He was flown back to London the very next day. It was then that his star began to wane and his privileges were curtailed. In a private meeting, Fogg pointed out that his failure to find the child was a "stain" on the Second Republic–his very words. Further, he was told that it was politically expedient to hide Peter's role in the affair in order to not give him any publicity, thus hopefully making him angry enough to make a mistake the next time he struck.

Publicly, Lord Fogg released a doctored report that supported the Bureau's own conclusions, pointing towards an unstable, paranoid man, probably a Russian.

Eventually, in September 1929, the Bureau fingered Sergei Gusev (born Ia. D. Drabkhin) who had come to America in 1925 to represent the Bolshevik International Alliance to the Workers Party of America. Gusev was tried, sentenced to death and executed on April 3, 1930.

In a memorable speech at Madison Square Garden the following month, President Colt suggested that all Americans of Russian origin should be interned in special camps. The eventual promulgation of the "Lindbergh Act" making any child kidnapping a federal crime was poor consolation.

Excerpt from Moony: The Life of Robert Goddard
Little Brown & Co., Boston, 1962

On the afternoon of October 19, 1899, I climbed a tall cherry tree and, armed with a saw which I still have, and a hatchet, started to trim the dead limbs. It was one of those quiet, colorful afternoons of sheer beauty, which we have in October in New Albion, and as I looked towards the fields to the east, I imagined how wonderful it would be to make some device which had even the possibility of ascending to Mars. I was a different boy when I descended the tree from when I ascended it, for my existence at last seemed to have a purpose.

A Small Place in the Sun

"Have you read *The War of the Worlds*, Detective?"

Professor Robert Hutchings Goddard from Clark University, Massachusetts, ignored the custard on the table before him and leaned towards the shaman. "A wonderful book. I read it when I was 16. It inspired my entire career!

"Right then, I decided to pay a return visit to Mr. Wells' Martians and I think we'll soon be able to do it."

It was about time, thought Holmes. Until then, they had discussed everything, from *Betty Boop* to the coronation of Haile Selassie, but not the Outer Space Exploration Program that, he was sure, was at the heart of the mystery.

Cavor gave out a long, skeptical whistle, but that did not deter Goddard who continued:

"My famous host appears to share with the American Press in having reservations towards the chemical approach. Someone at the *New York Times* has even dubbed me 'Moony,' or the 'Moon Man' after I promised to send a liquid-fuel propelled rocket to the Moon. I'm not ashamed of it. In fact, I'm quite proud that my dear friend Major Julian James has agreed to bear that nickname proudly and become our first American spacenaut."

"Are you saying that everything is going according to plan?" snickered Cavor. "Is the Gun Club likely to see dividends any time soon? I remember that fatcat Barbicane and his inane notion of somehow shooting a cannonball to the Moon. Your tests are no more conclusive."

Goddard swept away the objection with his hand.

"Come on, Professor. We've never tried to minimize the challenges we face. Yes, we still have a variety of problems to solve, like cooling the combustion chamber and finding the right kind of fuel, but I have no doubt that we'll prevail. At the end of the day, our OSEPM-1 rocketship is far safer, more efficient and easier to make than anything involving the use of your Cavorite."

Cavor wheezed loudly while wagging a bit of bread at the end of his fork.

"Poppycock! A child of five could grasp the advantages of Cavorite. I'll demonstrate it to you right now. See this piece of bread? If it was a spaceship, you'd merely need to plate it with a thin layer of Cavorite, no more than a pepper-grain's worth at this scale, and whoosh! It would be insulated from Earth gravity and zoom towards the Heavens."

Cavor threw the bun which flew straight into the air and knocked a vase over as it came down.

"A child of five, perhaps, but not me. You've just demonstrated that Cavorite is basically uncontrollable, in addition to being one of the most volatile explosives known to man. We could never guarantee the safety of a crew in a Cavorite-propelled vehicle. It could end up anywhere, or even blow up. There is room for Cavorite in our plans–to facilitate take-off from the Moon. But not here on Earth. Besides, the farmers of our heartland would never stand for it and as President Colt reminded me, 'That's where the votes are!' "

"You're testing your rockets in Kansas?" asked Holmes.

"No, that's just an expression. They'll eventually be launched from the Gun Club site in Stones Hill, Florida. But we're conducting all our tests in a small, isolated place in the sun: Los Alamos, New Mexico."

Excerpt from Memo No. 2 *by Eric Arthur Blair*
(September 1928)

Day by day and almost minute by minute, the past will be brought up to date.

New Art

Thus was born the Theater of Crime.

Upon his accession to supreme power in 1927, Fogg had asked the Office of Information Management to rewrite recent history, in order to cripple Peter Pan, his Resistance and his

Irish and Bolshevik allies, but also to sweep his own role in the last years of the Empire under the carpet.

Paradoxically, Lord Fogg envisioned his Second Republic as a stubbornly egalitarian society, entirely focused on productivity. There was no room any longer for colorful Heroes who stood above the Masses and, to the extent that people remembered a "golden age," it had to be diminished and made unglamorous.

A clever employee of the Office of Information Management, Eric Arthur Blair, had chanced upon the simple and effective idea of using the League of Heroes' own past to produce semi-fictional plays that would show that past to have been a lie. He called it "New Art." "Who controls the past," had stated Blair in his ground-breaking memo, "controls the future and who controls the present controls the past."

New Art consisted of commissioning plays loosely based on some of the League's old cases, using the archives and recordings of the Blue Room at the Reform Club. Any attractive or heroic elements were to be carefully excised in order to deglorify the "old days," and further, there would be a calculated emphasis on the decadent, wasteful habits of the old aristocracy.

The writer, a woman named Agatha Christie, had quickly found that most of Lord Kraven and Lord Greystoke's exploits were wholly unsuited to the purpose at hand. However, Holmes' casebook, properly rewritten, of course, would prove ideal. She had even managed to prevail upon the Detective, who idolized her, to play his own role on stage. He had agreed, not so much because he feared the other, worse fates that might have been in store for him had he refused to comply, but simply because, after the Lindbergh Affair, he despised himself.

Kraven and Greystoke had left the stage as real heroes. Holmes had stayed as a cardboard caricature of himself.

And in the Blue Room, Lord Protector Fogg smiled, taking satisfaction that the lie he had created passed into history and became truth.

Hamlet, Act 2, Scene 2

Hamlet - ...*What players are they?*
Rosencrantz - *Even those you were wont to take delight in, the tragedians of the city.*

Murder at the Castle

The Repertory Company of the Theater of Crime arrived at Lympne Castle the following morning.

Stage Manager Lodge had ridden ahead on his motor-bike. Having nothing better to do, Cavor's assistants, Spargus and Gibbs, had helped them unload, even though the metal-worker and the joiner were technically on exclusive loan to Cavor by the Second Republic.

The Professor left his laboratory and went to meet the company. Lodge, who was discussing room assignments with Virginia Buckley, shook his hand enthusiastically.

"You're going to be this evening's star," he said, refer-ring to the play, *The Mysterious Affair at Canterbury*, in which Cavor had been made into the grotesque Doctor Cavor-stein. "Not everyone has the chance to be immortalized while still alive, and at the Second Republic's expense to boot! Do you know where the Redskin is?"

"Last time I saw Mr. Holmes," replied Cavor stiffly, "he was walking near the pond."

The stage manager went around the gardens and along the canal up to the lake. Half-hidden by the reeds, the Detec-tive was there, smoking his ancient calumet.

"Hello there, Chief," said Lodge. "As you can see, I've come to entertain the egg-heads. Make sure that they keep their heads in the clouds, so to speak. But I also have a mes-sage for you."

Lodge took a paper from his leather jacket. It contained only one sentence: *Protect Cavor at all costs*.

"Since *Hamlet*, actors are *tragedians of the city*, my friend. Sorry, but no time off for you tonight."

Apart from the Double-0 agents who patrolled outside, everyone at Lympne was now gathered in the Great Hall. Holmes, wearing his feathered headgear, welcomed Zyd, who had traded her uniform for a simple, black sheath dress.

"You look stunning tonight, Chief Commissioner," said the Detective

"Merely a cover. You should wear this."

The young woman tried to pin a small iron cog wheel to his lapel. The symbol of the Second Republic.

"The Fairy Folk used a scarlet ribbon to show the way to the ball. Later, Peter used it as the symbol of the Resistance. I wore it then, but I was rarely worthy of it. So I'm not going to wear your symbol either tonight."

"A medicine man should know the value of talismans, Deputy Commissioner. It will protect you."

They sat in the second row, facing the stage that had been erected earlier that afternoon by Cavor's assistants. Robert H. Goddard and Bedford, in full evening dress, including white gloves, sat in the row in front of them. Seated behind them, Cavor moved restlessly in his chair:

"Holmes! Take that silly headgear off! Even if it's a travesty, I'd still like to see the play."

The stage manager dimmed the lights; the curtain opened. The play began.

Despite everything, the Detective always found it quite enjoyable to watch Paddy McKenzie playing Cavor(stein). He had become an expert in the art of disguise, a useful talent that would have been handy in the days of the League of Heroes.

The play was intercut with musical numbers written especially for the occasion. Holmes did not think much of Agatha's skill when it came to writing musicals. She was no Chorley & Sullivan.

The cast was singing about Dr. Cavorstein finding a lump of "Cavorstine" (*easier to rhyme*, thought Holmes) during a stroll in his garden, to the tune of some awful Charleston music.

"It didn't happen like that at all," growled Cavor behind him. "I synthesized the goddamn thing. It doesn't exist in nature!"

"You shouldn't question the new historical interpretation of the facts," said Zyd, only half-joking.

A later number portrayed Cavorstein almost as an alchemist, mixing colored powders in a cauldron.

"*Carbon bisulphite, A little bit of helium, That's how it's done,*" sang Paddy McKenzie.

"Incomplete but not altogether wrong," whispered Cavor to Holmes. "Not bad."

Unfortunately, the number soon turned into:

"*Alas and for our misfortune, Great Cavorstein is a sorcerer, A man friendly with Fairies, Clever but heartless,*" sung breathlessly by Virginia Buckley to the funeral tunes of a saxophone.

"Humph, I thought I'd paid for my errors," grumbled Cavor. "How long am I going to be persecuted for my past behavior?"

Indifferent to the scientist's complaints, Holmes looked at two empty seats. Taking advantage of the hurly-burly, Goddard and Bedford had left the room.

Finally, the play reached its finale: after Emily Inglethorpe's murderer had been exposed, Joris Lodge and Virginia Buckley returned, this time dressed as Uncle Sam and Boadicea to sing a final number to a ragtime tune:

"*America and Albion, United like brother and sister, Will go to the Moon, Taking a giant leap, For White Christian Nations...*"

The fireworks started as the curtain fell.

Suddenly, one of the Double-0 agents was there, at Zyd's side, whispering something in her ear. Holmes had not seen him enter.

"I see," she said. "Wait for us outside, 009." Then, she turned towards Holmes. "Deputy Commissioner, we're needed."

Robert H. Goddard lay at the foot of his bed, dead, an ice dagger stuck into his left eye.

Holmes took out his magnifying glass and examined the weapon.

"As you know, Chief Commissioner, once it has struck its victim, a Fairy Dagger becomes unstable very quickly. See how the blade is already melting? Considering the time it has taken to melt this much, I estimate the time of death to be about ten minutes ago. The American left before the end of the play; he was with Bedford. Has anyone questioned him?"

"We're looking for him. In the meantime, look at this."

Zyd pointed at five pounds nailed to the door frame with a crow feather. An Imperial note.

"What does it mean?"

"That our old friends are back," said Holmes.

He took the note. Written on it in red ink was:

It's a waste of time to open both eyes.

They searched the entire estate, and the neighboring woods, using special bloodhounds that had been trained in Dartmoor.

Eventually, they located Bedford, or rather his body. He had died from asphyxiation inside the OSEPM-2 prototype, Cavor's rival design that was competing against Goddard's rocket. It was a huge steel sphere that took nearly all the available space inside a warehouse adjacent to the Castle. With Spargus' help, Cavor activated the release system, letting air in and opening the machine in order to allow the agents to remove the body.

"Dear old friend," he said. "To have gone through all this with me just to end up dead. The Americans will never forgive us now. I fear our project is as dead as you are now..."

"I'd like to check something, Cavor," said Holmes. "Could you place the body on this table? Thank you. I didn't think I would ever have the opportunity to practice my skills again... You see, contrary to public opinion, Fairy weapons always leave unmistakable clues for one who knows how to detect them. The Ice Daggers, for example, burn the hands of those who use them. A bit of counter-magic, you might say. It's a small mark that disappears in minutes if you are one of the Fairy Folk, but can persist for days on human flesh. A simple examination under polarized moonlight will tell us if Bedford was connected to Goddard's murder."

"How dare you suggest such a thing!" said Cavor.

"Two men essential to the success of the American OSEPM have been murdered. Who benefits? Your own project. I must insist that you let me proceed."

Holmes took a carved opal from his pocket and quickly passed it over Bedford's hands.

"Look at that red rash on his right hand," he said. "And these marks between the inside of his thumb and his index."

"What does that prove?" said Cavor, angrily. "We spend our lives handling dangerous chemicals. Look at my hands. I could be just as guilty."

"Indeed. But I'm not finished yet. Look."

Holmes used a pair of tweezers to delicately remove a white fiber from the rash on Bedford's hand.

"Last night, Bedford wore white cotton gloves. Nothing like the rubber gloves used in your laboratory. Small fibers of cotton became embedded in his flesh when it came in contact with the dagger."

The audience gasped. *Just like the Theater of Crime*, thought Holmes. *But real.*

"I'm now fully convinced that Mr. Bedford murdered Robert Goddard. And possibly Alan Turing as well, but if that's the case, any older wounds from a Fairy Dagger would have disappeared by now. A pity I wasn't called in earlier."

Cavor was enraged; his head swayed from right to left.

"I see you haven't changed at all, Detective. Murder, for you, is just an excuse to indulge in dazzling displays of pseudo-logic. But you've conveniently forgotten that Turing's murder doesn't affect just the American project but mine as well. Bedford had no reason to kill him on my account."

"Yet that's what I believe happened," said Holmes. "Bedford, worried about the slower progress of your team, first killed Turing, who was mostly working for the Americans, in order to even things up. But, as that was not successful, he took advantage of Goddard's visit to kill him, as well. During the play, he probably suggested to Goddard that they meet outside to discuss some kind of technical breakthrough. He joined him in his room and struck the unsuspecting scientist. Then, knowing that he would eventually be caught, and not wanting to embarrass the project further, he locked himself inside your prototype–a fitting end."

The Shaman Detective turned towards Cavor.

"Could you describe the insides of this machine, Professor?"

"It consists of two concentric spheres. One is made of an alloy I designed, opaque to light, heat and gravity. The interior sphere is made of a special glass."

"Can one open or close the inside sphere from outside?" asked the Detective.

"Of course not! The spacenauts must be protected from any outside hazard."

"That is my point."

Holmes lit his calumet.

"Only Bedford, once inside, could expel the air from the interior sphere and create a vacuum. It was a double murder, followed by a suicide."

Cavor was strangely calm, his face not twitching.

"You're wrong," he finally said. "Bedford was totally incapable of violence. It's loathsome to even suggest that he killed two men. You've been wrong before, you know. You never found out who killed Kraven in the Antarctic. Have you ever asked yourself if, perhaps, ice doesn't impair your vaunted deductive powers after all?"

Excerpt from Be Prepared:
An Interview with Baden-Powell
by The Listener Magazine *(1937)*

So, instead of dying during the Great War, the Movement showed its vitality; it rose to the occasion and since then has gone on growing in strength and usefulness.

The Best and the Brightest

Holmes was walking alongside Zyd in the indifferent morning light of Lympne.

"Do you really think Bedford did it?" asked the young woman.

"Goddard, certainly. Turing, I can't be sure."

"Did he act on his own initiative?"

"A good question. The most important one, perhaps. A madman is capable of anything to protect something or some-one to whom he is totally devoted. With Goddard out of the way, and Cavor proven innocent, nothing will now prevent him from carrying on with his work for the greater glory of the Second Republic."

"What about the Americans?"

"Ah. I suspect interests might diverge there. They'll follow their own priorities. The Moon, Chief Commissioner, is like a big piece of cheese waiting to be swallowed by two fat rats."

The Shaman Detective picked up a stone and threw it across the flat surface of the lake. It skipped all the way to the other side.

"If you don't mind my asking, why are you involved in this tragic masquerade? I mean, the Republic, the black uniforms, the loyalty oaths towards butchers who don't deserve them..."

For a minute, the young woman hid her true self behind her official mask, then she exhaled with a deep sigh:

"My father was a barber in Pimlico. He was a poor but honest man, unable to guarantee me a decent life. I was rather gifted in math and very good at swimming, so the Young Republicans recruited me two years ago, right at the onset of the régime. You can guess the rest. The times are cruel; it's always the way during a time of transition, but our turn will come and things will change."

"*Our* turn?"

"When I was at the Young Republican Academy, I shared my room with another girl. She was First in every subject, but easy to live with despite her hot temper. We often argued for hours about a specific point of doctrine. She was my only real friend. On graduation day, Lord Fogg came to deliver a speech, a rather lyrical call to duty, the trust placed in us by the Second Republic, etc. Then, he offered to answer a few questions from the best students. My friend raised her finger. The Director was proud of her and let her speak. 'Lord Protector,' she said, 'do you remember when you used to command the League of Heroes during the Old Empire...?' I don't know why she did it. They immediately grabbed the mike. The Double-0 agents dragged her away, without waiting for the end of the ceremony. I never saw her again. But the Lord Protector isn't eternal. Soon, our generation will seize the reins of power. Then, we'll be able to change things, liberalize the régime... What about you, Detective? What made you leave Tiger Lily and side with Humanity?"

Holmes smiled while watching a black duckling paddling behind its mother.

"The dream of a world where different races could co-exist in peace and harmony, with freedom and justice for all. And the challenge, of course. Logic and science were like new, shining baubles that bought me off. I know now I was wrong. The time has come for me to face up to my past. I must return to London."

"You don't wish to question Cavor any further?" asked the young woman.

"No point in that."

The crow feather was lying in his palm, next to the neatly folded Imperial bank note.

"*It's a waste of time to open both eyes* was the motto of Old Solomon Caw, the Lord of the Ravens. I thought he was dead. He was one of Peter Pan's rivals in Neverland. When a young woman wanted to have a baby, she prayed to Solomon Caw to make her wish come true, then released a crow's feather to fly in the wind. Peter, on the other hand, steals babies from their cradle and leaves a five-pound note in their stead. The feather and the note–an impossible alliance, until today. They want to talk to me."

Excerpt from Daily Variety
(December 1930)

A mighty panorama of Earth-shaking fury as an army from Mars invades is on display in Sergei Eisenstein's War of the Worlds, *a Paramount production which opened today to boffo box office biz.*

Passages

Zyd dropped Holmes near the entrance of Kensington Gardens.

The place was surrounded by barbed wire. It had been closed to the public since the beginning of the Second Republic. Only a last remnant of fear and superstition had prevented the bureaucrats of the new régime from leveling the Gardens and turning them into flats.

Ignoring the glass shards, the barbed wire and the wrought iron fence, Holmes entered the grounds where, not so long ago, the Crystal Palace had proudly stood.

The Shaman Detective took the long way towards the Serpentine. No one was allowed to set foot on the little island that had once been the siege of the Neverland embassy.

He folded the Imperial note into the shape of a small boat, using the feather as its sail. Then, he blew it gently towards the island.

His task here was done, he reflected as he left.

In Baker Street, the smell of cabbage was unable to cover up the smell of death. Especially to one with a nose as sensitive as his.

Holmes saw a ray of light from under the Smiths' door, but instead of the familiar cacocophony of sounds, there was only silence. No marital strife, no children screaming, no concert of yapping recriminations.

He used his skeleton key to open the door and, holding up his breath, walked inside the flat. The first thing he saw was Mrs. Smith, lying in the corridor in a pool of blood, her face torn off. He stepped over the body and stepped into the living room. The teenage boy was hanging from the chandelier, strips of flesh dangling from his bones. The oldest daughter, who worked as a typist somewhere in the City, had been decapitated, and her head deposited obscenely in Mr. Smith's lap. His body had been nailed to his favorite armchair with harpoons, and a Jolly Roger spiked through his skull.

The babies were missing.

Their cradle was empty, but for a feather and a new Imperial note.

The Shaman Detective went back to the hallway, let out the putrid air that was filling his lungs and went up the stairs to his own flat.

Peter was waiting for him inside.

Excerpt from Wendy Darling: Memoirs
Hodder and Stoughton, London, 1912

Old Solomon Caw promised very kindly, however, to teach Peter as many of the bird ways as could be learned by one of such an awkward shape.

"Then I shan't be exactly a human?" Peter asked.

"No."

"Nor exactly a bird?"

"No."

"What shall I be?"

"You will be a Betwixt-and-Between," Solomon Caw said, and certainly he was a wise old fellow, for that is exactly how it turned out.

The Cleverness of Peter

Holmes woke up.

He was tied to a chair, under a spotlight. His body was in agony.

A man dressed in rubber overalls and wearing a gas mask was taking a needle out of his arm.

"So the great Shaman Detective has at last returned from the Land of Dreams?" said Peter Pan. "We can talk then."

Peter Pan, legs apart, hands on his hips, was facing him. Solomon Caw was perched on his shoulder.

"Please forgive us our little trick, but your house was under constant monitoring by Double-0 agents. We couldn't take a chance. We had to drug you and fly you out of there. I'm sure your attractive nursemaid, Zyd, can give you an aspirin later to rid you of your hangover. But I forget myself, I haven't made the introductions yet."

Peter indicated the men dressed in black and wearing gas masks.

"This is The Dullahan, Mr. De Valera and Mr. Kevin O'Higgins from Ireland, and these are members of the Underground Communist Party, even if I can't tell you their names because of their masks and their googly eyes!"

Peter laughed and stuck his face close to the Detective's—their noses almost touched. A think layer of slime covered his teeth and thousands of tiny wrinkles withered his once youthful face.

"You're probably asking yourself why I've asked them to dress up like this? To protect myself. The Consumption, Detective, that tumor that the humans have spread and which has decimated my people. I saw that American movie about the Martians recently. That chap Wells was right about a plague being the final solution to get rid of undesirables. And from what I gather, you haven't escaped unscathed either, eh?"

The Boy Who Would Not Grow Up grabbed the Detective's crotch.

"No little papoose to enliven your old age, shaman. By taking Sir Phileas' money, you've lost your balls, literally, and now you'll die alone, unmourned, unloved. All these deaths are on your conscience."

"You're hardly pure either, Peter," said Holmes. "I've witnessed your atrocities first-hand, remember?"

"What? The Lindbergh baby? He's better off dead. The Smiths? Snitches who would have sold their brood for a pound of sugar. Yes, I've killed my tens of thousands, but I have an excuse—I'm only seven after all!"

And he burst into a painful, maniacal laugh, with great tears of hysteria. *Great Goddess*, thought Holmes, *he's totally insane*.

Solomon Caw bit Peter's ear to bring him back to his senses. The Boy wiped the tears off his face.

"We've missed you, shaman," said the Lord of the Ravens. "Particularly Tiger Lily, right to the very end."

Holmes closed his eyes. *Tiger Lily, the very end*, he thought. *O, my Queen, what have I done?*

"Shut up, you bird of ill omen," said Peter, tweaking Solomon's beak. "I don't particularly object to making this more painful for him, but that's not why we're here, remember?"

"What do you want from me?" asked Holmes,

"From you? Nothing. A kiss and some honey, as we used to say in Neverland. No, quite the reverse in fact. We've come to help you solve your case. It was Tink's idea. You're entitled to the ritual three questions."

"Where are the Smiths' babies?" asked the Detective.

"In a warm place. Don't look at me like that. I'm telling you the truth. A baby in the mouth is worth two in the bush."

Pleased with his grim joke, the Boy clapped his hands, indulging in another fit of mad laughter.

Holmes then noticed that, if Solomon Caw had a shadow, Peter cast none. *Of course, Wendy was not there anymore to sew it back for him*, he thought. He wondered if losing his shadow was the cause of Peter's mental unbalance. It was like losing one's soul...

"Are the murders connected to the Outer Space Exploration Program?" he asked next.

"That's better, Detective. Yes, they are. You've got only one question left."

"Is Cavor guilty?"

"In many ways, yes. Guilty of having opened a pathway between our two worlds. Guilty of having supported a tragic farce. Guilty of many sins, indeed, but not of a triple murder. Besides, I'm quite fond of his knickerbockers and stockings."

"So who is?"

Peter's slap made his ear burn.

"Don't be greedy," said the Boy. "You must figure it out by yourself. You're the Great Detective after all, while I'm merely clever. How clever I am, though! Oh the cleverness of me!"

The last thing he heard was Peter Pan's laughter, like pearls of madness, slowly fading into the darkness.

"What I Want To Be When I Grow Up"
(Essay by Julian James, Age 10,
Slater Avenue School, Providence, RI)
(1905)

When I grow up, I'd like to travel to the Moon. I don't want to lord it over folks because my Da says we should all remember our proper station in life. I'd like to travel to the Moon because I could get together with all my friends and have a great adventure.

Excerpt from
The Moon Man: The Life of Major Julian James
by Edgar Rice Burroughs
AC McClurg, Chicago, 1929

At 16, he graduated from the Air School and was detailed to the International Peace Fleet, being the fifth generation of his line to wear the uniform of his country.

The Celluloid Toy

When Holmes awoke, he was back in his room.

The smell of death still permeated the house. He could not tell if the police had come to remove the Smiths' bodies or not, and felt too depressed to walk down to inquire. Peter's revelations still buzzed in his mind.

He decided to light a small stick of incense. As he fumbled around, he suddenly discovered a small celluloid toy figure that had been left behind on the carpet, next to him.

It was a crude representation of Major Julian James, the "Moon Man." Since he had been selected amongst much publicity to become the first American spacenaut, Major James had become a celebrity whose fame eclipsed that of even the greatest Hollywood stars.

Pulp magazines and movie serials were now based on his exploits, even anticipating his future adventures on the Moon. His purported biography, by Edgar Rice Burroughs, had already sold over 10 million copies. Everyone clamored for news of the Moon Man. Yet, he was being kept in virtual seclusion at the Los Alamos Space Center where, according to official spokesmen, he was said to be undergoing the most rigorous of training.

What the Press did not know, was that the great impetus behind the American Outer Space Exploration Program was entirely the result of President Colt's recent obsession with the words of the prophet Joseph Smith who, in 1837, had predicted that the Moon would be found to be inhabited by men and women who lived for thousands of years.

The prospect of discovering the secret of such a Methuselan lifespan had proved irresistible to the aging but still vital Colt. He dreamed of the day when he and a select few–all followers of Smith–would travel to the Moon and take their places amongst the Eternals who lived there.

Colt had gathered around him a coterie of Seven Seers and had turned into a recluse. Publicity photos still depicted him as a charming, blue-eyed, square-jawed, silver-haired, Southern gentleman, sitting with gravitas behind his desk in the Oval Office. But the reality was that Colt was now spending most of his time munching candy bars, a prophet's beard trailing down his chest, sitting nearly naked in a white leather chair in the operations center of Los Alamos. His long legs were often stretched out on a matching ottoman. He faced the control screens, watching one test after another, surrounded by his Seven Seers, babbling about their impending journey to the Moon.

Holmes studied the celluloid toy more closely. He took his magnifying glass and looked at it carefully. He found a series of dotted red lines all over its surface. *Major James*, he thought morbidly, *looked like a cow ready for the slaughter*.

Was it another of Peter's jokes or yet another peculiar clue to the mystery?

Excerpt from The Republican Times
(January 2, 1931)

Charles Moreau, Controversial Scientist, Dies at 73. Yesterday, noted biologist and controversial scientist Charles Moreau died. Dr. Moreau had been in declining health for several years. He passed away at his home in Down (Kent)...

Under the Carpet

When Holmes woke up, it was almost noon.

Downstairs, the police had come and taken the Smiths' bodies away. The door to their flat was now sealed with black tape.

Chief Commissioner Zyd was waiting patiently by the front door, smoking an Ardath.

"The conclusions of your investigation have been forwarded to the top and I can tell you that everyone's very happy with your work. But they'll tell you in person. Come on."

A half-hour later, Holmes and Zyd were led straight into Sir Oswald Mosley's office near Downing Street. The days of secret meetings in an obscure Ministry were obviously in the past.

After the First Deputy of the Lord Protector had exchanged a few patronizing pleasantries with Zyd, he turned towards Holmes:

"First, I want to express our appreciation for a job well done. The Second Republic has decided to make your temporary appointment as Deputy Commissioner permanent. Your life in the theater is over. From now on, you and Chief Commissioner Zyd here will be our permanent investigative team, assigned to the most delicate and sensitive crimes. I believe you will find the job most rewarding. Now on to the Turing matter.

"Our crime laboratory has confirmed your theory. Bedford was an extremely disgruntled man. He had to be carefully vetted when he was allowed to work on the joint Outer Space Exploration Program with Cavor, and came to resent what he perceived as an intolerable invasion into his privacy. He blamed the Americans and resolved to sabotage their project.

"Because of his past association with Cavor, he knew much about the Fairy Folk that is generally not public knowledge. He chanced upon a former Pirate named Cookson who had hidden his racial origins in order to get a job in the Program despite the Preference Act. Blackmailing Cookson, threatening to reveal his true nature, Bedford learned of the Fairy Daggers–and where to get them!

"He and Cookson forged identity cards and went to Aloysius Keys to get the Daggers. The costumier recognized their photos before succumbing to heart failure as an unfortunate consequence of the interrogation. A pity. We thought he might have had much more to tell us...

"Anyway, Bedford and Cookson–now partners in crime –went ahead with their plan. Cookson went to Cambridge and killed Turing, while Bedford stalked Goddard in Lympne. We believe, however, that Cookson, who has so far escaped our dragnet, conveniently forgot to warn Bedford about the effect of the blades on humans, thereby leading to the clues that enabled you to finger him as the murderer.

"When Bedford realized he was about to be caught, having accomplished his goal, he chose to end his life as a reconstruction has now established."

"What about Cavor?" asked Zyd.

"Perfectly innocent. The poor man suffered quite a shock, but we're sure he'll get over it and carry on with his portion of the Program. Ah! One last thing. Our investigation into the terrorist murders of your neighbors indicate that you have recently been in touch with the terrorists. Normally, we would have insisted on a thorough, er, debriefing, but due to your deteriorating physical condition, and your recent contribution, my Master has decided to be lenient. He only wishes to put a few questions to you personally. A car will come to fetch you at 8 p.m."

"Where to?"

"Where only a few of the most select can flatter themselves to have been received. The Blue Room of the Reform Club, of course."

Excerpt from
Neverland: A Scientific Theory
by John Ronald Reuel Tolkien
Oxford University Press, Oxford, 1925

And though I have not attempted to relate the shape of the mountains and land-masses of Neverland to what geologists may say or surmise about the nearer past, it is more likely that these people whom we have come to refer to as "Indians" or "Redskins" are, in fact, an extinct race, e.g., Neanderthals or Hyperboreans.

The Way to Dusky Death

St. Thomas Hospital had been requisitioned at the start of the century to deal with the poor and the sick from Neverland.

After a cursory health examination, each Fairy received a bar of soap, a blanket and a loaf of bread. At the time, the place was often mostly empty, often a mere way station before moving them to another destination in human society. It was no longer the case.

Placed under the authority of the Ministry of Ethnic Cleansing, the Hospital had now become a sanatorium for Fairy Folk dying of Consumption. Heaps of bodies were incinerated anonymously every week, no one wanting to know either the names or the numbers of the deceased.

Often, undesirable elements and illegal immigrants were sent to St. Thomas where they would steal the Fairies' Red Cross parcels, while abusing and mistreating them in many, horrendous ways. That, too, was not recorded in any ledgers or official documents.

Holmes arrived at St. Thomas just before sunset. With his brand-new identification as Deputy Commissioner, he did not have to wait long at the checkpoint before being admitted, and no one asked him any questions.

The Shaman Detective crossed the electrified fence and the heavy, reinforced walls topped with metal spikes and shards of broken glass, noting the snipers who, from their watchtowers, made sure no diseased patient could escape alive. The west wing of the Hospital had been turned into the crematorium, and the most awful smell hung over the court-yard.

Holmes had to present his documents again several times and sign a release before a surly orderly finally led him down to the third sub-basement. Most doctors being unwilling to work at St. Thomas, the Second Republic had recently turned to veterinarians.

"Just ring when you've finished," the man said. "Don't hesitate to kick any of them if they bother you. And if you'd like a quickie, well, I won't tell if you won't tell! Ha! Ha!"

The Detective began to walk down a series of dark corridors. The stench of urine and chlorine made him wince. Bowls of groats had been placed on the floors at just the right distance from the cells. The Fairies could barely reach them with their long dislocated arms and dip their fingers into them. A Pirate crawled towards the Detective, leaving his molting flesh behind as he advanced, and begged him to kill him. A Lost Boy was crying over the body of his brother, suffocated by muscular hypertrophy. He felt the brittle limbs of a desiccated Indian crunch under his feet. The Consumption killed each sub-species in different, yet horrible ways.

Holmes, overwhelmed by horror and sorrow, eventually reached the last cell. There, lying on a hard bed, indifferent to the vomit which stained the silk of her ancient dress, Tiger Lily scratched her abscesses while consoling Brave Little Panther. She was still alive and proud, despite everything, her ravaged face now hidden behind a metal mask.

The Detective who had once been the great shaman of her tribe bowed in front of his Princess and begged for her forgiveness.

When Tiger Lily's amber eye blinked her last command, he understood her at once and obeyed gratefully, smothering what was left of her life with a simple kiss.

Once out, Holmes went to the Turkish Baths to sweat out his agony and have his head shaven. He had the attendants pour and massage oil into his body, just as they did on the Island in the Olden Days, when he was not even a shaman yet. He had them paint the ritual eagle on his chest and the mark of the bear on his back, and most important of all, the single red line across his forehead that would guide him safely to the lair of the demon.

Then, he bought a knife.

Excerpt from Around the World in 80 Days
by Jules Verne
J. Hetzel, Paris, 1872

[Phileas Fogg] was one of the most noticeable members of the Reform Club, though he seemed always to avoid attracting attention; an enigmatical personage, about whom little was known, except that he was a polished man of the world. People said that he resembled Byron–at least that his head was Byronic; but he was a bearded, tranquil Byron, who might live on a thousand years without growing old.

The Price

The Double-0 agent died without a word.

The Detective wiped the blood from his Bakelite blade. He had not waited for the car that had been supposed to drive him to the Reform Club.

On his belt he wore a small bag filled with a powder made of tiger's excrement that would cause the dogs to run away. He moved through the darkness of the gardens of the Reform Club like a panther, silently avoiding all the hidden safety mechanisms, as he had once done in the Danger Room of the League of Heroes.

The Moon, who had made him her champion, answered his prayers and appeared. From his hiding place, inside a bush of trees by the pool, he saw a morbidly obese man come out of the Club and walk onto the terrace for a smoke. It was Sir Phileas Fogg. But the Lord Protector of the Second Republic of the Commonwealth was not alone. Three agents kept watch, each armed with Vickers machine guns.

Holmes screamed to the Moon and sprang. The Bakelite blade went through the jaw of one of the agents, nailing his tongue to his palate. In a convulsive reflex, the man pressed the trigger and his fire cut another agent in two. *The Moon was still with him*, thought Holmes. The Detective used the body of the agent as a shield, throwing it away at the final, surviving agent while removing the blade. He then lunged and, with one swift arc of the arm, scalped the man, who fell to the floor before he had time to realize what had happened to him.

"Not too bad for a dying Indian," said Fogg. "Those were three of my best men."

The former Master of the League of Heroes smelled of brandy and did not look that concerned by what had just happened. One might have guessed he had just lost a fiver at the races.

"I've come to kill you," said Holmes.

"I doubt that you will before you bore me to death with your explanations. That's one of the things I found the most unbearable with the League: to have to listen at dinner, each time, in excruciating details, to all your stories, yours, Kraven's.... That's why I authorized the Theater of Crime, so that it would make people hungry for heroes yawn with *ennui*. He who sleeps forgets his hunger. Please sit down, we have to talk anyway."

"Why did you assign me to the Turing case?" asked Holmes, remaining standing and wary.

"Believe it or not, I did not. I don't control everything, you know. It was the idea of that idiot Mosley. I found out only afterwards. He'll be punished for it, of course."

"Did you kill Turing and the others?"

"Not directly, of course, but you're getting hotter, like your Peter would say. Since you obstinately refuse to sit down, I suggest that we go into my office. I have things to show you, and besides, I'll be more comfortable in my chair. I like to tell my junior ministers that responsibilities weigh heavily on my shoulders, but the truth is that I'm not as young as I used to be."

Fogg got up with difficulty and, walking around the bodies of his agents, pushed the glass door that led into his office.

"We're going to enjoy a little movie."

He spoke aloud and ordered an invisible projectionist to roll the film. Holmes understood that he could just as easily summon help if he needed. But could they arrive in time before he struck?

A blur of black and white images appeared on the wall screen opposite Fogg's desk. They showed military barracks in the desert. The film jumped in places but the narrative sequence was clear. The first minutes were not interesting until Holmes saw a gate heavily guarded by American soldiers and a sign that read: "*Los Alamos, NM–Outer Space Exploration Program.*"

Then the film cut to some hangar–*Hangar 18*, it read. The next sequence must have been shot inside. Kid Colt was there. Holmes had seen photos, but had not set eyes on him since the Peace Conference in Paris. The American President was as insane and disheveled as the rumors had said. He was surrounded by seven men in white suits whom Holmes assumed were the Seven Seers.

Then Major James entered the hangar. He was as handsome and strong as the propaganda had made him out to be. *A hero's hero*, thought Holmes. A soldier handed him a cigarette before helping him into his suit. The latest generation of MechaMan armor was much lighter than the model once worn by Lord Kraven during the Great War, but it still took a good hour for the men to hermetically screw the different parts of the spacesuit together and install oxygen tanks.

During that time, James cracked a few jokes with the President, until they put his helmet on. The American spacenaut tried to scratch his nose through the double visor, then indicated that he was ready.

After that, he walked towards a tall rocket that had been erected inside the hangar. It was shaped like a cigar and rested on three metal fins. James climbed a retractable metal ladder and stepped inside the rocket. He locked the door behind him.

The roof of the hangar slid open, revealing a cloudless, starry night sky. The Moon shone brightly in the firmament above. The filmmaker zoomed back to Colt who now stood inside a control booth, his hand on a large, red button. Colt pressed the button.

A roaring geyser of fire erupted from the bottom of the rocket, lifting it into the air, but almost immediately, the pressure proved too strong and the craft exploded in a thundering fireball. The top of the rocket, where James had been, burst into a million fragments. Morbidly, Holmes recognized body parts of the armored spacenaut as they were thrown violently against the booth. His head, his right arm... He then realized what he had seen: the dotted lines on the celluloid toy that Peter had left with him exactly matched the dismemberment of the spacenaut.

The film went black, then the light was turned off.

"And that's how the great American Moon Man has gone to join the pantheon of heroes, to sit in company of Lord Greystoke and Lord Kraven," said Fogg.

"When did this take place?" asked Holmes.

"Last year. That's why Goddard came to Lympne to work with Cavor on a new design. It's been kept totally hush-hush of course. Colt pretends Major James is still alive, training in secret. They had too much invested in him. They've recorded a few fake telephone interviews and used an impersonator hired in Vegas."

"Was it an accident?"

Fogg waited a long moment before replying.

"Does anything ever happen by accident, Detective? Ever since Cavor *accidentally* discovered Cavorite and the Fairy Folk *accidentally* arrived in Kensington Gardens, all our lives seem to have proceeded according to a Grand Design even *I* cannot see, but which I nevertheless know to be real. I am the master schemer, yet here is a scheme that is beyond even my powers. Turing's machine had the potential of unraveling that Grand Design, you see? That–*computer*–could see farther and deeper than I could fathom. It couldn't be. It had to be stopped. The Grand Design–whatever it is that I serve–had to be preserved, do you understand, now?"

Goddess! thought Holmes. *He's gone mad too, just like Peter.*

"When your friend Kraven tried to set up a world government," Fogg continued, "he became a threat to the Grand Design. So I set up the Christensen expedition–the alien tale was a cover story invented by a Frenchman–and I arranged for the explosion of his airship. Going to the Moon was another threat to the Grand Design. Maybe Colt's Seers are right and there are Immortals who live there, though I doubt it, but I know something for certain: we are not meant to know. That's why I joined Colt's insane Program, to better bury it. Bedford was a Double-0 agent, one of the best. He did what he had to do. What I told him to do. Now that Goddard is gone, only Cavor remains, and his craft will never fly. I've already seen to it. Tomorrow, Lympne will be a smoking crater that will inspire even greater fear in the population and throw them into the waiting arms of my Second Republic."

"Was the League a threat to the Grand Design as well?" asked Holmes

"Not at first, no. People need dreams, they need heroes, as I learned from you all. But heroes, like dreams, must serve a purpose; they must be subordinated to the Grand Design, and not depart from its goals. The League of Heroes outlived its usefulness, just as the Outer Space Exploration Program had, when it tried to undo the Design. Tomorrow, the people will blame its demise on Peter Pan, and the Grand Design will have been repaired and life will go on as before. Do you have any other questions, Detective?"

"Yes. Only one more. Where is the third Dagger?"

Fogg smiled.

"You're as good as ever. You remembered Keys mentioned *three* Fairy Daggers..."

He took a box from under his desk, put it on the table and opened it. The third Ice Dagger was in it, resting on a bed of red velvet.

"Here it is. Now let me explain how I intended to finish our chat. You are now in the early stages of the Consumption. And I'm old, likely to die soon. So you either kill me out of a misguided sense of loyalty and others will pay dearly for it while the Grand Design will go on unimpeded; or you kill yourself now and leave the stage with honor, and let our young Commissioner Zyd take care of the future, whatever it might be."

The first lights of dawn were shining on the gardens of the Reform Club, long streams of scarlet clouds that spread across the horizon like a Fairy invitation to the dance. Elsewhere in the city of London, children drank their milk, workers prepared to go to work and millions of lives continued doing their everyday tasks, impervious to fate, as if to prove Fogg right.

Holmes did what he had to do.

PART FOUR

The Grand Design

"Not doubt but certainty drives one mad."
Nietzsche

"Any truth is better than indefinite doubt."
Sherlock Holmes

The Rehearsal

"Right! Let's rehearse one last time," said Kraven.

With all the delicacy of a Bonsai gardener, George pulled a case that had once contained his fishing rods out of the trunk of his old Vauxhall and delicately deposited it on the workbench.

The four of them were working in George's garage. A low-wattage bulb hung from the ceiling; it occasionally swayed from side to side just like in the title sequence of *Callan*. Empty bottles of beer and half-eaten sandwiches were everywhere and the Glen Miller Band played *Moonlight Serenade* on the record player.

"Can't we switch that thing off?" whined Syd. "Just give me a poodle and some chocolates and I'd feel like I'm at my auntie's."

George sighed.

"Shut up, Syd. The music helps me concentrate."

George opened the case. Inside was a rocket launcher.

"This is a *Fauspatrone 2*, also called a *Panzerfaust*. It fires a hollow-charge grenade and can easily be handled by a single man. Its maximum range is less than 50 yards, but that ought to be enough for us. It was designed by the Nazis as a basic close-combat antitank weapon, but can also fire smoke

216

grenades. In fact, they used them on the Eastern front to blind Soviet tanks, except that after a while, the Russkies learned to drive right through the smoke. And this," he added pointing to a metal, egg-shaped canister with a stubby knob at one end, "is an *Eihandgranate 39* smoke grenade. Both in great condition."

Kraven whistled in appreciation.

"How did you get your hands on these, George?" he asked his son-in-law.

"I blow up houses all day long, so I've got... acquaintances in the explosive trade. There's an awful lot of military surplus around if you know who to ask. And young Syd here was a big help in making a deal for these."

"It only cost me a full run of *Playboys*–mint, of course– plus a signed first edition of *Mein Kampf*," added the hippie.

Kraven lifted the launcher.

"Who's going to fire this?"

"I will," said George. "It's in great condition but it's not brand new either. And we can't very well test it here, so it needs to be handled with a certain tactile sensitivity."

"Tactile sensitivity? La-dee-da! Did I really hear you say that, George?" mocked Syd. "Where did you pick up words like that? In your wife's *Woman's Mirror*?"

"Shut up, Syd! You should be out practicing with the van. You're the driver, remember? You better not mess up."

"Why should I mess up?" complained Syd.

"Because you ain't no Sterling Moss, that's why," snickered George.

"Are you taking any drugs right now?" asked Kraven.

"No. Only Vitamin C. I've been clean for two weeks."

"Good. What about the security? Bobby?"

"Every Wednesday afternoon," English Bob said, "*he* travels in a chauffeur-driven Rolls-Royce from the Reform Club on Pall Mall to the PM's residence on Downing Street and back. I've followed the car and checked the security at every point. The best time to take *him* would be when *he* returns to the Club, late in the day. There's virtually no security there and traffic won't block our getaway."

"Funny. I'd have thought that, after that last IRA scare..." remarked Kraven.

"I've taken a few photos as well," added English Bob, pulling out several snapshots from his pocket.

Kraven looked at the photo of a fat man getting out of a car while a chauffeur held the door.

"It's *him* alright," he said. "Sir Phileas Fogg in the flesh. I don't understand. He should be long dead. It's impossible..."

"And you should be, what, over 90?" said George. "That's why we're doing this. To find out the answers. In the last two weeks since we clobbered those creeps from Social Services–Social Services, my ass!–we did find that your Sir Phileas Fogg really exists. He even has an entry in the *Who's Who*! He lists his hobbies as 'history, medieval churches, chess and architecture.' The Foggs are an old family from Kent, where they were seated from ancient times, some say well before the Norman Conquest. This Fogg appears to be the last of the line. His parents must have had a wicked sense of humor, naming him Phileas, after that Jules Verne character."

"I remember the novel well," said Kraven.

"But I thought you told us your Fogg was real?" said George.

"He was. When he was young, he managed to go around the world in just under 80 days, which got him his first promotion in Military Intelligence. That trip became a legend. News of it filtered throughout Europe and inspired that Frenchman, Verne."

"OK. Well, as far as I can tell, our Fogg hasn't done anything like that. He went to Eton, joined the Royal Military Academy at Sandhurst, served honorably during the War, then joined the counterintelligence section of MI6, eventually rising to the position of director-general. He was forced to resign in 1952 after the Philby scandals and retired to his family estate in Kent. Single. No kids. He comes to London once a week and stays at his club..."

"The Reform Club."

"Yes, the Reform Club, on the south side of Pall Mall. It's *the* leading club for politicians. During that week, he visits the PM's office. That's when we'll grab him."

"Let's run through the plan again," said Kraven.

"OK," said George. "When I see the Rolls-Royce come down Lower Regent Street, I give the signal to Syd here."

"I'll be parked with the van on Waterloo Place and start the engine," said Syd.

"Just as Fogg gets out, I'll fire the smoke grenade," said George.

"Then English Bob and I will rush out and use the cover to grab Fogg," said Kraven.

"I'll pull the van over," said Syd, "you all jump inside and we're out of there before anyone is the wiser."

"Then you drive to George's site in Holborn," finished Kraven. "By then, all the construction workers will have already gone home. George has a key. We can dump the van there and switch cars. Any questions?"

"Only one: when do we do it?" asked English Bob.

Lord Kraven watched each member of his new League of Heroes and replied:

"The day after tomorrow."

The Day Before

Syd drove the van through Central London, from Piccadilly to Holborn, up the Strand, down Whitehall, through Oxford Street, along the Embankment and over any streets he might have to take on the night of the kidnapping. He knew that the success of the enterprise relied entirely on their ability to get away safely. That's why he stayed focused on the traffic, ignoring any of the myriad distractions that were part and parcel of everyday driving in Central London. *Plan for every possible contingency*, he thought. After all, unlike what that twat Scarlett O'Hara said, tomorrow was not going to be just another day.

Syd was enjoying the role the Old Man had given him. No more of this Syd-find-me-this-for-tomorrow, Sid-find-me-that-for-next-week crap, no more being enslaved by the tokens of consumerism. If only Bolo could see him now! He had become a true revolutionary. He was going to strike at the heart of the system. And he would get answers. He would break through the walls of reality and take a peek at what lie behind.

Along at the wheel of the van, he began singing:

He's a real nowhere man,
Sitting in his nowhere land,
Making all his nowhere plans.

He would find out what had really happened to Paul. Oh yeah.

George, for his part, did not think about Paul, or John, or Ringo. George did not think at all.

If he had thought about the next day, he would have been forced to consider the madness of the enterprise and admit to himself that, all things being equal, the odds of success were not particularly high. What he had to look forward to was a pair of striped pajamas and a steady diet of porridge. So it was better not to think.

Why had George so readily embraced his father-in-law's madness (for inside himself, he still thought of it that way)? One day, he was an Old Man making his life miserable; the next, a Lord High-and-Mighty who had been James Bond's granddad in the days of Queen Victoria. Madness!

But inside George was another George, one who liked to blow up houses, who had uprooted his family to come to the big city to find a better life, and who, most of all, did not appreciate being humiliated in front of his wife and sons by two wankers whose salaries he paid with his taxes. No, siree, he did not.

It was that George who had devoted himself body and soul to his father-in-law's mad enterprise, borrowing a van from work, stealing supplies, even taking entire days off despite his wife's complaints. That George was not striking back just at Fogg, M, Hunter, Control, No. 2, but at all the faceless men and bureaucrats, building surveyors and supervisors who had pulled the strings of his life. George's participation in his father-in-law's madness was George screaming, *I'm not a number, I'm a free man.*

Still not thinking, George rummaged in his closet to find the right set of clothes for the following day. He had lost weight recently, which was an indication that he was happy (or happier) since he tended to eat when he felt miserable. He looked at the family photo on the nightstand. *I am doing this for them too*, he allowed himself to think.

Besides, he didn't really dislike porridge all that much.

Robert Hammerstein looked at himself in the bathroom mirror.

The Union Jack jacket that Syd had found for him somewhere in Carnaby Street was a little like his mind. The three crosses of St. John, St. Andrew and St. Patrick parceled out the flag just as the strands of recovered memories divided his mind. There was still so much he couldn't remember or understand. But the Old Man had given him a reason to live. A sense of purpose had replaced the mindless drifting, the realization that he was nothing but an automaton going about his programmed existence.

He didn't know what to believe. Had he really been "English Bob" or was that just another delusion? Still, even if that's all that it was, he enjoyed it more than his previous life. He embraced his new existence and glorified in it; it was his lifeline to something bigger and greater.

Before he left, tomorrow, he intended to have a full breakfast of scrambled eggs, sausages and bacon. The first one in more years that he could remember. And he knew that, this time, he wouldn't be needing any bicarbonate afterwards.

English Bob looked at himself in the mirror and smiled.

Lord Kraven sat on his bed in the attic, in the dark, so as not to be able to see the walls. Why look at images from the past when one is trying to create the future?

Besides, he now remembered all too well the moments of glory and the tragedies. His duels with Prince Spada and the bombing of London, his defeat of Doctor Fatal and his coming face-to-face with the Sow. He remembered what Lord Greystoke had told him, that night before he disappeared:

"Don't you find it all rather ridiculous?" he had asked. Had the League's entire existence really been justified by the need to fight a Boy? Or was there another reason for its existence?

A *Grand Design*, perhaps?

The words made him shudder involuntarily.

He took his daughter's copy of Barrie's novel and read an excerpt that he had underlined earlier:

But Solomon Caw was right; there is no second chance, not for most of us. When we reach the window it is Lock-out Time. The iron bars are up for life.

D-Day

Kraven, George and English Bob were sitting at the back of the van, shoulder to shoulder, looking like parachutists waiting to be dropped into occupied France in a Hollywood film.

They remained mostly silent; unlike Hollywood soldiers, they did not crack jokes, exchange photos or sweethearts' letters. They rehearsed in their heads the tasks they had to accomplish and planned for what lie ahead of them.

It was the end of the afternoon. A Wednesday afternoon. If English Bob's information was correct, and Sir Phileas remained faithful to his schedule, his black Rolls-Royce would be driving up Whitehall and turning left into Pall Mall before stopping in front of the Reform Club in less than a half-hour.

Syd stopped the van a little before the Club's entrance and parked unobtrusively. He checked the surroundings and saw nothing suspicious. He knocked on the glass and told the others to get out.

Kraven and English Bob were first to step out of the van. They were dressed as City bankers or lawyers, carrying copies of the *Guardian*, and would not attract any undue attention.

After they had gone, positioning themselves between the Travellers' Club and the Canton Club, George got out. He carried a bunch of tools and dumped them across the street. He had selected a place that had a direct line of sight to the entrance of the Reform Cub. In only minutes, he had erected a reasonably convincing simulacrum of the kind of site that workers repairing a sidewalk would leave behind at the end of the day. Finally, he took the case that no longer contained fishing rods and waited.

Inside the entrance of the Reform Club, Robert Meadows-Taylor stood proudly in his brand-new hall porter uniform. He knew all of the members' habits and had taken his station near the doors because he expected Sir Phileas to arrive any minute, and wanted to be there to welcome him personally. Sir Phileas was a generous tipper at Xmas.

During the war, Robert had been captured by the Japanese and forced to work building a bridge in Burma. He had been lucky to come out alive with only a gamy leg to show for it. After he had been demobilized, he had mostly gotten bored doing odd jobs, until a former Regiment C.O. had remembered him and gotten him a cushy position at the Reform Club.

He had spent a good 20 years there, relieving people of their coats and hats and, almost as an afterthought, guarding their secrets. All in all, not a bad job. *It's going to rain*, thought Robert. Still anticipating Sir Phileas' imminent return, he grabbed an umbrella so as to be ready. While doing it, he noticed a city worker across the street. The man was smoking a cigarette and looked fidgety. There was a big case at his feet. Robert wasn't aware there was work being done in the street.

Besides, the man should have gone home an hour ago. What was he still doing there? Waiting for someone to pick him up perhaps? But something deep within Robert's mind–perhaps some kind of instinct gained in the Burmese jungle all those long years ago–felt uncomfortable. There had been an IRA scare recently. What if?... Hesitating no longer, Robert pressed a small button on the underside of the front desk.

At the neighboring Travellers' Club, Rear Admiral Sir Miles Messervy had finished entertaining his granddaughter, Alice. A flower child of 18, who hated the Establishment in all its manifestations, Alice had felt the need to flaunt what she perceived to be the Club's stodginess by inviting to dinner her best friends, who happened to be the fellow members of the band in which she was presently lead singer, the *Hawklords*.

However, she had been very disappointed when the Hall Porter had barely registered any surprise when a lithe young Venus, her hair dyed with henna, dressed in low-cut jeans and all too obviously braless under a cowpoke fringed leather jacket, had shown up accompanied by a long-haired dandy with sideburns, a top hat and a frock coat with a garish em-broidery on the back, and a bare-chested, red haired youth wearing bouffant Turkish pants. To tell the truth, the Four Horsemen of the Apocalypse themselves would have elicited no more surprise from the Hall Porter, who had seen much worse during his years as a porter at Cambridge.

As a result of this, Alice had been in a bad mood all night and, after realizing that her grandfather was not likely to finance the band's proposed tour to America, was about to leave. As a lark, and in a last ditch, desperate effort to attempt to elicit a reaction from the Hall Porter, she decided to steal his cap.

Just then, Sir Phileas' Rolls-Royce turned into Pall Mall.

Syd, who had seen the car approach in his rear view mir-ror, tensed up.

Kraven and English Bob, simulating an energetic discussion between two gentlemen, stepped forward, timing their steps to coincide with the arrival of the car.

George flipped open the case and, in a smoothly rehearsed movement, affixed the smoke canister to the end of the *Panzerfaust*.

The car stopped, right in front of the Reform Club's entrance. But the car door remained obstinately closed and Sir Phileas did not get out. George remained there, holding his launcher, uncertain about what to do.

Suddenly, a few yards away, a manhole across the street opened up and two men sprang out like jacks-in-the box. George recognized them at once: they were the men from "Social Services." *If I don't struggle, it'll go easier for me*, he thought. *Porridge*. He lowered the Panzerfaust.

Then: one of the men pulled out a gun and aimed it at him.

From the van, Syd had seen the two men come out of the sewer hole. *My God! They're going to shoot him*, he thought when he saw the man point the gun at George.

At once, he started the van and, the engine roaring, barreled down the street, aiming straight at the attackers.

Then: the *Hawklords* rushed into the street.

Lord Kraven and English Bob took in the scene with a quick glance: George's attackers (whom the Old Man immediately recognized for who they were) and Syd's driving into the street.

But then a young blond girl rushed out of a building and ran past them and into the street, laughing and proudly holding a cap in her hand.

Another fellow in a top hat followed, then a third youth with a mop of red-hair. The latter saw Kraven and stopped:

"Hey, mate, has anyone ever told you that you look just like Richard Harris in *Camelot*?" he said. "Are you looking for the Grail too? Would you like to be our *guru*?"

Kraven's attention was momentarily distracted by the young man. During that instant, Robert Meadows-Taylor stepped out of the Club and opened the Rolls' door.

Then: Sir Phileas stepped out of the car and inside the Reform Club.

George realized he was about to die. He raised the *Panzerfaust* and fired. The recoil knocked him to the ground and the smoke grenade went on to hit the facade of the Reform Club (designed by Charles Barry, R. A.) where it began to spew heavy billows of acrid grey smoke.

On its way, it also hit Robert Meadows-Taylor, who had been lucky enough to come back from Burma with only a gamy leg, but had been unlucky enough to have pressed a small button on the underside of the front desk of the Reform Club, and even unluckier to have come out to help Sir Phileas Fogg out of his Rolls-Royce.

The first man from Social Services turned around and muttered an "Aw shit" under his breath.

George took a craftsman's hammer which he had been carrying under his jacket and sprang on the agent, knocking the gun out of his hand, then with a backhand blow sent the man sprawling to the ground.

But the other agent had had time to pull out his gun and shot. Once. Hit in the arm, George collapsed on the dirty sidewalk. For the first time in his life, he was grateful for being overweight. The bullet seemed to have only pierced the fat of his arm. Whirling his other arm around, he still had the presence of mind to hit the agent's ankles with the hammer. Hard.

The security man dropped to the ground, screaming. George crawled towards the asshole who, one day not so long ago, had dumped an Old Man and some carbon receipts on his doorstep. *How much better things would have turned out if I hadn't answered the bell that day*, he reflected, *but it's too late for recriminations now*. He twitched in pain when he felt the bullet in his arm, but managed to get up.

Then, he noticed a long-haired dandy running across the street. He wore a top hat and a frock coat with garish embroidery on the back. It represented Captain Marvel giving a message of peace at the United Nations. George stopped to look at it. Exactly the same as on his lunchbox. *What are the odds?* he thought.

Then: the first agent, who had now gotten up, shot George through the heart and he died.

Syd swerved madly to avoid the crazy blonde who held a cap in her hand and her top-hatted boyfriend (so he thought).

The vehicle careened through the street, drove onto the sidewalk and, moving blindly through the billows of smoke that now enveloped the Club's entrance, hit Sir Phileas' Rolls-Royce head on. A smell of burnt rubber and car paint spread through the air.

Syd was knocked out by the collision. His head lay on the wheel. The blaring sound of the horn added to the pandemonium. A new, more deadly smell slowly seeped into the air: that of gasoline. A tense silence fraught with drama hung in the air. One could almost hear the silent ticking of a clock.

Then: the van exploded and Syd died.

English Bob saw the van burst into flames and rushed forward to help Syd. Meanwhile, Kraven, who had seen Fogg enter the Club seconds before the chaos erupted, rushed inside through the smoke and the debris.

The shock of the explosion threw English Bob down on the sidewalk. He looked around. Kraven had disappeared. The smoke made it impossible to see a few feet away. He felt something wet on his head, and by pitting his hand to it, realized it was blood. Whether it was his or someone else, he could not tell.

There was still dust and rubble falling all around him. He got up, ignoring the charred body of Robert Meadows-Taylor and bravely moved forward. Even though he had no remembrance of being the legendary Hero Kraven had told him about, something within him stirred. It was like a secret symphony being played inside his mind for himself alone. Still looking for Kraven, he stepped across the gaping ruin that had been the Reform Club entrance. He felt dizzy. Blood loss, he thought. He caught a reflection in a piece of broken glass. It had been his blood after all. The right side of his skull looked as if it had been scalped.

Then: Robert Hammerstein collapsed; he finally recognized the music he had been hearing in his head: *Albion Ascendant*, the Queen's own anthem. He closed his eyes and, a few seconds later, he was dead.

Lord Kraven stepped boldly inside the Reform Club. When he heard the explosion outside, he had already climbed the grand marble staircase leading to the first floor hallway. He recognized the layout from his previous visits during the time of the League of Heroes. It seemed as if the Club had not changed much.

As expected, the way to the Blue Room was barred by the Roster Officer on duty.

"State matter. I'm here to see Sir Phileas," said Kraven, impeccably pulling out a business card from his elegant City banker suit. Then, as the officer extended his hand to take the proffered card, in an elegant swipe, Kraven used its sharpened edge to slice through his jugular.

The man collapsed to the floor, bleeding profusely. Quickly, Kraven searched him and removed a sub-machine gun and a revolver. Then stepping over the now-dead man, he proceeded along the corridors.

He recognized the same classical paintings that adorned the walls last time he had set foot there, on January 10, 1919.

Finally, Kraven reached the door to the Blue Room. Bizarrely, it was painted blue and a sign was posted on it, which read: "FOR THE ATTENTION OF SIR PHILEAS FOGG: MASSACRE PLANNED FOR TODAY AT 7 p.m."

It was 7:30. How could he have known? thought Kraven. He shook his head, as if to chase away an annoying insect, then opened the door and stepped inside the Blue Room.

Behind the Blue Door

The room was in total darkness.

Kraven groped for the light switch, found it and turned the lights on.

He recognized the familiar room where Sir Phileas had so often received him in the past, but it was different while also being the same. It had none of the luxurious comfort and Old Albion charm that the real Blue Room had. It was as if a clumsy artisan had tried to build a replica of the real Blue Room with crudely printed plywood and cheap draperies.

He walked across the imitation desk to the French windows. He could see the gardens beyond, but they were not real gardens, just a *trompe l'oeil* painted background.

Kraven stepped out onto the balcony, which turned out to be a concrete corridor with stage lighting to complete the illusion. Baffled he looked around. He gripped his gun and, hearing noises to the right, followed the corridor in that direction.

He arrived at a vast, brightly-lit room that looked like a self-service dining hall. It appeared to be filled with Indians and Fairies, Pirates and Lost Boys, Spada's mercenaries and the Jade Mask's Dacoits, German soldiers and Tommy Boys. They all turned towards him and someone shouted: "Surprise!"

As if in a dream, not altogether in control of himself, Kraven started to open fire, shooting indiscriminately. They dropped to the floor like leaves in the wind, slowly, not suddenly. Even the blood seemed to flow in slow motion and the shards of Wedgwood china floated through the air like triangular soap bubbles. Then Kraven heard the repetitive clicking sound signaling that he had emptied the charger and that his gun was now empty. He discarded it and stepped across the bodies, noticing almost despite himself that the Fairies' wings were not real but made of cellophane and that the Indians' skin color was due to makeup.

The dining hall was now unnaturally silent: no gasps, no cries for mercy, no moans of pain, not even a death rattle.

At the other end was a set of swinging doors with round glass windows. Kraven looked through one of them. The other side was bathed in a greenish light, like that of an aquarium. There were Men-in-White walking calmly about, carrying trays with what looked like a mix of electronic components and surgical instruments.

Kraven grabbed his revolver and pushed the door open.

No one stopped when he entered. One of the Men-in-White put his right index to his lips in the universal gesture asking for silence, while pointing at a corner of the room with his left hand.

There stood a sarcophagus-like contraption from which sprouted a dozen cables and tubes. Some contained different liquids, the colors of which he could not guess since they were all bleached by the ambient green light. A low hum emanated from it. There was a round glass window where the face should be, and in front of it, a circular, panoramic screen, the back of which was also connected to the sarcophagus through its sides.

Kraven stepped around the machine to examine it closer. He looked at the screen first. On it, he saw Kid Colt, but not as he knew him. Now he looked old, insane and disheveled. He was surrounded by seven men in white suits.

A young man Kraven had never seen before entered the frame. He stepped inside what looked like a futuristic version of the MechaMan armor Kraven himself had worn during the Great War. The young man then walked to a rocketship, entered it and locked the door behind him. Colt pressed a large red button. The rocket exploded.

Kraven turned around to look at the glass window to see who was inside the sarcophagus. At first he could only see a humanoid shape suspended in some kind of mysterious solution. He briefly wondered if it was the same as the solution designed by Moreau that had made him into Lord Kraven.

Then he saw the man's face.

It was Sherlock Holmes.

"We have to talk."

Lord Kraven wandered aimlessly through the concrete corridors of what was obviously no longer the Reform Club.

Opening door at random, he came across the Danger Room. He briefly wondered what it was doing there instead of at the League's Headquarters but had to focus his attention on avoiding its deadly traps to come out alive at the other end.

He was old. He no longer had the speed and reflexes of his youth. A pendulum blade was going to slice him in half when it crumpled against his body harmlessly, barely tearing his clothes. It was made of soft plastic imitating steel.

He walked out of the fake Danger Room unscathed.

And stepped into the Cairo Lunatic Asylum.

Four Prussian soldiers wearing gas masks came at him with flame-throwers. Kraven grabbed his revolver and shot four times. The four bodies crumpled. *At least I haven't lost my marksmanship*, he thought.

He stepped across the iron door that should have been the cell of the Egyptian psychic and found himself on the *Lusitania*.

Leaning over the railing, he could see that the ship was on rollers simulating the waves of the North Atlantic.

"You've made quite a mess, haven't you?"

The man who had spoken to him was Prince Spada, but a Prince Spada who was dirty and badly shaved, dressed in grubby overalls. He also had quite a beer belly—but maybe the Spada he knew had worn a girdle.

Kraven did not reply. Nothing made sense anymore. He just waited to see what would happen next.

"This way," said Spada. "Follow me."

They walked off the bridge and down the metal corridors. Spada opened a door and stepped aside to let Kraven go through.

He felt that the end of his quest was near.

On the other side was the Special Studies Cabinet (where no student ever went) at Christ's College in Cambridge.

Where it had all begun.

Three men were waiting for him. One was Professor Cavor. Another was Sir Reginald Plumdritch. The third man was hugely fat and was busy toasting a muffin in the fireplace, under a plaque commemorating Darwin's stay at the College. It was, of course, Sir Phileas Fogg.

Sir Reginald walked towards him, holding a syringe. His intentions are clear.

"Not this time," said Kraven, nonchalantly delivering a powerful uppercut to the man's jaw that sent the scientist sprawling against the library wall. The *trompe l'oeil* partition collapsed, revealing a scaffolding behind which Kraven saw a vast hangar not unlike a motion picture sound stage. Out there, there were other scaffoldings, hinting at other "sets."

Kraven turned towards Cavor and Fogg. Cavor, embarrassed, avoided his eyes and pretended to look elsewhere.

Fogg turned around and slowly said:

"We have to talk."

Kraven passed out.

The Hospital

He woke up on a hospital bed. His neck was immobilized by a leather strap that prevented him from turning his head. His sleep patterns were intermittent: he would wake up suddenly, then fall back to sleep. The only thing in his field of vision was a white door and a dusty ventilation shaft. He knew he was in a hospital because of the smell.

He needed the sleep, not wanting to remember, or even simply to think, but even in his slumber, rest eluded him. The dreams would catch up to him, a jumble of unreal images and sensations, snippets of two very different lives, that of Lord Kraven, Savior of the Empire, and of the Old Man.

Each, in turn, would fight for prominence in his mind, claiming to be the legitimate reality, and yet, deep within himself, he now realized that neither was.

He was looking forward to gradually becoming himself at last, instead of being a made-up phantom, an illusion.

Then, the others came. Since he could not see them, and they did not speak to him, he recognized them only by the sounds they made. A muffled knock against a wall. The creaking of a trolley cart. A door opening or closing. The sound of an IV bottle being replaced.

He felt someone giving him a sponge bath and, between artificially induced sleeping periods, he would spy an arm wearing a wristwatch or holding a moist towelette, but never more. And they still would not speak to him.

Eventually, after days, perhaps weeks, of this treatment, boredom became almost unbearable. He had no fear of dying because he knew he was being fed intravenously. There was no pain either. But where was he? Who was he? What did they want from him? How long were they going to keep him there?

Finally, one day, when he woke up, he discovered that the strap that had kept his head immobilized had been removed during his sleep. Flexing his neck, he relaxed his muscles, oscillated his head from side to side and began to look at his surroundings.

To his left was a nightstand with an empty plate on it. There were no flowers, no cards, no clocks and no calendars. Across the room, despite the bad lighting, he recognized a water fountain with paper cups. To his right was a strange and complex machine made of metal and tubes, not unlike what he seen in the green room of his dreams, the one that Holmes had been connected to. If he, too, had been attached to such a machine, he now understood why his head had been immobilized.

"Would you like some water? Don't try to talk, just blink."

Sir Reginald Plumdritch sat by his bedside, offering him a glass of water with a straw in it. His mouth felt as if it had been packed with cotton. He blinked. The scientist brought the straw to his lips and, awkwardly, he managed to sip in some water. It tasted like plastic but he did not care. He immediately began to feel better.

Plumdritch was dressed in a faded blue overall; he looked more like a repairman than like a sinister mad scientist. He tried to speak, ask a question, but could not. Plumdritch took the glass away and put it back on the nightstand.

"Sleep now," he said. "You'll feel better in the morning. You'll have plenty of opportunity to talk then."

Plumdritch then left the room and he began to drift back to sleep.

A few days later, he had settled into a new routine. The passing of time did not seem to matter since he lacked any reference points other than the serving of meals, the taking of medication and the sleeping periods.

A nurse took care of him. She was a small young woman with shortish red hair cut in a boyish style. Her name was Zydblinski and he had never seen her before. She fed him with a spoon: fruit jelly, mashed potatoes and other soft foods. He drank milk, juices and high protein drinks. She also shaved him with an old-fashioned hand razor, telling him that he had to look at his best because he would soon have visitors. When he was finally able to stand on his feet, she helped him to the shower cubicle just outside his room.

Nowhere were there any mirrors.

Zyd (as he had nicknamed her) would cannily avoid answering his questions, limiting herself to innocuous chatter or a vague "later." So he had nothing else to occupy his mind than to once more review what he thought had been his life: his friends, his enemies (not such an easy distinction now) and past and recent events, the history of Albion and the geography of Neverland. He had plenty of time to go over every shred of his existence as he regained his strength.

Finally, the day came when Nurse Zydblinski said: "You're ready to receive visitors now."

The Visitors

The first person who came to see him was English Bob.

Or, rather, the first two persons.

There was Young English Bob as he had known him in the heyday of the League, with his infectious broad smile and wavy hair, and Old English Bob, the slightly confused older man with a stomach ulcer.

Both were dressed the same, wearing the Union Jack. But one wore a beautiful, tailor-made tunic, whereas the other had to make do with a creased jacket found on Carnaby Street.

"Glad to have you back, sir," said Old English Bob. "This time, we thought we might have lost you for good."

"It didn't go too well, did it?" he replied. "You got killed when the van exploded."

"Well, yes, the scenario went totally out of control. But I'm told it's nothing that can't be fixed."

"I wanted to tell you, sir," interjected Young English Bob, "it was an honor to be working with you. I'll never forget the time when you jumped off the *Lusitania*."

"Yes, quite an honor," added Old English Bob.

Nurse Zydblinski entered the room with his dinner.

"Visiting hours are over, boys," she said. "Our great man needs his rest."

"I've come to apologize," said Syd.

Except it was not Syd the hippie but a handsome young officer dressed in a uniform he didn't recognize. His hair was cut quite short and he looked exhausted. He held his cap in his hand, kneading it in embarrassment.

"My real name is Lieutenant Syd Barrett. Syd the hippie was meant to be a reassuring sidekick that would buttress your Level-3 persona with his harmless comic book fantasies, but instead it tapped into fragments of the Level-2 persona which we thought had been safely buried. I tried to make those seem outlandish by giving you even more lurid comics, but it only added to the problem. Everywhere you looked, you found a clue. Finally, I thought mentioning the ludicrous Paul McCartney conspiracy would finally make you realize this was all a product of your imagination–which in many ways, it was–but it only made you more eager to access the truth. Nothing seemed to work and our carefully built scenario completely careened out of control."

The young officer looked so mortified that he could not help but provide some encouragement.

"I'm sure I'd have found out anyway," he said reassuringly, not knowing exactly what he was supposed to have found out.

"Very kind of you to say so, sir, but I take full responsibility for my mistakes and the failure of the second scenario. Without me, we might have succeeded. Please forgive me."

The next visitor was Professor Cavor.

"My real name is not Cavor, of course," he said. "You're making a tremendous recovery. We're all thrilled."

"Who am I?" he asked.

"Ah, well, I'm afraid that's a question for later. You have to learn how to walk before you can dance, as they say. I've come to give you these."

The man who had been Cavor took a bunch of paperbacks from his briefcase. They bore colorful covers and were all part of a continuing series entitled *The League of Heroes*.

"Before we can answer your questions, you should read these first," said Cavor. "Besides, Dr. Plumdritch tells me you're not quite yet ready to move about on your own two legs. Don't think of this as a reading assignment, more as a little vacation."

After Cavor had left, he began thumbing through the books. Their titles, while lurid, reminded him of his own life: *Prisoners of Baron Samedi, Robotor, The Sons of the Phar-*

aoh... The books had been written very quickly (you could tell from the style) but carried an undeniably seductive power. There was no author's name–just a generic publisher's credit.

He began to read the books in random order. They featured a quartet of stalwart heroes, Lord Kraven, English Bob, Lord Greystoke and Sherlock Holmes, protecting the Victorian Empire of Albion against the forces of evil, often represented by Peter Pan and various villains from Neverland.

He did not need to read them cover to cover to recognize carefully edited and overly dramatized chunks of his life. *Had this been my life?* he thought. *Am I nothing more than a pulp hero made flesh?*

When Nurse Zydblinski came to serve him dinner that night, she found him engrossed in reading *The House on the Edge of Tomorrow*. She removed the books to make room for the food tray.

"Can you picture that?" she said wistfully. "All our scientists powerless, the military overwhelmed in less than a week. And yet, in those books, they won. They always won."

He pressed her with questions, but she refused to say anymore.

He had been doing physical therapy for a week and reading *The League of Heroes* series when Dr. Plumdritch (it was still hard to not think of him as the deadly Doctor Fatal) came in.

"You've made tremendous progress," he said. "Next week, you'll be ready to go out. But first, I wanted to test your cognitive patterns."

He pulled out a stash of 8x10 glossy photographs.

"Just tell me what you recognize."

In succession, he quickly saw, and identified, photos of George's house, its living room, the attic, covered with comic book cuttings, its garden with its rusty swing, its garage, Syd's trailer and even the room at *The White Hart*.

"Very good," said Plumdritch, when he had finished. He then took his blood pressure and tested his reflexes. "Everything appears to be working wonderfully," he finally pronounced. *"Mens sana in corpore sano.* You'll be ready next week."

"Ready for what?"

Plumdritch did not answer and just left the room. The black-and-white glossies were still spread over his bed. His eyes fell on the photo of his attic with its colorful collection of cut out pictures and he reflected that he was finally about to find the truth.

As Plumdritch had promised, the day of his liberation finally came. That morning, Nurse Zydblinski brought a nondescript set of grey overalls and helped him put them on, after he had put on real underwear and socks and a pair of surgical gloves. He was given flat-heeled shoes that looked like grey tennis shoes. He was no longer shaky on his feet, but he could not have run much of a race. Walking steadily, he finally left the room which had been his entire universe for an unknown number of months and emerged in a corridor very much like those he had seen beyond the Blue Room in his last incarnation. Plumdritch was there, waiting for him.

"Excellent," he said. "Are you ready?"

"I am," he said, putting as much determination in his voice as he could.

"Then follow me."

Life at 24 frames per second

They walked through a maze of tunnels with windows opening to the outside.

There were crates of canned food and boxes of prepared meals piled at each intersection, with no attention paid to tidiness or organization. He did not met anyone, but he could hear sounds of life and the hum of generators through ventilation shafts.

They reached a metal door marked "CONTROL" and entered the room behind it.

Gone was the luxurious office, the plush surroundings. Fogg and Cavor, dressed in similarly non-descript overalls, looking tired and mildly unkempt, sat on ordinary plastic chairs in a Spartan office painted grey.

Plumdritch motioned him to an empty chair and himself went to sit behind a bare desk, which was nothing more than a table with a telephone, a computer and some files.

Fogg and Cavor looked at him for what seemed to be a long time without saying anything.

Then, Fogg spoke:

"I knew we had chosen the right man."

Maybe they expected some kind of reaction from him, but he strived to remain impassible. He watched them in turn, noticing the drabness and the worn-out state of their clothes. He observed that Cavor was no longer twitching, and Fogg was not nearly as obese as he remembered him.

"Where am I?" he finally asked.

They looked surprised. Fogg looked at Plumdritch, who shook his head. Cavor jotted something down inside a note-book.

"In London, of course," Fogg replied. "Is that the only thing you've forgotten?"

He swallowed to give himself time to think. He decided to not answer the question. How could he know what he did not know?

"What part of London?"

Cavor whispered something in Fogg's ear. The former Master of the League nodded.

"My colleague suggests we need to bring you fully up to date. It's an excellent idea. So to better answer your question, we're going to take you on a little tour. But in the meantime, suffice it to say that, like all of us here, you're in Hell."

Everybody seemed to have been waiting for him at the cafeteria. He recognized the dining hall from the last bits of his surreal dream-like journey.

Unsurprisingly, George was there, with his wife and sons. He recognized the Llewelyn-Davies brothers, but also Baron von Tod and Queen Victoria, Dean Putnam and Kapitan Mors. Many faces, some known, others unknown.

They served a tepid bubbly in Styrofoam cups and everyone, it seemed, felt compelled to congratulate him and tell him a story about themselves.

"It took us hours to build the Crystal Palace set," said George, eating some crackers. "Even with forced perspective, it took half of Stage 18. The biggest set we've ever built."

"The *Lusitania* came close," added Kaiser William. "The engine room, with icy water up to my chest, I almost caught my death!"

"Nothing compared to the aerial dogfights," said Baron von Tod, who really was a mechanic named Toddle who spoke with a Yorkshire accent. "When I think I used to get vertigo just climbing on the roof! I crapped my pants in that simulator!"

"We ate, slept and lived our characters," explained the woman who had been his daughter. "We dressed as they did, spoke as they did; we did everything exactly as if it had been real. And all to help and support you."

"And I did all the costumes," said the man he had known as Aloysius Keys. "I was so happy when they wrote me in."

They all were genuinely happy to see him again. Joy spread from group to group as he proceeded across the room, under Plumdritch's supervision, Cavor and Fogg observing him like silent shadows.

Nurse Zydblinski dragged him by the hand to a table where, she said, an "old friend" was waiting for him.

Unlike the rest of the crowd, the tall man was dressed in some kind of battle fatigues and wore guns. He was drinking beer with other armed companions.

He was the man who had been Lord Greystoke.

"Hi, mate, join us for a beer," said the former Lord of the Trees, handing him a can. "You richly deserve a cold one!"

Plumdritch pushed back the beer.

"He shouldn't be drinking yet."

"And how are you planning to stop me?"

There was a tense moment, which he broke by just grabbing the beer and drinking it slowly. Plumdritch looked at Fogg and Cavor, but they remained mute. He enjoyed the cold, frothy liquid as he had never enjoyed another drink in his life.

"Sorry I couldn't visit you earlier," said Greystoke, "but I just found out you'd been let out when I returned from my last mission. I wanted to tell you in person that I was always against this idea of his," he continued, indicating Fogg. "Do you recall our last 'conversation' in that pub during the London Burning? The League is and always was bullshit. It's a dream, an illusion, a colossal waste of time and I'm sorry they dragged you into all that shit. Win or die, that's our only choice; anything else is a distraction we can ill afford."

The other soldiers approved, nodding silently. Fogg said nothing. Plumdritch took him by the arm and led him away.

"Don't let him confuse you," he said. "You still have much to see."

They took him to the room that he had seen when he had gone beyond the Blue Door. The one bathed in greenish light, with its humming, sarcophagus-like contraption attached to tubes, pipes and cables. There was the same round glass window behind which he had seen Sherlock Holmes, except that it was now empty, as was the circular, panoramic screen in front of it.

Almost as if he had read his thought, Plumdritch said:

"He's somewhere else. This one was yours."

Carefully filed on shelves across the room were digital recordings of rock and Victorian music, and visual recordings labeled Ingolstadt, Cairo Asylum, London Bombing, Paris Peace Conference, Dean Putnam's Office... Even minor events had their own recordings: Breakfast, Exercise Practice,

Watching TV... He could see his life in a single glance, watch it unreel at the speed of 24 frames per second.

"What does this all mean?" he asked.

"I'm quite tired," said Fogg. "The Theater of Crime scenario has been exhausting. Do you mind if we sit down?"

Without waiting for a reply, he pulled out a chair and sat down. Cavor and Plumdritch remained standing.

"If there's a man who deserves the truth, it's you. But first, I've got to explain what all this is," he continued, embracing the room with a gesture, "and tell you what we did to you..." After a pause, he continued: "You know that specialists don't agree about the workings of memory. Some think that our mind chooses to retain only those events that it finds useful or significant. Others believe that everything is stored in there," he lightly tapped his forehead with his finger, "a coffee stain on a paper, the smell of a flower, a couple of French words heard across Oxford Street... Even if it's not readily available, it's all there. It provides the background information that helps the conscious mind make sense of the bits we do remember. So in effect, you don't have to entirely brainwash a man to change the contents of his memory. You only need to supply new significant events, and the background memory will do the rest and fill in the blanks, as it were. With this technology, we could take anyone and with a few, well-prepared scenarios, give him an entirely new life."

Fogg asked for a drink. Cavor took a decanter and filled a glass. The fat man drank it before going on:

"In your case, we had to proceed in two phases. First, we had to erase the significant events of your previous memory. That was done with LSD and Amobarbital. Then, we had to insert the new memories, scenarios we had carefully constructed. We hesitated a little before deciding to use Ketamine, because at very high doses, it not only create hallucinations, which was, in effect, what we sought, but it sometimes even affects the background memory. The subject almost becomes another man entirely; the experiment goes out of control..."

"Is that what happened to me? I was inside that tank, living your scenarios?"

"Yes. We didn't scrimp on the details. We built sets to shoot the scenarios, which were then fed to you through this screen. We used every means of simulation available to create the world of the League of Heroes. And I must say, we succeeded admirably. You became Lord Kraven, Savior of the Empire, your Level-2 personality."

"Unfortunately, a few anachronistic details went by unnoticed at the time," added Cavor. "The *Eleanor Rigby* poster from the Beatles at the Alhambra, your Dunhill 1900 fast car, in fact an American model from the fifties. But, overall, everything was very coherent..."

"Up to the moment of the Paris Peace Conference and your project of a one world government and independence for the Fairy Folk. That's when, despite all our efforts, Lord Kraven began to escape our control. So, we simulated your death in the Antarctic and aborted the experiment."

"Why did you put me through all that?" he asked.

"I'll show you," said Fogg. "But first, let me finish. Confronted by the failure of our first scenario, we decided to abort it and launch a new simulation. We created your Level-3 personality and put you in the skin of an older man in London, 1969. We gave you a family. We thought that an ordinary existence, made of little nothings and carefully managed, would restore the tear in your background memory and eventually enable us to restart the project., Unfortunately, the very opposite happened. Your choice of reading material reawakened memories from the Level-2 personality. First, vague remembrances, then actual memory fragments. You acquired the certitude that, in another life, you had been a Victorian superhero. We desperately tried to regain control of the scenario, but everything we did only reinforced your beliefs. Ultimately, we decided to abort and let it run its course to its ultimate conclusion."

"People died."

"No, no one died. It was all part of the simulation, designed to bring you out step by step."

They were interrupted by Kid Colt arriving. Like Greystoke, he was dressed in military fatigues and looked tired and dirty. Fogg introduced him as Major Kit Coltrane, without any other details.

"The grounds are clear," he said. "As clear as can be, anyway."

"Very well," said Fogg. "Inform security that we're arriving." Then, he turned around and said: "I told you before that we all were in Hell. Now you can see for yourself."

Hell

He followed Coltrane, Fogg and Cavor down the corridors. Men and women with tired faces and covered with grime stepped aside to let them pass. On the way, they picked up two armed men. He recognized them: they were the men who had claimed to be from Social Services.

They arrived in a concrete bunker with flak jackets, a variety of guns and crates of ammunition.

"We have to hurry. We don't have much time," said Coltrane, handing him a bulletproof jacket. "Kevlar underlining. I don't know if it's enough, but it's better than nothing."

Everyone put on a jacket and grabbed a gun, except Fogg. They then walked towards a freight elevator that was waiting for them.

"Not more than five minutes," said Fogg. "And let's be especially careful."

Coltrane pressed the UP button. The machine rose slowly, ponderously but without a shudder. It was obviously maintained properly.

They arrived in another bunker, opposite a huge airlock that reminded him of a bank safe. Three armed men also wearing flak jackets were waiting for them by the airlock.

Before signaling to the men to open the airlock, Fogg repeated his instructions:

"No more than five minutes. We all stay together and return at the least sign of danger."

"What is there to fear?" he asked.

"You'll soon see."

At his signal, Coltrane punched a code on a keypad, offered his thumbprint to a scanner and the soldiers released the airlock.

The same maneuver was repeated on the other side and, eventually, they stepped out on Piccadilly Avenue.

The first thing he noticed was that they were inside a gigantic dome. London was trapped inside a monstrous Crystal Palace, like a monument in a snow globe. It was impossible to tell how large the dome was, but he thought it must have covered at least all of the West End, and maybe a little bit more.

Piccadilly Avenue was empty; the road littered with all kinds of garbage, men's and women's shoes, Louis Vuitton luggage, old newspapers, various items of clothing and even a policeman's helmet leaning against a lamppost. There were a few overturned cars and one was a burned-out husk. The impression was that people had ransacked the place, then left in a panic. There was no noise, no wind to rustle the bits of newspaper lying about, only a deadly stillness. There were no visible signs of life as they walked on. They came across a fast food restaurant. There, too, panic had left its unmistakable mark: uneaten cheeseburgers still in their silver wrappings, and unfinished sodas. As they proceeded slowly past Leicester Square, he noticed that they were being watched by snipers posted at the windows and on the rooftops.

They passed by the real Reform Club (no traces of explosion) and reached Trafalgar Square. He saw another group of armed men sitting on the steps of the National Gallery. He recognized Greystoke and his fellow troopers. They waved at them as they continued down towards the Thames.

Above, the sky was darkening. A storm broke out but the rain didn't reach him. It was odd being in the middle of a storm, hear the pinging of the rain on the Dome, but not feel its wetness.

"We should go back," said Coltrane.

"No," said Fogg. "I want him to see them. We owe him that much."

They reached the Embankment and the inner wall of the Dome. He noticed that the soldiers looked increasingly nervous and were checking their guns. One of them, his finger on his earpiece, reported to Coltrane.

"The lightning hit the Dome near St. Paul's. Caused a fissure. There was contact with the enemy, but penetration was stopped and the area is being decontaminated."

"We should go back," repeated Coltrane. "This is extremely dangerous."

"They're here," said Fogg.

He had thought Hell was the abandoned city under the Dome. He had been wrong.

Hell was on the other side of the glass.

They were glued to the Dome. He could almost hear the rustling of their membranous wings, see his reflection in the impenetrable, multi-faceted eyes that stared at him, smell the fetid sweetness of their kitin shells. There were thousands of them, pressed against each other, smacking their mandibles, clutching with their claws, their soft, putrid bellies contracting and expanding, expelling miasmic, yellow vapors.

"We've learned to identify various sub-species," said Coltrane. "These," he added, pointing towards a gaggle of taller creatures whose heads resembled a three-cornered hat, "we've dubbed the '*Pirates.*' "

Outside, the creatures swarmed against the Dome, new ones crunching, eating, digesting and excreting the ones before them. Some were reddish in color, with strange markings all over their bodies, and feather-like antennae. "*Indians,*" he guessed. Then there were the coleopter-like "*Fairies*" with their wings striated with pulsating veins and their dilated egg-sac cavities from which issued strange, larva-like things, that were just gobbled up by the others. But the most fierce-looking were the "*Lost Boys*." From a distance, they might have looked almost human with their proportions and raccoon-like masks, but close-up, he saw that they were a mass of vermiform parasites that, out of a predatory reflex, clung together in a parody of the human form. There were bodies without skeletons, seeking to embrace and consume anything they touched.

"You're in luck," said Fogg. "Their leader is here. The one we've called *Peter Pan*."

He was only as tall as a small boy, with two arms and legs connected to a green body articulated in three segments, with wings on his back. He stood up on his clawed feet, his arms folded like those of a praying mantis. His face was both the color and texture of dried tobacco leaves. It had the finer features of a boy's face, but its tiny teeth were all very sharply filed and its eyes were pools of inky blackness lit only by some undying, malevolent evil.

"They appear to obey only him."

A swarm of tiny *Fairies* hovered around his head. At his silent command, they dashed straight on towards the Dome and crashed against its glass, like gnats on a windshield.

"Sometimes, they manage to crack the Dome open. They have no regard for their own lives; the stronger ones eat the weaker ones. When they do, they eat us–after a little play... Otherwise, most of the time, they seem content to merely watch us. Watch us die, I suppose."

Neverland

"What happened?" he asked.

They were back in the CONTROL office. No one had spoken to him during the return journey. He did not mind because he needed to collect his thoughts. Now, Fogg, Cavor and Plumdritch sat across from him. The door was open. Some people had gathered outside, as if this was some kind of momentous event. Perhaps it was.

"They appeared out of nowhere one morning in Kensington Gardens," said Fogg. "At first, we mounted an effective resistance. We had the superiority of numbers, and our weapons are more than adequate to kill them. But we had not counted on... What you might call the *Consumption*. They carry a parasite in their bodies that spread and eradicated nine-tenths of the human race in just under a month. It was horrible. They flew all over the world, spreading their filth, killing us all and feeding on the remains of Humanity. We, here, in London, were in the eye of the storm, as it were. We found ourselves trapped under this dome. *Neverland*, we call this place. For all we know, we may be the last survivors, or there may be other isolated pockets elsewhere on the planet. We don't know. We tried sending messages but we haven't heard anything back, and we got tired of sending messengers who never returned. Maybe they did it to keep us here, alive, to satisfy their curiosity."

"Where do they come from?"

"We don't know. Another dimension? Another universe? Out of time, perhaps? Being better read than my scientific colleagues, I was struck by the similarities with Barrie's tales, and I came up with the idea of using the nomenclature of *Peter Pan*–and perhaps another notion that might still prove to be the only salvation for our benighted species."

"You're talking about me, aren't you?"

"Yes. I said we would explain..."

Nurse Zydblinski suddenly walked past the crowd and entered the room.

"The subject has just killed himself, sir," she said. "As you predicted."

Plumdritch rushed out. Fogg sighed deeply and rose out of his chair.

"You might as well come with me. This will help explain things..."

He followed Fogg into the room with the other sarcophagus, the one inside which, in his drug-induced delirium, he had recognized his old League ally, Sherlock Holmes.

But this time, looking through the round glass window, he saw that the thing inside the steel machine was not the Great Detective. It was one of *them*. One of the creatures they called "*Indians*."

He was floating, his double eyelids opened forever on dead, golden eyes, his inhuman face turned upwards, surrounded by Medusa-like tendrils, his feathery antenna shattered. His shell-like body had lost its brilliant colored markings and was slowly eaten away by the various fluids in which he had been immersed.

"We captured him on the morning of the first day of the Invasion," explained Fogg. "He looked as if he might have been someone important. We were never sure. There's so much about them we don't understand... After debating the pros and cons for a long time, Dr. Plumdritch managed to reprogram him. We were never quite certain of the effects our drugs would have on him, but we decided to take the risk and incorporate him into the scenario we had built for you. He became Sherlock Holmes, the Great Detective, the Logician, still loyal to a queen, Queen Victoria, still part of a collective, the League of Heroes, but this time working against his own species. It was a unique opportunity to try to fathom the way their minds work and see if, maybe, we could work with them. Then, when we had to abort your experiment, we decided to try another tack. First, we kept him on ice, as it were. The 'Theater of Crime' was his equivalent of George's house. Later, we built a new scenario in which we turned the tables: it was the Fairy Folk who died from the Consumption. He was forced to serve an evil Empire. We threw clues about space travel and extra-dimensional exploration. We hoped to learn something from him. We thought he might turn against the Empire and show us some of their weaknesses. Nurse Zydblinski tried to prod him in the right direction. But in the end, we failed. He chose to kill himself rather than serve humanity... Another failed experiment."

"I see," he said. "What about me then?"

"You remain our last, best hope. In more ways than one, you *are* what we made you: Lord Kraven, the Savior of the Empire."

"Why this focus on the League of Heroes?"

"We believe the novels hold the solution."

"But why?"

"Because you wrote them."

The League of Heroes

They were back in the CONTROL room.

"To give credit where credit's due, it was the Professor's idea," said Fogg pointing at Cavor. "Right after the invasion, while we were still debating the origins and nature of these creatures, he remembered a series of science fiction adventures he had read while in college: *The League of Heroes*. It was most fascinating: the author had drawn upon a variety of sources, J.M. Barrie, Sir Arthur Conan Doyle, Edgar Rice Burroughs, Jules Verne and many others, to invent a world which had been invaded by creatures from the fictional Neverland. The parallels were striking. But, in the novels, mankind thrived, whether it absorbed, thwarted or defeated the invaders. We quickly located the author and, with his consent—yes, it was you and you did volunteer—we began to conduct a series of psychological experiments to find out where you had gotten the inspiration for the books."

"We never discovered whether you had some kind of precognitive power that had enabled you to see the future," Plumdritch continued, "or your mind had somehow been able to tap into that other dimension or universe from which the creatures originate. Perhaps a bit of both? However, while you were unconscious, we came to realize that, as we fed your brain information about the creatures' behavior, habits and modes of attacks, you came up with counter-plans, solutions and, like in the books, the most reckless, desperate plans always worked! *The heroes always won!*"

"Most of what you've seen here exists only because of you," added Fogg. "It is your imagination that led us to organize the force commandos led by the man you came to know as Lord Greystoke. We owe you much already. You're the architect of the Grand Design,"

"We haven't been able to determine yet if this is a natural consequence of your imagination as a writer," continued Plumdritch, "or if, somehow, your mind is able to affect certain elements of reality on a sub-atomic level, causing probabilities to shift at the crucial moment to insure success."

"That's why we eventually decided to embark upon an even more ambitious plan and recreate *The League of Heroes*," said Cavor.

He watched them for a long moment, these men with weapons, scientific knowledge, these last survivors of the human race, realizing that their hopes for survival were pinned on a series of pulp novels written by a hack writer. (*Don't be so tough on yourself*, he thought. *They were quite enjoyable.*)

"You really hope to save Mankind by finding a way out in a drug-induced series of hallucinations featuring a bunch of comic book characters? That is pure insanity."

"Not entirely," said Fogg. "As I said, we've already found some very good ideas in Lord Kraven's methods."

"But it'll take years to find a solution, assuming there is one."

"We're not going anywhere," replied Cavor with a smirk.

"Trust us, we've tried everything else," said Fogg. "Yes, our methods are unorthodox, but they have produced results. Somehow, you foresaw the crisis we face and, through your fiction, you resolved it. Now, we can but hope to harness your abilities–whatever they are–and resolve the same crisis in the real world as well."

"How do I know this is the 'real world' and not another of your scenarios? I don't even know what my real name is, or what I look like."

"You can't, of course," said Plumdritch. "And it's better that way. For the scenario to become fully operative, there must be as little conscious awareness as possible of your Level-1 personality. The writer must be erased in order for his creation, Lord Kraven, to become dominant. It is he who will be our Savior."

"You're planning to put me back inside that coffin, aren't you? Make me live through more goddamn *League of Heroes* adventures? Forever and ever, until I find the magic bullet that you seek."

"Yes," said Fogg. "It's our hope that, having shown you the situation we face, you will volunteer again and that, this time, Lord Kraven will prevail."

"But what if there *is* no magic bullet? What if I'm stuck in there forever? What will happen to you? What will happen to me?"

None of the three men said anything. Nurse Zydblinski pressed his shoulder affectionately.

"I know we're asking a lot from you. But you're the only hope we've got left."

Behind her, he saw children with dirty clothes, grimy faces and hope still in their eyes when they looked at him.

"Before you, er, go under, would you be so kind?...."

Cavor was presenting him with a well-read copy of *The League of Heroes* No. 1 ("*Lord Kraven, Savior of the Empire*") and a pen. He wanted him to sign the book. At heart, he was still a fan.

He grabbed the pen and, at once, felt stupid.

"What name do I sign?" he asked.

"Kraven, of course," said Cavor. "You are he, as he is you."

With such devotion to a fictional hero, how could he not prevail? For the first time, he felt a whiff of optimism. Perhaps this was not such a fool's errand after all. Lord Kraven could still save the Empire!

Then, he slowly lowered himself into the salty solution. He felt the cold contact of the electrodes and the sting of the needle.

He was starting to feel the effect of the ketamine. He heard the film unreel in the projector just as they closed the lid of the sarcophagus.

"You'll enjoy this," said Fogg. "This is a roaring good story."

The League of Heroes was waiting for him.

APPENDIX

The League of Heroes
(1898-1920)

1. *Lord Kraven, Savior of the Empire*

At Sir Phileas Fogg's request, Lord Kraven begins to gather the future members of the League of Heroes. But some do not wish to join it…

(*First appearance of Sir Phileas, Lord Kraven, Lord Greystoke and Sherlock Holmes. English Bob is not yet part of the group.*)

2. *Albion Mourning*

While he is working on his metaconditioning program, Lord Plumdritch becomes Peter Pan's latest victim. Can the League survive?

(*First appearance of the Danger Room. At story's end, Lord Plumdritch becomes Doctor Fatal.*)

3. *Grand Prix*

Lord Kraven takes part in the Paris-Amsterdam car race to save Lady Darling from the clutches of Professor Diabolas.

4. *Mañanitas*

Sherlock Holmes, Kid Colt and the Navajo Rangers cross the Mexican border to rescue George Patton from La Chupacabra.

(*First appearance of Kid Colt.*)

5. *The Venice Affair*

The *Mona Lisa* has been stolen! Lord Kraven goes to Venice and faces Prince Spada, Monarch of the Calabrian thieves.

(First appearance of Prince Spada, Kraven's arch-enemy. Robert Hammerstone has not yet become English Bob.)

6. *The Tragedy of the Yiddish Theater of Kentish Town*
    The Impossible Club meets every week in an abandoned theater to watch a mysterious puppet show.
    (Deaths of John Bull and Lady Guernsey of the Original League of Heroes.)

7. *The Mouths of Demonia*
    The Archbishop of Canterbury collapses during a charity event. Sherlock Holmes' investigation takes him to the dark recesses of the mysterious Uncertain Ballet.
    (Professor Cavor replaces Lord Plumdritch.)

8. *The Return of Lord Kraven*
    The Diamond Consortium of Antwerp begs for Lord Kraven to come out of retirement and investigate the beautiful yet deadly Enchantress known as Madame Vulpinia.
    (First appearance of Madame Vulpinia.)

9. *The Strange Case of the Living Dead of Caldwell*
    Colonel Plumdrake, an Indian Army veteran, decides to suddenly change his will, but his heirs argue that he is already dead...
    (Holmes uses one of Cavor's inventions for the first time–and lives to regrets it.)

10. *The Jewels of Abdulhamit*
    Prince Spada steals the Pink Elephant diamond from the Palace of Topkapi. Lord Kraven investigates...

11. *The Giant Gorilla of Sumatra*
    Lord Greystoke lands on Skull Island, off the western coast of Sumatra. But its native cannibals are the least of the threats that await him...

12. *The Prisoner of Ingolstadt*

Aboard the *HMS Albion Ascendant*, Lord Kraven and English Bob go to rescue the Prince of Wales from the clutches of Prince Spada.

(*Kraven and Spada fight their last duel.*)

13. *Prisoners of Baron Samedi*

The entire League is sent to Haiti to stop an enemy who has the power to summon the dead. English Bob gets initiated into the Capoiera.

14. *The Blue Terror*

The Jade Mask arrives in London, and with him, The Living Terror That Walks.

(*First appearance of the Jade Mask.*)

15. *The Case of the Extroverted Autophage*

The Reform Club holds its Annual Banquet, but will Sir Phileas be on the menu?

16. *Robotor*

Anton Banacek's strange toy store is the theater of a series of grisly murders.

(*First mention of the Shangri-La Electric Company.*)

(*This issue was pulled because of complaints from parents' associations and is very rare.*)

17. *Shadow of the Horla*

In France, Sherlock Holmes must defeat a legendary renegade Fairy Lord or face the Curse of Eternal Madness.

(*First appearance of the Horla.*)

18. *The Eyes of the Moon*

Lord Greystoke returns to the Congo on the trail of international gun merchant Turckle Darksmith.

19. *The Ghost of the Hudson*
    Lord Kraven joins Lord Greystoke in America to capture Turckle Darksmith before the death-dealer can unleash the power of the Moonstone.
    (*Kid Colt guest-stars.*)

20. *The Mystery of the Ubiquitous Killer*
    Lord Kraven and English Bob investigate the case of schizophrenic Siamese twins.

21. *The Invisible Viking*
    Lord Kraven travels to Thule to investigate a series of mysterious deaths that have plagued that Arctic research outpost.

22. *Murder in Crimson*
    The entire League join forces when Sir Phileas Fogg is kidnapped by a deadly enemy...
    (*Doctor Fatal returns.*)

23. *The House on the Edge of Tomorrow*
    Peter Pan takes Madame Vulpinia to a mysterious house which exists in a different dimension of time.
    (*First mention of the House and death of Madame Vulpinia.*)

24. *Murder in Berlin*
    In Berlin, Lord Kraven investigates the mysterious hunts of Baron von Tod.
    (*Kraven meets Baron von Tod for the first time.*)

25. *The Wharves of San Francisco*
    English Bob is prisoner in Chinatown. Lord Kraven must challenge the Trilogy Triad to free his young assistant from the clutches of the Jade Mask.
    (*The Jade Mask returns; Kid Colt guest-stars.*)

26. *The Case of the One-Armed Marquis*
The Marquis of Charançolles is found dead at his desk, his right arm cut off, but a left arm lies on the rug!
(*Kraven learns French with the Quick-Read method.*)

27. *The Deadly Doctor Fatal*
During their annual congress, the members of the Royal Academy of Science take off their clothes and waltz. Lord Kraven suspects an old enemy is back...
(*First "death" of Lord Kraven.*)

28. *Dancing a Deadly Tango*
Who poisoned Lord Shamwell? Was it the curry? Who left a small blue marigold bottle in the library? And what really happened in the gazebo? So many mysteries for Sherlock Holmes to solve...

29. *The Black Idol*
Lord Greystoke finds himself trapped in the Roman Catacombs, at the mercy of the Mother of Tears.

30. *The Claws of the Horla*
The renegade Fairy Lord returns to challenge Sherlock Holmes to a new duel.

31. *The Sow*
Lord Kraven is forced to return to the House and join forces with Peter Pan to prevent a dark goddess of chaos from crossing the bridge between the Netherworld and Neverland.

32. *The Eggs of the Roc*
The ships of Albion are attacked by a sea monster–or are they? Lord Greystoke teams up with Lord Hook to challenge Captain Sinbad and his electric submarine, the *Siddhârta*.
(*The Shangri-La Electric Company returns.*)

33. *The City of Ultimate Fear*
Lord Greystoke and Sherlock Holmes travel to Tibet to thwart the Jade Mask's plans to take over Central Asia.
(*First appearance of Auguste de Grandin.*)

34. *Death at 3,000 Fathoms*
Lord Kraven challenges Kapitan Mors over the sunken ruins of ancient Atlantis.
(*First appearance of Kapitan Mors.*)

34b. *The Adventure of the Harrowing Harem*
The Sultan of Jarawak asks Lord Kraven to investigate mysterious happenings in his harem.
(*Special limited edition sold only to collectors.*)

35. *The Werewolf of Gibraltar*
Someone is hijacking Abion's ships off the coast of Morocco. Lord Kraven investigates...

36. *The Sons of the Pharaoh*
Albion's interests in Egypt are threatened by a strange new sect. After undergoing brain surgery, Lord Kraven is admitted to the Cairo Lunatic Asylum.
(*Auguste de Grandin returns.*)

37. *The Metamorphosis of Sir Phileas Fogg*
In Prague, Sir Phileas suddenly changes into a giant cockroach. Sherlock Holmes must find a cure...

38. *The Frightful Four*
French crime lord Fantômas issues a challenge to the League of Heroes.
(*First appearance of Fantômas.*)

39. *Return of the Sow*
The House is under assault from the Undying Ones; Lord Kraven must cross the Everlasting Bridge or see Albion destroyed.
(*Second "death" of Lord Kraven.*)

40. *The Night of the Black Freighter*
Lord Hook enlists Lord Greystoke's help to travel back to Neverland to face a threat from the pirate's past.

41. *The Red Tiger*
Sherlock Holmes is accused of murder in Washington.
(*Kid Colt guest-stars.*)

42. *Influenza*
Albion is threatened by an invisible enemy. For the first time in its history, the League is powerless, unless...

43. *The Son of Walpurgis*
A coven of German Mystics attempts to resurrect the legendary Wode. The League faces the Siegfried Legion...

44. *The* Lusitania *Affair*
Naval plans are missing. Lord Kraven and English Bob board the *Lusitania* to recover them.
(*First mention of Kraven's war effort; last appearance of English Bob in the series.*)

45. *The Strange Case of the Symbiotic Cartel*
A young nurse suspects her employer of stealing his patients' eyes. Sherlock Holmes investigates...
(*Fantômas guest-stars.*)

46. *Albion Is Burning!*
Lord Kraven tries to stop Kapitan Mors from launching his deadly Flying Dragon armada.
(*Last appearance of Lord Greystoke in the series.*)

47. *The Hammer of Portsmouth*
Lord Kraven stops the Prussian army before it can advance towards London.

48. *The Eagle Has Crashed*
Lord Kraven fights Baron von Tod in a duel to the death in the skies over the Somme.

49. *Brave New World*
The Great War may be over, but some of Lord Kraven's enemies have not disarmed... Enter: The Karnophage.
(*Last appearance of the Shangri-La Electric Company.*)

50. *The Ice Tomb*
Lord Kraven joins an International Expedition searching for mysterious aliens that might have secretly landed in Antarctica.
(*Last issue of the series.*)

The Theater of Crime Plays
(1929-1930)

1. *The Mysterious Affair at Canterbury*
　　Loosely based on *League of Heroes* No. 7. The Uncertain Ballet is replaced by the Canterbury Cricket League.

2. *The Murder in the Cemetery*
　　Loosely based on *League of Heroes* No. 9. The *Necronomicon* is replaced by the *East Sussex Railway Guide*.

3. *The Big Five*
　　Loosely based on *League of Heroes* No. 38. Originally entitled *The Big Four*, the play was rewritten and expanded to make room for Laurence Olivier to play Fantômas.

4. *The Mystery of the White Train*
　　Loosely based on *League of Heroes* No. 45. The collection of eyes is replaced by a diamond collection.

5. *The Murder of Roger Shamwell*
　　Loosely based on *League of Heroes* No. 28. The play was cancelled before the end of its run.